BELLE

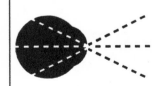 This Large Print Book carries the
Seal of Approval of N.A.V.H.

AN AMISH FAIRYTALE

BELLE

AN AMISH RETELLING OF BEAUTY AND THE BEAST

SARAH PRICE

THORNDIKE PRESS
A part of Gale, a Cengage Company

Farmington Hills, Mich • San Francisco • New York • Waterville, Maine
Meriden, Conn • Mason, Ohio • Chicago

Copyright © 2017 by Price Publishing.
An Amish Fairy Tale.
Thorndike Press, a part of Gale, a Cengage Company.

**LIBRARY OF CONGRESS CIP DATA ON FILE.
CATALOGUING IN PUBLICATION FOR THIS BOOK
IS AVAILABLE FROM THE LIBRARY OF CONGRESS**

ISBN-13: 978-1-4328-4545-2 (hardcover)
ISBN-10: 1-4328-4545-4 (hardcover)

Published in 2017 by arrangement with Zebra Books, an imprint of
Kensington Publishing Corp.

Printed in Mexico
1 2 3 4 5 6 7 21 20 19 18 17

BELLE

CHAPTER ONE

Sunflowers always made Belle happy. Very happy. Perhaps it was the way their large, oversized heads seemed to follow the sun. Or perhaps it was how they looked like bright, sunny yellow faces, smiling at her. Or maybe it was just because she favored the color yellow. Regardless of the reason, whenever she walked to town, Belle always paused to look at the small patch of tall, happy sunflowers that greeted her from the Troyers' front garden. Today, with the sun shining overhead and the sky as clear as the day was long, would be no different.

Her friend Ella lived there with her two stepsisters and her stepmother, but they were most likely all working at their store in town. In their absence, Belle admired how Ella had planted their garden with the sunflowers lining the back rows and book-ending the cornstalks that appeared almost ready to be harvested. She stood on the sidewalk and gazed at the garden, her hand on the white picket fence that bordered the Troyers' property and the main street that led to Echo Creek. The warmth of the summer's day on her back was almost as comforting to Belle as the sunflowers. She loved summer, even when it was hot and humid.

A male cardinal flew off the porch of the house and landed on top of a sunflower. Belle watched it for a few long seconds, admiring its red feathers and wondering why it was alone. They usually traveled with their mates.

"Hello there, Annabelle!"

Surprised, Belle turned to see who was greeting her from the porch. She lifted her hand to shield her brown eyes from the sun. "Is that Ella, then?"

Ella Troyer leaned against the white railing as she reached over to pluck the dry laundry from the line. She was a fetching young woman who, unlike Belle, had blond hair and a pretty face that mirrored her sweet personality. Even now as she worked, Ella smiled. "*Kum* visit a spell, Belle," Ella called out.

Belle hurried down the sidewalk toward the house. "Not helping at your *maem*'s store today?"

"*Nee,* not today." Ella unpinned a white

towel and began to fold it. "Too much work at home, *Maem* says." Ella laid the folded towel into the basket and leaned against the porch railing. Her smile broadened. "And isn't that fortunate for me? Now I can be outside by myself, with no fear of *Maem* chastising me again or my *schwesters* bothering me. I like it when they're all at the store."

Belle did not respond, preferring to keep to herself what she wanted to say. She knew that Ella's stepsisters had never been very kind to her, especially after Ella's father had passed away the previous year. Often Ella was asked to work while her stepsisters went to singings and youth gatherings at the different Amish farms in Echo Creek. While Belle was just as happy to stay home with her nose buried in a book, she knew that Ella would have liked a bit more of a social life. But Linda, her stepmother, catered to her own daughters first and foremost, and that often meant that Ella stayed behind at home alone.

"That's where I'm headed. The store," Belle said at last.

Ella laughed, her blue eyes sparkling. "The new books arrived a few days ago. Just this morning, *Maem* was wondering when you'd stop by."

Books. That was the only thing Belle loved more than sunflowers. Each month, she knew exactly when the new shipment was to arrive and usually was there at the Troyers' store, waiting with anticipation. But yesterday it had rained, and this morning her father had needed her to help him in the barn. He was always trying new things or improving on something, and his latest invention would surely help the family regain its financial footing.

"I meant to *kum* last evening, but *Daed* was finishing his new grill. He's taking it to Liberty Village on Wednesday morning to see if Schrock's General Store will sell it to the *Englischers*." She paused. Her father had tried to get Linda Troyer to carry the grill in her store. But Linda had been adamant that no one in Echo Creek would buy it. Belle didn't want Ella to think that she was complaining about her stepmother's rejection, so she added, "They have more tourists there, you know."

Ella nodded. "*Ja,* I reckon they sure do. I'll say a prayer tonight that his trip is successful."

"*Danke,* Ella." Belle glanced down the road that led to the center of town. "I best get going." She waved at her friend and continued her journey to town.

10

Echo Creek was a small town with just a handful of stores. Ella's stepmother had inherited Troyers' General Store from her late husband. There was also a large feed and grain store, as well as a hardware and lumber store. Those were the main businesses on the strip that constituted the town center. Along a side street, the Lapp brothers built sheds that they sold to *Englischers.* Twice a month, a large truck came to town to pick up the sheds and drive them to the shed dealership in a neighboring county. And Joshua Mast had a blacksmith shop, where he shoed horses and repaired wheels for farm equipment and buggies.

Unlike most of the other families in Echo Creek, Belle's family wasn't from there, but the town was the only place Belle knew as *home.* She had been just six years old when her parents had moved to the farm on the outskirts of town. Her older brothers and sisters often spoke of their previous home in Trinity Falls, a neighboring community located just south of Echo Creek. Belle's siblings frequently reminisced about how life was better then. The farm was larger and the soil richer. But their father wasn't a very good farmer, at that, and three years of bad crops forced them to sell the farm and move to a more remote area. Then, two years later, their mother unexpectedly died.

Today, just over ten years later, Belle barely remembered her mother.

Now that her two brothers were older and married, both of them having returned to Trinity Falls with their wives, only Belle and her two sisters remained at home. Without the boys to help with the farmwork, her father had fallen on tough times. Again. If only one of her older sisters would marry someone who might move onto the farm to help *Daed*! But that was looking less and less likely with each passing season. The fields were overgrown, and the only crops that seemed to grow on their farm were debt and dreams.

The bell rang over the door as Belle walked into the store, careful to close it behind her so that the midday heat didn't tag along with her. She glanced around and immediately saw the bookcase. She hurried over to it, eager to discover what new books had arrived the previous evening.

"Good afternoon, Belle Beiler!"

She turned toward the front of the store, where Ella's stepmother stood behind the cash register. "Good afternoon, Linda." She hesitated before stepping away from the bookshelves to properly greet the older woman. "I just saw Ella, and she said the new books arrived yesterday."

"*Ja,* that they did. Drusilla just unpacked them an hour ago. Thought you might be in today." Linda pointed toward the bookshelves. "She set them toward the front of the display. I think you'll be rather pleased with the new selection. Plenty of romances and a wonderful selection of those devotionals you like. The one on the end cap looks like something you'd enjoy."

"*Danke.*"

Without waiting, Belle hurried back toward the shelves and began to peruse the different titles. While she was especially fond of romance novels, she looked for the devotional that Linda had mentioned.

In the Book of Matthew, Jesus tells us to judge not lest we be judged, if not by others than by God. Often I wonder how it is possible to not judge others? There are no two people who are exactly alike. That is the beauty of God's creation in mankind. The very fact that everyone is different can create the urge to compare others to our own set of values and standards. When people fall short of our own expectations, how can we not judge them?

The answer to this is simple: remember that the ruler you use to measure other people's shortcomings is nothing compared to the ruler that God uses to measure ours. Accept the differences in other people with compassion and understanding. Realize that you, too, are different from everyone else who might measure your imperfections. Release the urge to judge and instead embrace the differences, even those you disagree with, in order to be right with God.

For a moment, Belle simply sighed, pressing the book against her chest. If only others might live the Word of God as much as they preached it. However, far too often, people tended to tout the Golden Rule as a measure of how others should behave, rather than how they themselves should behave. Why, if only people switched their way of thinking, how much kinder the world would be! But Belle wasn't necessarily concerned with the world. Her concern lay mostly with her community in Echo Creek. And, to be even more specific, with her father.

Just as Belle was about to read the next passage, she heard a commotion outside of the store. Loud footsteps and voices interrupted her peace.

"*Maem! Kum* quick!"

Belle looked up as Anna and Drusilla ran through the front door. They were out of breath, and Anna's prayer *kapp* was askew on her head. Drusilla shut the door and bent down, peering through the window. "Did you see him?"

"See who, *Dochders*?"

"Adam Hershberger."

At the sound of the name, Belle lost interest in the book. Instead, her attention was fully riveted to the conversation.

"Adam Hershberger? How would I have seen him?" Linda sounded irritated as she walked around the counter and joined her daughters.

Belle stared over the top of the bookshelf toward the door. Excited and pushing at each other, Anna and Drusilla were peering through the glass panes of the door. Linda, however, quickly ended their struggle to have a better look by shoving her way between them. Though she had tried to sound uninterested, Linda's attention to the main street of Echo Creek was a clear indication that her curiosity was as piqued as that of her daughters.

"Are you sure you saw him, Drusilla?" Linda asked, standing upright when she realized that the main street was empty. Her two daughters stood before her, the one looking flushed in the cheeks and the other looking disheveled. "*Mayhaps* you were mistaken?"

Drusilla reached over to straighten her sister's *kapp*. "*Nee, Maem.* We both just saw him as he drove through town in that odd-shaped buggy of his."

"Really!" Once again, Linda peered through the door's windowpanes. Anyone would be hard-pressed to mistake Adam Hershberger's buggy. While the other Amish in Echo Creek drove plain black buggies with lighter-colored tops, Adam drove a completely black buggy that had a narrow window in the back and only slightly bigger ones in the doors. "I wonder what on earth he's doing in town? He usually only *kums* at the beginning of autumn and spring."

"And it's summer!" Anna gushed.

"We know it's summer, goose." Drusilla nudged her sister's arm.

"How that man survives, I'll never know." Once again, Linda stood up. "It's not normal for a man to live alone like that. Although I must confess that I sure am glad he only visits here twice a year for his supplies. It's unnerving to be in his presence, that's for sure and certain."

"I couldn't see his face." Anna sounded disappointed.

"And why would you want to?" Drusilla made a face, scrunching up her mouth and nose. "He's so ugly with that scar!"

16

"You've never seen his face, either!" Anna snapped, giving her sister a sharp elbow to her side.

Belle frowned. She, too, had never seen Adam Hershberger, but like the rest of the town, she had certainly heard of him. Ever since she was a child, the other children had made fun of the elusive man who lived five miles from town, on one of the largest farms in the church district. Belle never understood why this was permitted, even though she understood the reasons behind the ridicule.

As a child, Adam had been caught in a fire; a fire that had left his face scarred. The fire had happened five years before her family moved into the town, and, since the Amish rarely spoke of tragic events, no one ever discussed the events of the actual fire. The only reason Belle had even learned that much was from overhearing an occasional comment, usually just a whispered reference to the fire, from other people whenever Adam's name was mentioned, which wasn't very often.

When Belle had been younger and still attending school, the other students often played a made-up game called "The Beast." One student, usually a boy, would pretend to be Adam Hershberger and would scrunch up his face and chase the others, trying to capture them. Once his prey was captured, the Beast would pretend to eat the loser. It was a game that Belle despised and refused to play. Thankfully, Teacher had found out about the game and put an end to it. But the children had still whispered about Adam and his horrible face. Belle had always wondered how the children knew about Adam, since they certainly did not see him at church or in town. She suspected that they overheard their parents talking about the Hershbergers at home.

And yet Belle knew almost nothing about the Hershberger family.

Instead of chastising either of her daughters — something that Belle thought any good Amish woman should have done — Linda said, "It's a wonder that Bishop doesn't shun him." She spoke mostly to herself but with a heavy distaste lingering on her words that Belle found rather strange.

At this, Belle could no longer remain a silent observer.

Slamming the book shut, Belle frowned at them. "Why on earth should Adam be shunned?" Belle folded the book under her arm and walked toward the gathering at the door. "He's done nothing wrong."

"Well," Linda started slowly, a slight hesitation to that one word as if she was trying to find a valid justification for her comment. "Let's start with the fact that he doesn't attend church service. I'd think the bishop would care about that, being that Adam is baptized and all!"

That was the first Belle had ever heard of Adam being baptized. Of course, Adam was a great deal older than Belle — probably ten years or more — so, had he ever been baptized, it would have happened long ago.

Casually, Belle shrugged her shoulders. "I don't blame him for not attending service, the way people talk about him so. Surely everyone would simply gawk at him!" Belle glanced at the back of Anna and Drusilla's heads as they continued staring out the windowpanes. "I'm sure the bishop has taken that into consideration. His presence would be a distraction from worship and fellowship, don't you think?"

"I heard the bishop goes out there once a month to provide him spiritual leadership." Drusilla seemed pleased with herself for having this tidbit of knowledge.

"That's something, at least." Belle started to walk toward the counter, wanting to pay for her book and return home. It would take her a good forty-five minutes to walk there, and she wanted to get supper started early so that her father could retire for the evening. He needed to get up extra early the next day to prepare for his journey after doing the morning chores. And on Wednesday morning, he would leave at five o'clock in order to get to Liberty Village by eight, when the store opened.

"I'm ready to pay now," she said when not one of the Troyers left their post at the door.

Reluctantly, Linda returned to the counter to ring up Belle's purchase.

The entire community knew about Adam Hershberger and how he lived a reclusive life. Belle couldn't understand their fascination with the man. As far as she knew, he never bothered anyone, rarely came to town, and seemed set in his ways. But for some reason, at the beginning of autumn and spring, those two times a year when he came to town, usually early in the morning, to stock up on dry goods for the upcoming season, everyone talked about it for weeks. The stories usually changed, too. If he bought two forty-pound bags of flour, after two weeks it grew to twenty bags! If he spoke to someone, another rare occurrence, by the time two weeks had passed, it had become an agitated argument. Belle merely rolled her eyes whenever she heard Adam's name and the ridiculous stories people told. She had better things to do than participate in such folly.

She was halfway home, the road having changed from macadam to dirt and gravel, when she heard a buggy approaching her from behind. She stepped onto the grass, the road being more narrow here. A quick glance over her shoulder caused her to catch her breath. It was a strange-looking buggy, the top black instead of the regular gray color that the other Amish in their community drove. And the undercarriage was tapered, not square. As the buggy approached, Belle knew that it must be Adam Hershberger driving it. The doors were shut and there were hardly any windows — just narrow slits so that the driver could see his side mirrors.

But Belle could see enough to catch his eyes, at least one of them, staring at her.

For a moment, she felt oddly uncomfortable. A chill went down her spine, and she almost wrapped her arms around herself for warmth. But just as quickly as it happened, the chill vanished.

She stopped walking, and as she kept her eyes on that small window, she lifted her hand to wave at him, a small smile on her lips.

For a moment, the driver seemed to slow down the buggy, and from this vantage point, she could see inside the larger front window. He kept staring at her, a shadow of a man, dressed in all black except for the front of his white shirt. She couldn't imagine that anyone would be wearing a dark jacket and heavy hat in such weather. It must have been terribly hot inside the buggy.

As the buggy passed her, she thought she heard his voice, and she definitely saw him lift the reins to slap upon the horse's croup. The buggy lurched forward as the horse began to canter down the remainder of the road toward the bend that would lead past Belle's home and toward Adam's own farm, several miles down the same lane.

Once he was gone, Belle continued walking along the road, wondering what sort of man wouldn't even open the doors of the buggy in order to let in some fresh air on such a hot summer day.

By the time she made it back home, it was almost three o'clock. She set her bag on the counter and hurried over to where she had hung her apron. After tying the apron around her waist, she set about her daily task of preparing supper for her father and sisters, the strange but brief encounter with Adam Hershberger long forgotten.

CHAPTER TWO

"*Kum,* Belle!" As he stood on the other side of the opened kitchen window, Melvin excitedly motioned with his hand for her to join him outside.

"What is it, *Daed?*"

He grinned. "*Kum* see what your *daed* has made! This one will make you proud."

Belle wiped her hands on her apron. "You know what the preachers say about pride, *Daed.*" But she smiled anyway as she crossed the floor to where he waited for her, by the back door. She was always proud of him. His passion for creating something new or more practical was certainly a gift from God. If only other people would start believing in him as much as she did. "Are you finished with the new prototype then?"

"I am indeed!" He grinned at her, his lower lip partially hidden by his mustacheless beard. It was so gray that it was almost white. But he always kept it neatly trimmed rather than letting it grow shaggy, like some of the other older men in their church district. And his eyes, so dark yet so full of life, sparkled as he gestured for her to walk faster. "I want you to see this, Belle. It's finally ready and just the way I imagined it."

His joy was contagious, and Belle hurried to follow him down the warped porch steps and over the patchy yard to the barn. It was a newer barn, which always puzzled Belle since the house was in such disrepair. And yet what should have housed forty cows in any other Amish farm now was home to only six cows and a horse. The rest of the barn was filled mostly with rusty farm equipment and piles of metal that Melvin used to make his grills. He loved soldering and fixing rakes, hoes, and other items for some of the farmers in Echo Creek. The only problem was that the larger equipment rarely broke, and the smaller items were often disposable; it was more expensive to repair them than to simply replace them.

"Just think, *Daed,*" Belle said as she walked behind him, trying to keep up with his eager footsteps. "It's only been a year since you started building this."

"A year, Belle!" He laughed and tugged at his gray beard. "It seemed that I started this design so long ago but now, looking back, it really wasn't. Oh! How I pray this changes our lives. I won't be greedy and hope for more than we need, though. I just want enough. That is all. Enough for you and your *schwesters.*"

Belle slipped through the doorway into the back room of the barn, where her father built most of his inventions. Scattered throughout the dusty room that would normally have been filled with bales of hay were discarded dreams: a better-designed buggy wheel, a less-expensive clothesline pulley system, a nonbreakable kerosene lantern. Each item was useful, solving a problem, items that so many people in their community could use. Unfortunately, most of the Amish already had these items, even if they were inferior versions, so they had no reason to buy another, even if it would make their lives a little bit easier or more comfortable; that would be, after all, in contradiction of the principles of the simple and more austere lifestyle, devoid of luxuries and modern amenities, decreed by the *Ausbund,* which contained their articles of faith, as well as the pragmatic ways these were to be applied by their community.

And that was precisely why the Beilers never had enough of anything. Without people buying the products that Melvin made, there was little income to pay bills and feed the small family.

"*Ja, Daed,* that's all we ever needed. Enough. So even if this doesn't sell, we'll find something else to fall back on."

In the middle of the room stood her father's latest invention: a grill. But it didn't look like any type of grill Belle had ever seen. Instead of being raised from the ground, it actually *rested* on the ground. The main part of the grill was a sturdy metal rectangular box. That was where people would burn wood or coals. On either side of it were metal poles and a pulley wheel. The grill hung from the support poles, and the pulley wheel allowed it to be raised or lowered. Belle also noticed that there was a hook attachment in case people wanted to cook with a cast-iron pot, the old-fashioned way. At the top of the pulley, there was a lever that could stop the grill from being lowered farther than it needed to go. And the grill tilted so that the fat from cooking food would drain into a special holding compartment, either to be discarded or used for cooking or brushed over the meat.

"Oh, *Daed*!" Belle could hardly contain her delight. *This* invention made sense. *This* invention was practical. *This* invention might actually sell. "It's so different from the last one you made!"

Like a small child eager to show off, Melvin ran over to the wheel, moving the lever to spin it slowly, up and down. "It took me a while to get the tension on the wire just right, but look at this!" He turned the wheel so that the grid lowered to rest just over the wood box. "Even when it's all the way down, it is still tilted. And the wheel doesn't get hot! I had to use a special metal."

Belle remembered far too well the last time her father had created a grill — it was round and had swung in and out, rather than up and down. He had burned his hands quite a few times, once quite seriously, and Belle had had to put salve on them until they healed. "I daresay that the rectangular shape is much better than the round one, don't you think?" She reached out her hand to touch the top of the grill. "The design will dispense the heat better, anyway."

Her response made Melvin smile at her, pride in his eyes. "That's my girl. Always thinking. I wish I had known that before I started working on the round one. *Ja, vell,* this one is better anyhow. The lowering of the grill is much more efficient than the swinging arm contraption. Much better for controlling the cooking temperature. And it looks much sturdier, wouldn't you say?"

"It does indeed!"

He clapped his hands together. "Tomorrow I'll ride to Liberty Village, Belle. I may not return for a day or two, so I'm going to need you to take charge of the *haus*."

She nodded her head. She knew only too well what he was thinking but not saying: her sisters would not be apt to do much while their father was gone. They would see it as a time to go visiting with friends or even sneak over to the lake to wade in, perhaps up to their waists! Belle would have to make certain that the cows were fed and milked and the garden weeded and watered. She didn't mind having to do the work for her sisters, but she often wished they would show a little more responsibility. It would be hard to find proper suitors for them if people suspected how little they helped around the farm.

"Of course, *Daed*."

Melvin reached out and touched her cheek. "I know I can always count on you, Annabelle. Reckon I don't even have to ask, do I now?" Dropping his hand, he sighed. "So much like your *maem*. Kind, thoughtful, considerate . . ."

Belle blushed. "No more so than others, I suppose."

Her father gave a soft laugh. "And modest, too, *ja?*" Together they moved out into the yard, and he turned toward the house, shielding his eyes from the sun. "If the stores in Liberty Village agree to carry my grill, sell it to the *Englischers,* Belle, *mayhaps* we'll have more than enough. *Mayhaps* I'll finally be able to fix up this place."

Following his gaze, Belle tried to see what her father saw. The house needed a fresh coat of paint. The shrubs around the front door were overgrown and tired-looking. And the driveway needed some new gravel to fill in the ruts and cover up the worn areas of dirt. But to Belle, it was home, and perfect just the way it was. "You know what they say about putting the cart before the horse . . ." she quipped in a light tone.

Melvin glanced at her. "And sensible, too, I reckon. Might as well add that to my list of your best traits." But he smiled, clearly taking no offense at her words. "I best go on to town, then. I need to pick up some feed for the cows."

Belle watched as her father wandered back to the barn. She could hear him moving about, talking to the horse in a soft voice as he brushed down the mare in preparation for harnessing her. Sighing, she returned to the house, knowing that she needed to complete her kitchen chores before heading out to the garden. There was always so much work to do. But working in the garden was her favorite chore. She loved feeling the dirt beneath her fingers and watching the progress of the vegetables as they grew.

With autumn just around the corner, Belle knew that her days of gardening were winding down. She had already canned tomatoes and beans for the winter months. But there were still pumpkins and squash to tend. After the last of the vegetables were harvested, Belle would prepare the soil for the next spring planting. And then she would be finished working outside for the year.

"Mornin', Belle," her sister said when Belle walked into the kitchen.

"Morning? It's almost afternoon, Susie."

Susie made a face at her. "You know I wasn't feeling well yesterday."

"Oh, *ja*! I almost forgot." Belle tried not to smile as she poured coffee into a mug for her sister. "And Verna? I reckon she's feeling poorly, too?"

"Danke." Susie ignored Belle's quip as she took the mug of coffee and sipped at it. "You sure do make good coffee." Setting

down the mug, she looked at Belle. "What's on our list for today?"

Belle glanced around the kitchen. She had already made breakfast and cleaned those dishes. Susie would have to make her own meal if she didn't want to wait for dinner. And the bread was almost finished baking in the oven, as attested by the rich fragrance permeating the entire house. "Not much left inside. But the garden needs work."

This time, Susie waved her hand at Belle. "Season's almost over, Belle. You don't need to work the garden."

But Belle was adamant. "We need to prep the soil for next year. You know that. Planning and preparation are the two most important tasks for a farmer."

"Whatever you say, Belle." She glanced up when she heard the sound of the buggy. "Is *Daed* going somewhere, then?"

"*Ja,* to town. He finished his prototype and intends to go to Liberty Village tomorrow morning."

At this news, Susie immediately jumped up and hurried to open the screen door, calling out, "*Daed! Daed!* I want to go with you!"

Belle sighed as her sister disappeared. Once again, Belle was left alone to do all the chores. There was no point in reminding Susie that many hands made light the work. Instead, as the buggy pulled out of the driveway, Belle wandered outside to the garden, deciding that if she had to do the chores alone, she'd at least start the one she preferred the most.

It was almost an hour later when she heard someone approaching from the lane.

"Good day, Belle."

She didn't have to look up from her hoeing to know that Gabriel was walking down their short driveway and headed in her direction. She rolled her eyes before she stood up and turned around, forcing a pleasant smile on her face. "Hello, Gabriel. What brings you this way?"

He wore his Sunday pants and a clean white shirt. It was clear that he had not been working on his parents' farm this morning. And from the pleased expression on his face, she knew that his visit to their farm, which was some distance from his parents', was of a social nature. After he sauntered up to the gate that surrounded the family's garden, he leaned against it, and one of the vertical slats came loose. Quickly, he reached down to wedge it back, shoving the rusted nail back into the too-wide hole in the post.

"Thought it was a nice day and wanted to

see how you're doing all the way out here."

Belle laughed. "All the way out here?" She gestured toward the main road. "We might be the last house in Echo Creek, but we're certainly not so isolated. Town's only two miles from here, and with plenty of farms along the way."

Gabriel raised an eyebrow at her. "We sure don't see much of you in town."

"I was just there yesterday."

Gabriel seemed surprised to hear that. "No one told me."

She reached for her hoe and began picking at the weeds once again, her toes digging into the soil. Like most Amish women (and some men, too) she preferred the freedom of not wearing shoes and quite often went barefoot, even when she went into town. She was glad that she wasn't wearing any now, otherwise, Gabriel might have tried to ask her to go walking with him. Even he would know that no respectable woman would go walking with a man without wearing her shoes! "Can't see why anyone would, Gabriel. It's hardly news worthy of repeating."

He puckered his lips and kicked at a stick on the ground. "Aw, Belle, why are you so standoffish to me?"

She could think of a million responses to

that question, but she had always been taught good manners, and that included not always speaking her mind. "You know how much work we have to do here on the farm, Gabriel."

"Farm." He snickered and glanced around.

Reason number one, right there. "Is something I said funny?"

"Nee, nee." Still, he wore a smirk. "Not much of a farm now, is it, though?"

Belle pursed her lips and shot him a stern look. "It does well enough for us, Gabriel. Might not be as fancy as some other farms, but we make do. And I don't appreciate your insinuating otherwise."

He ran the back of his hand across his mouth, almost as if he were wiping away the smirk. "Aw, Belle, I'm sorry. It's just . . ." He paused and looked around. The fields were full of weeds, and the barn was in need of a fresh coat of paint. Even the windmill was rusted. "Your *daed* sure could use a man around the house to help him fix this place up. Why! My own *daed* remembers when this here was one of the most productive farms in Echo Creek!"

She focused on a stubborn weed, smacking the hoe into the soil. "That must have been long before we moved here."

For as long as she could remember, the Beiler farm had never been very fertile. As her older sisters told the story, their father had bought the farm for their mother. She had always wanted to live on a farm. Melvin wanted nothing more than to please her. But after she passed, Melvin began to lose interest in farming. Instead, he tried his hand at raising dairy cows. For a while, that had been successful, until he began building things. His preference for working with metal surpassed his interest in milking cows twice a day. Slowly, he began to sell off the cows to purchase new tools for welding, as well as supplies to make his inventions, leaving only six cows to help feed the family.

And that had been the beginning of the end to farm life for the Beiler family.

"Why don't you rest a spell, Belle?" He reached over and grabbed the top of the hoe. Surprised at his forward gesture, thinking that he would take over, Belle stopped trying to work and looked at him. But he gave her a small smile and added: "Let's go for a walk. Just you and me."

Belle shook her head. The string of her prayer *kapp* fell over her shoulder and she reached up to push it back. "*Nee*, Gabriel. *Daed* is leaving tomorrow, and he needs my help before he leaves."

"Leaving?"

She nodded. Everyone in town knew that her father was trying to build something — anything! — that he could sell. It wasn't a secret. In fact, too many times, she had overheard people snickering when Melvin tried to talk to Linda about carrying his inventions in her store. But the Amish weren't interested in grills or new pitch-forks, in self-standing fancy hayrack-feeder combinations, in insulated water troughs that would never let the water freeze. They were perfectly happy with what they already had, thank you very much. "You know he was making that new grill, Gabriel. Since Linda won't carry it in Troyers' General Store, he's traveling to Liberty Village to-morrow."

Gabriel nodded. "Oh, *ja,* I remember now. That grill with the wheel thingie."

Wheel "thingie." Belle smacked another weed. She didn't like the way Gabriel spoke of the invention, his tone almost mocking her father's device. "It raises and lowers the grill. And it doesn't get hot like the rest of the metal on the grill. It's ingenious."

"Ingenious or not, Amish don't need that."

"*Mayhaps* not," she admitted. "But I bet the *Englischers* will buy it."

He laughed.

"It's not funny, Gabriel." She leaned against the hoe and gave him a stern look. "Not all Amish men are meant to be farmers. No one made fun of Ella's *daed* when he wanted to open that store in town. In fact, all of us shop there, don't we?"

"That's a bit different. Linda Troyer carries things we all need . . . like flour, sugar, hardware, and tools."

Belle tried to mask her emotions, not wishing to offend Gabriel but feeling the strong urge to defend her father. "Someone, somewhere, will be needing a new wood-burning grill, Gabriel. And when my *daed* finds the right people who want to carry it in their stores, no one will be laughing, for sure and certain."

"Aw, Belle," Gabriel said somberly. "I didn't mean anything by it. One of these days, your *daed* will make something people want, I'm sure."

I just hope it's this time. She kept that thought to herself as she glanced up at the sun. "*Ja, vell,* I best get going. *Daed* will be home soon, and he'll need help with the afternoon milking."

Gabriel looked disappointed that their visit was cut short. While Belle felt bad that Gabriel had walked all that way from town, she knew better than to encourage him by talking with him for any longer.

"If you must," he said. "But I'll be stopping by to make sure you and your *schwesters* are getting on all right while your *daed*'s gone, Belle."

She forced a smile at Gabriel. "No need for that. We'll be just fine, I'm sure." Then, before he could argue, she lifted the hoe and placed it against her shoulder. "*Danke* for your visit. Say hello to your family for me." Without another word, she started to walk toward the barn, dreading the thought that Gabriel might follow through on his promise to visit while her father was traveling to Liberty Village.

CHAPTER THREE

On Thursday morning, Belle awoke to the sound of thunder. In the early-morning light, she opened her eyes and saw that the room was darker than usual. A few seconds later, a flash of lightning filled the room, followed by another loud rumble of thunder.

Good thing her father had left on his trip yesterday morning. Rain would have delayed his progress and made travel a misery. Some of the roads leading from Echo Creek to Liberty Village weren't paved. Inclement weather meant puddles and potholes. She wondered if he would be delayed coming home.

Once again lightning flashed and thunder rumbled, as if to remind Belle to get going.

"Oh, help!" she muttered as she tossed back the covers. Rainy days were not her favorite, that was for sure and certain. While she knew that rain made the garden grow, she wasn't ready for a long day of complaints from her sisters. It was hard enough getting them to help with the outdoor chores on sunny days, but on rainy days, they usually sat around the kitchen table and complained about how damp and depressing everything felt. It was true that the house was more humid on rainy days. But Belle always pointed out that complaining did nothing to make the situation any better.

After getting dressed and fixing her hair, she quickly made her bed and hurried down to the kitchen.

She paused at the door and looked outside. The sky was almost black with dark clouds quickly moving through in succession, water pouring out of them and drenching everything underneath. She was surprised to see that it was almost six o'clock. She had slept late, and the cows needed to be milked. With a sigh, she reached for her father's rain slicker. Slipping her arms into it, she realized that her father did not have any protection from the rain. Hopefully the rain would stop before he started his journey home that afternoon.

The rain drenched her hair and face as she ran from the house toward the small barn. Once inside, she shook off the jacket and wiped the raindrops from her cheeks.

"Good morning, girls!" she sang cheerfully as she walked down the aisle in front of the cows. "Sorry I'm late this morning. And I hate to tell you, but it's going to be a long, wet day. Might not send you out until the afternoon."

The only response she received was a gentle moo from one of the cows.

"I know, I know. Your udders are full. I'll be along shortly with the pail." She hurried into the back room to get the milking stool and bucket. Most farmers had automatic milkers that were run with diesel machines, but her father's herd was too small and the milk production too little to justify the investment. Besides, Melvin didn't *want* to be a dairy farmer. The milk that was produced on the farm was used by the Beiler family for drinking, baking, and making cheese, which Belle sold to Linda Troyer to sell to other families in the area. Besides gardening, making cheese was one of Belle's favorite things to do, and today was a perfect day to do just that.

As she started milking, she hummed "Jesus Loves Me," her cheek pressed against the flank of the cow while she gently coaxed the milk from her teats. There was something about working with cows that brought joy to Belle's day. She loved their musky smell (although she could do without the pungent odor of the manure!) and the sounds of the cows chewing their cud. Each cow seemed to have her own personality: one was feisty and liked to kick at the bucket; one was calm and sweet, sometimes trying to lick Belle's neck or nuzzle her hair; and yet another was always impatient, eager to get the milking finished. Belle remembered the days when their dairy herd had been much larger than just six cows. But over time, they had needed to sell off cows and, occasionally, slaughter one or two for winter food. Now the small herd was all that they could afford, and Belle worried about what they would do for the upcoming winter. If they slaughtered another one, they'd be down to five cows, and that would not produce enough milk for her cheese making. And they needed that money to buy dry goods.

Almost an hour passed before Susie ran through the barn door. She shook off her shawl and tossed it on a pile of hay. "Why, it's raining cats and dogs out there!"

Belle glanced up from the last cow she was milking. "That it is!" She sighed, worry etched in her face. "I sure hope the rain lets up before *Daed*'s trip home."

"Oh, but he'll stay another night, don't

you think?" Susie hurried to grab a shovel and began cleaning the cow manure. She scooped it into a wheelbarrow, one shovelful at a time.

"Where's Verna? Still sleeping?" Belle returned her attention to the cow without waiting for the answer.

"She never was a morning person," Susie quipped. "And why bother getting up when it's such a miserable day! I've half a mind to go back to bed myself."

But chores needed to be completed. Truth be told, Belle was grateful that Susie had joined her at all. She wasn't usually one to step up to the occasion without being prodded a bit.

By eight o'clock, the cows were milked and fed, their stalls were clean, and both young women were trying unsuccessfully to dodge the raindrops as they carried buckets of milk into the house. Belle hurried to light the lantern that hung over the table, the soft glow creating a cozy warmth in the room.

She was just about to make coffee when a loud clap of thunder caused her to jump. "Oh, help! That's awfully close. I reckon it's just as stormy at Liberty Village, *ja*?"

Susie sat at the kitchen table, her head bent over a piece of paper as she wrote something on it. "I'm sure I wouldn't know." She scribbled something and then paused, looking thoughtfully at the kitchen wall.

"What're you writing?"

"A list." Susie gave a mischievous smile.

"A list of . . . what?"

"A list of all the things we need if *Daed* starts selling these grills to the *Englischers.*"

Belle should've known better than to ask the question. Still, the gleam in Susie's eyes made Belle laugh. "Well, I sure hope a new buggy is at the top on your list!"

"*Nee!*" Susie frowned at her younger sister. "Why on earth would *that* be on *my* list!"

Now Belle's curiosity was piqued. The farm needed so many things: repainting, a larger workshop for their father, repairs to the barn — and there was a leaky roof that needed to be fixed before winter came. And, of course, a new buggy for their father to fetch his supplies from town. "If that's not on your list, what is?"

For a moment, Susie did not respond. Her eyes quickly scanned her list. Finally, she answered Belle. "New fabric for a Sunday dress. New boots. Mine have a hole in the sole. Material to make a new prayer *kapp*. You can see how yellow mine has gotten."

"Bleach it."

Susie scowled. "There's nothing wrong

with wanting to make a new prayer *kapp.* I can hardly expect anyone to ask me for a buggy ride wearing this old thing." She swiped at the limp strings of her prayer *kapp.*

"Starch it."

But Susie shook her head. "*Nee,* a new one is in order. Oh, and we need to have a picnic here. We haven't hosted a youth gathering in years."

Belle knew that was an understatement. She couldn't even remember when they had *ever* hosted a youth gathering. Besides the fact that their home was the farm farthest from town, it was also in the worst shape. It was embarrassing to not be able to host youth gatherings like everyone else in their church district. But Belle also knew that her father couldn't really afford to feed all of those people. It was increasingly hard for him to feed his own family!

"What're you two doing?" Verna trudged down the stairs, her long brown hair hanging down her back. She walked over to the small cabinet near the door and retrieved a brush.

"Making lists."

Belle shook her head and pointed to Susie. "Not me."

Verna began to twist her hair into a small bun. "Lists of what?"

"Things we need." Susie began to read off her list once again.

"Oh!" Verna hurried over to the table. She forgot about her hair and sat down next to Susie. "I need new dresses, too. Put pink fabric on your list! I've always wanted a pink dress. And not that pale pink. I want a bright pink one!"

Susie scribbled on the paper.

"I'd love a red dress!" Verna added.

"Oh, I don't think the church leaders have said we can wear that new color yet," Belle pointed out.

Verna ignored her. "And a new coat for winter."

Belle frowned. "What's wrong with your old coat?"

Verna shot her a look of disdain. "Just that, Belle. It's old!"

Unfazed by Verna's sharp tone, Belle retrieved some pins from the cabinet and then stood behind Verna to fix her hair. "Seems you both are mixing up your wants and needs."

"Oh, Belle!" Verna rolled her eyes. "No one wants to marry a poor girl! I'd be helping out *Daed* if I got married, now wouldn't I? One less mouth to feed."

Placing her hands on Verna's shoulders, Belle leaned over and whispered in a teasing voice, "The dress does not make the girl. A man should fall in love with what's on the inside, not the outside."

Angrily, Verna swatted at her. "*Ach,* Belle! What would *you* know about love, anyway!"

Ignoring Verna, Belle picked up the brush. She was used to being taunted by her sisters. It was just something that Susie and especially Verna did. Long ago Belle had learned to take their goading with extra patience. So instead of commenting about how cruel Verna's comment was, Belle listened to her sisters as they discussed other items that they'd ask their father to purchase when he returned from Liberty Village. Belle merely shook her head and continued with her morning chores.

She had three work dresses and her nice dark blue dress for Sunday service. There was nothing more that she needed. As for bleaching and starching her own prayer *kapp,* as well as her Sunday apron and cape, she did not mind. Too much of anything was always bad to have, she reminded herself, with a quick glance at her sisters to reinforce the thought.

"*Kum* now, Verna and Susie," Belle said at last. "I hate to break up your plotting and scheming to capture the hearts of every available young man in Echo Creek, but we do have a few chores that must be done today."

Verna acted as if she did not hear as she got up to pour herself a cup of coffee. Susie, however, being the more practical of the two, sighed and hurried to fetch her apron.

"What do we have to do today?" she asked Belle as she tied the apron strings behind her waist.

"We've cheese to make and cleaning to do."

"Cleaning?" Verna scoffed as she stirred sugar into her coffee.

"The bathroom needs a thorough scrubbing, since someone" — Belle glanced at Verna — "chose to go visit a friend last week rather than clean it when it was her day."

"Verna!" Susie tossed a hand towel at her sister. "You best do it then!"

"It's not *my* week."

"But you didn't do it when it *was* your week!"

Belle reached out and touched Susie's arm. "Regardless of whose week it is, it must be done. Unless *you'd* like to make the cheese and milk the cows, I suggest one of you get started."

Verna scoffed at her. But, after finishing her coffee in one long gulp, she set down her mug and, with an overexaggerated sigh, fetched the cleaning supplies and headed to the bathroom.

For the next few hours, Belle worked in the kitchen, not just making cheese but also baking some fresh homemade bread, knowing that her father would appreciate a nice warm slice whenever he arrived home. Susie took advantage of the time to sweep the upstairs and dust the furniture, Verna joining her when she had finished cleaning the bathroom. On a rainy day in Echo Creek, inside chores were about the only thing that anyone could do.

By early evening, the sky was still pitch-black, with the exception of the occasional lightning strike. Belle stood at the window and stared outside. Earlier, both Susie and Verna had helped with the late-afternoon milking, for which Belle was grateful. The rain had continued to fall so hard that Belle almost expected to see Noah's ark floating down their driveway. Fortunately, their property sat upon a slight hill, so the overflowing creek across the road didn't threaten to flood the house.

"Oh, I'm sure that *Daed*'s staying over in Liberty Village, don't you think?" She spoke mostly to herself, not expecting either one of her sisters to answer. "He wouldn't be foolish enough to travel in this weather, now, would he?"

"Daed?" Verna looked up from her needle-point. *"Nee,* he wouldn't risk it. Not with that old buggy we've got. Why, those wheels would just break if he got stuck in the mud."

With a heavy sigh, Belle forced herself to turn away from the window. It wouldn't do her any good to keep fretting about their father. She could only pray that he had enough common sense to stay in Liberty Village. "Anyone feel like playing Scrabble?" She didn't wait for their answer as she went to fetch the red box from underneath the cupboard.

Setting down her needlepoint, Verna reached out for the box. "I sure do hope the rain stops. It's going to be awful wet for our next volleyball game."

Belle frowned. "I'm more worried about *Daed* than a youth gathering."

Verna winced at the reprimand. "Of course, Belle. But, like *you* said, *Daed* would *never* try to get home in such weather."

Belle frowned at her sister's lack of concern and cast one more look out the window. "I sure hope not."

As they set up the board game, Belle's thoughts returned to her father. Ever since their mother had died, long before Belle was

51

old enough to remember her, he had been the sole provider for the family. Unlike other Amish men, he hadn't remarried, choosing to raise his daughters by himself instead of finding a replacement mother. Some days, Belle wondered if that had been a wise decision. Despite being the youngest of the three children, Belle had grown to take on more of the household responsibilities than her sisters. And with that role came the realization that, if anything happened to their father, there would be a lot of problems for the Beiler girls. Or, more likely, for Belle. Neither Verna nor Susie would work the farm, and it wasn't as if there were excess part-time jobs in Echo Creek for young women. The mostly Amish town was self-sufficient, with the exception of any non-Amish-produced goods brought in from the neighboring town of Liberty Village.

Another bolt of lightning flashed through the window, illuminating the room.

"Oh, help!" Belle whispered. "I can't concentrate."

"Me neither! I hate thunderstorms," Susie said, pushing her Scrabble tiles into the center of the table. "I think I'll just go to bed. All that rain is making me blue, anyway."

Verna sighed. "And just when I was winning!" But she, too, began cleaning up the table.

Belle waited until both of her sisters disappeared upstairs. Only then did she turn off the kerosene lantern that hung over the table. Cloaked in darkness, she made her way to the staircase, feeling the railing beneath her hands before she took that first stair. In the distance, she heard the low roar of thunder and, within seconds, more lightning lit up the sky outside the windows.

"Please, dear Lord," she whispered. "Take care of *Daed.*"

Only then did she ascend the stairs and disappear into her dark bedroom for the night.

CHAPTER FOUR

The next morning, the sound of a horse and buggy pulling into their driveway distracted Belle. Getting up from the table where she had been folding laundry, she hurried to the kitchen sink to peer out the window. It was still raining, and she could barely see the buggy as sheets of water poured down the window. The buggy stopped by the porch and Belle squinted, trying to make out whose buggy it was. But she couldn't tell anything except that it wasn't her father's.

Concerned, she ran to the door, opening it and stepping outside onto the small porch. Rain cascaded down the broken gutter, and she was almost instantly drenched. But from the porch, she immediately recognized the buggy.

Adam Hershberger.

The left door slid open, and, to her surprise, her father emerged. He reached behind the front seat for his bag and leaned inside as if saying something to whoever was driving the buggy — most likely Adam! — before he shut the door and ran through the puddles and into the house.

"Daed!" Belle let him inside. "You're soaked clean through!"

He mumbled something as he passed her. But Belle did not immediately follow him. She stood there as the driver turned the horse and buggy around, heading back down their driveway toward the main road. For a split second, the driver paused the buggy as it passed the house and Belle saw that, indeed, it was Adam Hershberger driving it. While she couldn't make out the details of his face, she saw him stare in her direction, dark curls sticking out from beneath his hat and covered his eyes, before slapping the reins onto the horse's back, urging it to move faster — whether to escape the rain or her scrutiny, she did not know.

Shutting the door, Belle hurried over to her father. He stood shivering, still holding his bag, in the middle of the kitchen. "What on earth!" She ran to the cabinet near the bathroom door and retrieved a large towel. Wrapping it around her father, she helped dry him. "What's happened? Where's your buggy? The horse?"

Abruptly, Melvin stepped away from her, clutching the towel closed at his throat. He didn't meet her concerned gaze. Instead, he slid into a chair at the head of the kitchen table and stared at the floor. He wore an expression of sorrow, one that Belle had never seen before. Even when his inventions fell apart or he had to start over from scratch, Melvin always remained upbeat and hopeful. His faith that God had a plan for him kept him in good humor, even during the worst of times.

So what, now, could have brought her father so low?

"Talk to me, *Daed*. What's wrong?"

He lifted his gaze to stare at her, his eyes swollen red as if he had been crying. "Oh, Belle! What a disaster!"

"We've been worried sick about you, *Daed*. What happened?"

He shut his eyes and nodded his head. "And rightfully so. I never thought to check the weather, *Dochder*."

"Please tell me, *Daed*. What has you looking so forlorn?" She took the edge of the towel and rubbed his wet hair. "Surely it cannot be *that* bad." Even without him talking, she knew that something downright awful had transpired on his journey. "Did you make it to Liberty Village?"

"I did not."

Belle gasped. "Where've you been for the past two days, then?"

For the first time since entering the room, he raised his eyes and looked at her. But the moment their eyes met, he lowered them. "Adam Hershberger's farm."

A gasp escaped her lips. She could hardly believe her ears. Besides the preachers, she knew of no one who went to the Hershberger farm. It was as mysterious a place as the man himself. "Where is the horse, *Daed*?"

"Dead, I'm afraid."

Oh, help! Belle shut her eyes and said a quick prayer. *Please, God, make* Daed *be mistaken.* Without a horse, her father couldn't travel to town to get supplies. Without a horse, they wouldn't be able to go to church. Without a horse, they'd be hard-pressed to survive. And she knew that they could not afford to replace it. "Oh, *Daed* . . ." she offered with teary eyes.

But he held up his hand. She could see the pained expression on his face and immediately stopped herself from saying any more.

"I'm afraid, *Dochder,* that you haven't yet heard the worst of the story." He shook his head, his dark eyes still downcast.

Sliding onto the bench next to where he sat, Belle touched his arm. "Tell me, *Daed.* Tell me what could possibly be worse."

Their conversation was interrupted as Susie and Verna ran down the stairs, happily calling for their father's attention. When they joined Melvin and Belle in the kitchen, the two young women practically pranced around the room.

"Oh, *Daed*!" Verna smiled with delight. "You're home! What did you bring us?"

"Did you get any new fabric for our dresses?" Susie asked cheerfully, clearly unaware of the somber mood in the room.

"How many of your grills will the store in Liberty Village purchase?" Verna asked, spinning on the floor as if she were already wearing a new dress, not her faded green one with the torn hemline. "I can't wait to make my new dress for the singing this weekend!" She turned to look at Susie. "*Mayhaps* Jacob Glick will finally ask me to ride home in his buggy!"

Susie glared at her. "Jacob Glick? Is *that* who you've set your sights on? Oh, help, Verna! His family's almost as poor as we are!"

"*Nee!*" Verna snapped defensively. "He's a *gut* man! Set to inherit his *daed*'s farm!"

"And will continue spending all his income supporting those cousins that live outside of town!" Susie made a face to show her displeasure. "Seven brothers and not one of them married! Can you imagine?"

Melvin slammed his hand down on the table. "Enough!"

Immediately, the room became silent. Belle stared at her father in surprise. He had never been one to raise his voice. Both Susie and Verna stood in the middle of the kitchen, their mouths hanging agape, clearly startled by their father's reaction. Slowly, he pressed his hands against the tabletop and rose to his full height. For the first time, Belle realized that his shoulders were stooped over and he appeared fatigued. Raising his three daughters alone, without the benefit of a mother to help him, had clearly drained him of energy, and the enthusiasm of his two older daughters was taxing his last nerve.

"The horse died," Belle explained in a soft voice. She noticed the shocked expressions on her sisters' faces. "And *Daed* never made it to Liberty Village."

"*Ach!*" Susie rushed to the table and sat down. "You never made it there?"

Melvin shook his head and walked over to the sink. He leaned against the edge of the counter and stared outside at the rain that pelted the window. "I never made it there, *nee*. I missed the turn. I don't know how, but I did." Once again, he hung his head, his wet hair matted against the back of his neck. "Then the road became rough, and there was a pothole. I didn't see it, and the buggy wheel dented. The horse spooked and started to run. I couldn't stop it, and the next thing I knew, I awoke in a strange house."

Belle caught her breath. "Adam Hershberger's?"

Susie gave her a confused look. "Why on earth would you mention that crazy old beast of a man?"

Belle was about to chastise her for such an uncharitable comment when she realized that her father's shoulders were shaking, just enough to indicate that he was sobbing. Quickly, she arose from the bench and hurried to wrap her arms around him. "It's going to be fine, *Daed*. Everything will be fine. We'll find a way. *Mayhaps* I can work in town . . . or I could make more cheese. We will be all right."

But he shook his head. "No horse. A damaged buggy." A sob escaped his throat, and he covered his face with his hands. "I've no way to provide for you girls."

Out of the corner of her eye, Belle saw Verna grimace and reach for Susie's hand as if for comfort. Frowning at them, Belle tightened her hold on her father. "God always has a way of providing for us," Belle whispered as she leaned her cheek against her father's shoulder. "You'll see."

"He already has." Melvin's whispered words were barely audible. Susie and Verna had not heard him, but Belle did.

"Well, that's right *gut* news!" She forced a smile. "See? Good things often follow the bad."

But her father merely shook his head. "I'm not so certain of that, dear Annabelle. You see, I've sold the farm."

Stunned, Belle loosened her arms from around her father. "You did what?" Belle pulled away and stared into her father's face. "You didn't just say that you sold the farm, did you, *Daed*?"

To her further dismay, he nodded his head slowly. "*Ja*. I had no choice." He pulled away from Belle and raised his hands to his face, rubbing at his pale flesh. "Last night, Adam Hershberger brought me a plate of food. He sat with me in his kitchen and asked me what had happened. I told him. Told him everything."

"What do you mean, 'everything'?" Belle

asked cautiously. "What haven't you told us?"

Melvin avoided looking at any of his daughters. "That grill . . . I invested the last of my savings in it. And I haven't paid the mortgage on this place in months." He shuddered as if trying to ward off another sob. "Now, without credit, I can't buy a new horse or fix the buggy. We'll have to slaughter another cow, and even *that* won't see us through another winter. And the bank . . . why, they'll be banging at the door any month now to foreclose on this place."

"You mortgaged the farm?" Belle made her way to the bench, too dazed to stand anymore. "When, *Daed*?"

In a defeated whisper, he answered her. "Last year."

"Why?"

He shook his head as if to clear his thoughts. "Oh, Belle, I had no choice. We had no money!"

Despite the devastating revelation that her father had mortgaged the house, Belle felt even more disappointed that her father had not shared this information with her.

"Adam offered to buy the farm. Pay off the mortgage and give me some money which, thankfully, will help us find a new place to live, perhaps in another town.

Maybe near your *bruders,* until we get back on our feet."

Verna gasped. "Another town? But all of our friends live here!"

Susie shot her a dark look. "You mean *Jacob Glick* lives here."

Ignoring Susie, Verna's eyes flashed angrily, and she turned to face Belle. "You! If you'd only accepted Gabriel's attention, why! We'd be fine. You know he would live here and work the farm. He wants to be a farmer. And he'd never let us starve! His family has money, too. They'd see that *Daed* wouldn't have to struggle. Such a selfish girl! Putting *Daed* in this position!"

"Verna!"

Despite her father's quick reprimand, Verna did not stop there. "Always thinking of yourself instead of the rest of us."

Belle's eyes widened as she listened to her sister's tirade. "That's not true, and you know it."

"*Nee!* You could marry him and we could keep the farm." Verna turned toward her father. "Tell her, *Daed.* Tell her to marry Gabriel."

A pale-faced Susie sank into a chair at the other end of the table. "Oh, why didn't Gabriel want to court *me*?" she lamented. "*Mayhaps* he'll still help us. I'll accept him!"

63

Verna rolled her eyes. "You'd accept anyone! Even one of those short Grimm brothers who live together!"

Susie gasped and started to argue back.

But her father held up his hand, interrupting them. "Girls, that doesn't help me any. Besides, I'm afraid that the farm *is* sold. Whether or not Belle would accept Gabriel now, it's too late. Adam offered me a decent sum of money. I can pay off my creditors and hopefully find a place to rent in Trinity Falls and *mayhaps* I can rebuild my grill prototype." He sighed and tried to force a soft smile at his three stunned daughters. "This is God's will, I suppose. He wants us to go somewhere else. I should have seen the signs long ago."

"Why would Adam want this farm?" Belle asked. "Isn't his own farm one of the largest in the district? Doesn't he have enough to do there?"

Melvin shrugged. "I don't know the man's reasons, but at least you won't have to marry a man you don't love just so that we can stay here . . . on a farm that has been nothing more than a hardship to me ever since your *maem* and I moved here."

"The fields have horrible soil. Why, that back field is nothing more than a mess of weeds, brambles, and rocks!" Belle couldn't understand what interest Adam Hershberger would have in their farm. He lived such a solitary life that she couldn't imagine he wanted to live closer to town. In fact, from what little she knew about him, he preferred being as far away from town — and people! — as possible. "This just makes no sense, *Daed*."

"What's done is done." He reached out for her hand and gave it a tender squeeze.

There was a deeply sorrowful look upon her father's face. Seeing it broke Belle's heart. After all of his hard work to create and sell something that could support his family! How could such a terrible thing have happened? And the result was not just the destruction of her father's dreams, but the realization that the family would have to, once again, relocate to a smaller, more manageable place, most likely far away from Echo Creek.

Belle stared at her father, wishing she knew what to say. She so wanted to comfort him, but the thought of leaving Echo Creek, her friends, and the only memories she had of her mother — however few remained! — created a tightness in her chest. She simply could not imagine packing up and shutting down the house. And to turn the keys over to Adam Hershberger, a man who already had more than enough, especially considering he was the last of his family line?

"Surely Adam would reconsider, *Daed*. Perhaps if the bishop were to talk to him?"

But her father shook his head. "*Nee, Dochder.* I gave Adam my word, and I won't be going back on it." He gave a long, mournful sigh and stood up. Slowly, he straightened his suspenders and looked around the room as if drinking in his own memories. "Going back on my pledge, why, that's akin to lying, and we all know what God thinks of liars."

"Oh, *Daed . . .*" Her voice trailed off, and she found herself at a loss for any further words.

"It'll be all right, Belle," Melvin said, although she was certain he didn't truly believe that. "We'll make a fresh start of it somewhere else. *Mayhaps* in Liberty Village." That, too, didn't seem believable. Property was too dear in the area. That was one of the main reasons hanging on to their Echo Creek farm had been so important.

"*Mayhaps,*" she whispered softly, not convinced but wanting herself to wish for the best.

"Now, I'm terribly tired." He shuffled toward the door that led to his bedroom. "I reckon a good long nap will do my body and mind some good." As he opened the door, the hinges squeaking from lack of maintenance, he turned to look at Belle. His lips twisted into a forced smile that was meant to reassure her that everything would be fine, but failed. "You'll see, Belle. We'll bounce back from this and things will be better than ever. God has a plan for us. Never forget that."

And with those words, he slipped through the open door and shut it behind himself.

Ja, Belle thought. *God does have a plan.* If only she knew what it was.

CHAPTER FIVE

"He did what?" Ella's blue eyes widened as she stared at Belle, the disbelief more than evident in her expression and mirrored in her friend's.

With a feeling of defeat, Belle shook her head, letting her fingers play with the edge of the saucer on which her cup of coffee was resting, still untouched. She noticed that her hands were trembling. Even after three days, she hadn't been able to come to terms with it herself. Just the thought of having lost the farm made her ill at ease. So she understood Ella's surprise; she felt the same way as her friend. "That's right. *Daed* sold the farm to Adam."

"Sold it?"

Belle sighed as she nodded her head in affirmation. "Sold it."

"To . . . Adam Hershberger?" Ella asked, as if making certain she had heard her friend correctly.

"Ja."

"The man who lives in that isolated place north of town?"

Somehow Belle managed to smile. "I know of no other Hershbergers in the area, Ella."

"*Ach!* This is right terrible." Ella pushed away her own cup and saucer as if too disgusted to even drink her coffee. The color had drained from her cheeks. "The farm is gone?"

Just hearing the words spoken from Ella's lips hurt Belle's ears. It was too painful to fathom, but she knew that it was time to accept the facts. "So it appears."

"Oh, Belle." Tears welled up in Ella's eyes. "You simply cannot move away."

"We are. We're to pack and leave in two weeks."

Ella gasped. "Two weeks? Why! You've been there almost twenty years!"

"Fifteen years."

"Your *maem* died on that farm. You grew up on that farm. Your family has years and years of memories of living on that farm. And these are things you can't pack!" A tear fell from Ella's eyes, trickling down her left cheek. Belle wondered if she was remembering the loss of her own mother, just a few short years after Belle's. Perhaps that was one of the reasons they had become such *gut* friends. And then, of course, their friend Sadie Whitaker had lost her mother, too. They were a trio of motherless girls who had leaned on one another for support during their youth. But there had always been an extra-special bond between Ella and Belle, perhaps because they lived closer to each other and, therefore, spent more time together. Or perhaps it was that they both had to work twice as hard as other girls to make up for the flaws of their respective families. While they really never talked of the latter, it was something they knew only too well about each other.

The front door opened, and Ella's stepmother marched into the room. There was a fierce look of determination on her face as she glanced around until her eyes landed on Belle. "Ah, Belle! I was hoping to find you here," she said as she crossed the room. "What is this I hear? Moving!"

Slowly, Belle nodded her head. "*Ja,* you heard correctly."

"Ella, go make me some tea," she commanded as she sat in the chair at the head of the table. "And is it also true that Adam Hershberger bought the farm?"

"*Ja.* That's true, too."

Linda shook her head, clearly upset by

the confirmation of this news. "Outrageous, that man! We're supposed to help one another, not steal one anothers' properties and leave families homeless!"

Belle gave a weak smile. How quickly stories changed when passed along the Amish grapevine. "He didn't really . . . *steal* the property."

But clearly Linda was not listening. "That Adam. Now what on earth would he want with your *daed*'s farm anyway? He has his own property, doesn't he now? Surely that's enough for one man to handle. Now, to steal your farm? Such a terrible thing."

Despite being distraught at having to move, Belle felt compelled to correct Linda. "Linda, *Daed* sold it of his own volition."

Linda gave a disapproving grimace as she clicked her tongue: *tsk, tsk, tsk.* "Your *daed*'s a might too proud, I'd say. He should've come to the church for help. But he never asked!"

There was nothing that Belle could say to argue Linda's point. On numerous occasions, she had encouraged her father to do just that: ask for help. The *g'may* always took care of their own. Such was the way of the Amish. But he *was* too ashamed. While Belle understood his reluctance to ask for help, she wished that he hadn't been so determined to make it on his own when it was evident that he couldn't. If that was pride, she better understood the proverb "pride goeth before a fall."

Of course, Belle also realized that Linda and several of the other members of the community *could* have helped her father by supporting his efforts. Why, Linda could have carried one of his grills at her store. Helping a man earn a living was certainly much better than forcing him to ask for financial assistance, something that would make the recipient feel beholden to the givers and the givers feel self-satisfied for helping out. Certainly pride could work both ways, she pondered.

But she would never say such a thing.

"Too late now." Belle sighed. "We're to vacate in two weeks."

"Two weeks!" Another *tsk, tsk, tsk.* "I have half a mind to go speak to the bishop! Stealing your farm! Now," she said, pointing a finger directly at Belle, "this is nothing short of a shunning offense if I ever heard one." She barely looked at Ella as her stepdaughter set the cup of tea before her. "Reprehensible, that's what this is!"

"Something has to be done," Ella said as she sat down next to Belle. "You can't move."

But Belle knew that they could and, apparently, would have to do just that. "I can't imagine leaving for another town, I'll admit it," she replied. They'd have to start over in a new place, with new people. Certainly her sisters would need to work, and that was not something she anticipated being a pleasant adjustment for them or for her or her *daed*.

Linda sipped at her tea and practically spat it out. "Ella! This tastes like swill!" She shoved the cup and saucer across the table. The liquid spilled onto the table, but Linda made no move to clean it. "Honestly! You'll never attract a husband if you can't even make a *gut* cup of tea or coffee!"

Belle averted her eyes, embarrassed about how Linda spoke to her friend. But Ella appeared unfazed as she apologized to her stepmother and then hurried to make a new cup of tea. Belle knew far too well that this was not the first time Ella had been spoken to in such a manner.

"Now, Belle," Linda said, leaning forward, apparently unaware of her guest's discomfort. "There is a simple solution, I'm sure."

"Oh?"

Linda nodded. "*Ja.* If the bishop speaks to this Adam . . . Talks some sense into him. I understand he goes out that way from time to time. And, like I said, what on earth would Hershberger want with another farm anyway? He has no one to pass along his own farm to. Now he wants another? How will one man manage both places with no help?"

As Linda spoke, Belle felt the tightness return to her chest. *Of course!* she thought. Linda was right. Someone needed to talk to Adam Hershberger and explain the situation. Certainly he did not know the true depths of the Beiler family's despair. The bishop might bring it up with Adam, but only a Beiler could explain their true situation. Besides, the bishop would surely not go speak with Adam unless her father requested it, and Belle knew that such an outcome was highly unlikely.

So, who better to speak to Adam than herself? She pondered the idea.

She would go to his farm and talk to him. Explain to him how all of this was a big mistake. As Linda said, there was no logic to his acquiring their farm. From what little she knew about Adam, the Hershberger farm was more than large enough for multiple Amish families. And to think that he farmed it all on his own!

Another idea popped into her head.

Living all alone, why! Adam must need

help in the house. She had never heard of anyone working on his farm or at the house. It must be terribly neglected. She could clean the house and cook some of his meals. Yes, Belle would approach him with a barter arrangement: let them continue to live in their house in exchange for her help. It wasn't as if her father *wanted* to farm anyway. Even Adam Hershberger couldn't argue the logic behind her idea. Of course, Belle did not want to be around Adam any more than the next person did. But she would make that sacrifice if it meant her family did not have to move.

With this realization, her heart began to beat rapidly and she became excited. It was actually a fine solution all the way around for her and her family. If the Beilers could actually live rent-free and have use of the workshop while Adam did whatever he wanted with the land, everyone would win. Her father wouldn't have to worry about a mortgage or paying property taxes! With Belle helping Adam, her sisters would have no choice but to start helping out more around the house, and that would humble them, perhaps enough to finally attract husbands!

She jumped to her feet.

"Oh, Ella! Linda!" Her cheeks were

flushed with excitement. She didn't want to share the idea with them just yet for fear that they might try to talk her out of visiting Adam. His reputation as a gruff, unkind man was common knowledge. But that did not matter to Belle, and even made her more determined than ever to speak to him. "I . . . I have to go! I forgot about something important that I must do!"

Ella looked bewildered. "But you only just got here a few minutes ago!"

"I'm so sorry, Ella." And she meant it. Belle could sense Ella's disappointment. She knew that Ella enjoyed not only her company but also the fact that Linda treated her a little better when Belle was around. As soon as Belle left, Linda would begin barking out orders and a whole list of chores for Ella to finish. But Belle couldn't help that. Not today, anyway. She had her own family woes to worry about. "Truly, I must excuse myself."

A few minutes later, she walked alone down the road, role-playing out loud what she would say to Adam to try to convince him. As she walked, her bare feet kicking up dust along the way, she extended her hand as if he stood right before her. "Good afternoon, Adam. My name is Belle," she said aloud and forced a smile. "And I'd like to discuss some business with you."

Nee, she thought. That sounds too professional and not friendly enough.

"My name is Belle Beiler and I want to talk to you about my father's farm . . ."

Nee! Too aggressive.

"Hello, Adam. I'm Belle Beiler. *Mayhaps* we could help each other with a troubling situation?"

Hmm. *That* sounded softer. More pleasant. Belle wondered if it might actually do the trick. Even intrigue him enough to engage in a useful discussion with her. Besides, she argued with herself, just because he preferred to isolate himself didn't mean that he was as disagreeable as Linda Troyer and some of the other members of her community claimed.

She continued talking to herself, trying to find the perfect opening that would pique Adam Hershberger's interest without sounding too pushy or aggressive. The right tone of voice. Despite what Linda Troyer thought, Adam had done nothing wrong in purchasing the Beiler farm. Pointing the finger at him might make her feel better, but Belle knew the truth. The blame for the loss of the farm lay on one person's — and *only* one person's — shoulders: her own father's. However, she suspected that the only person who could get Adam to improve the situation was herself.

With a new spring to her step, Belle hurried away from town. When she approached her father's farm, she quickly passed the driveway, hoping that no one would see her. Of course, neither one of her sisters was outside, and her father was probably in his workshop, lamenting the loss of the property and his inability to provide for his small family.

Dear Lord, Belle found herself praying, *please guide my tongue as surely as you are now guiding my feet down this road. I know that this is the solution to our problems. Now if only I can speak the right words to appeal to Adam's sense of compassion. Please help me find the right words, Lord.* Her prayer grew stronger with each step she took, and she knew that it was God, not her own feet, that carried her down the road to Adam Hershberger's farm.

CHAPTER SIX

Belle stood at the door, her hand aching from knocking against the weathered wood that was so in need of a fresh coat of paint. Could it be that Adam, too, was a tad short on motivation for maintenance? It was not a large home by any standards, at least not from the outside. It appeared to be a typical older farmhouse with a porch across the front and, from the looks of it, another, smaller porch just outside the back door. She had seen it as she approached the house from the road.

The front of the house had two windows on both the first and second floors. The front door wasn't in the middle of the house but was set a bit off center to the left. She wasn't sure if its strange placement was by design or because of a later addition to the floor plan.

Taking a few steps toward the first window, she peeked through the glass. It was so dirty that she had to rub a spot with the back of her hand in order to see inside. There was a sitting room with a sofa, a rocking chair, and a small table. The room was small and probably where the family would gather in the evening . . . That is *if* other people lived at the Hershberger farm. But Belle knew that Adam lived alone, and she was convinced that this room hadn't been used in years.

Turning back to study the front yard, she noticed that it was littered with garbage, old damaged furniture, and broken tools. It resembled more of a junkyard than an Amish farm, or at least, any Amish farm that Belle had ever seen.

As far as the landscape, everything appeared overgrown: bushes, trees, weeds. If there were any former flower beds, Belle couldn't distinguish where they might have been. She could, however, just barely make out the remnants of a vegetable garden. Overgrown, of course, as everything else was.

Just beyond the house was a patch of pine trees that hid most of the dairy barn. It was larger than any of the barns she had seen on the farms in Echo Creek. And the cows, a mixture of Holsteins and Jerseys, wandered through the plush green fields that were visible behind the barn, beyond another patch of pine trees. At least the animals appeared to be healthy and cared for.

Sighing, Belle turned and knocked one last time at the door, hoping that someone would answer, but to no avail. There was still no answer.

Boldly, she reached for the doorknob, her fingers touching the worn metal that didn't even have a lock in it. Instead, there was a large, old-fashioned keyhole just beneath it. With one simple turn of the knob, the door swung open, and she took a step backward as if half expecting someone to be standing there ready to admonish her for entering the house.

But the room was empty. In fact, the entire entrance room was empty. Of furniture, at least. But there were crates on the floor, each one filled with sticks and logs, stacked in such a way as to create a path down a long hallway beside the staircase that led to the second floor. The hardwood floor was littered with leaves and dirt. Clearly the house had not been cleaned in years. The odor of time and neglect struck her nostrils and she shut her eyes, repulsed that her father had actually spent the night at such a house.

"Hello?"

No one responded.

Cautiously, as if the floorboards might crack beneath her feet, Belle stepped inside. She tried to breathe through her mouth, but the air tasted as bad as it smelled. She called out again and was answered with silence.

She followed the path down the hallway. With the windows facing the north and south, the house was dark. She saw no lanterns to light, even when she stepped into the kitchen. If she had been appalled at first at the condition of the entrance room, she was even more horrified when she entered the kitchen. Not only was it dirty and congested with crates of timber but the counter was covered with dirty dishes and rubbish. The sink dripped, the noise of each drop reverberating in the silence of the room. She thought she saw a small gray mouse scurry across the back of the stove, which had clearly not been used for cooking in such a long time that there was no fear in the mouse at making such a bold journey.

The back door was open, and the screen door, meant to keep out flies and other small creatures, banged gently in the soft breeze that had followed the storm. She stepped over to it, careful not to trip on a bag of garbage on the floor. She thought she heard a noise coming from the stable, which was in between the house and the dairy barn. Taking a deep breath, she left the house and hurried across the yard toward the small building where she imagined the horse and mules resided.

Upon entering the barn, she let her eyes adjust to the darkness. Despite the fact that all of the windows were unopened, everything appeared immaculate. Fresh hay was on the floor, the walls were cleared of the typical cobwebs that adorned corners and ceiling, and few flies bothered her.

"Hello?" she called out one last time. A horse nickered in response. She walked over to the stall and reached out to touch its nose. "Where is your owner?"

"People don't *own* animals!"

The deep voice startled her, and Belle spun around, taking a step away so that her back pressed against the stall door. She could see no one, yet she knew that she had heard a man's voice.

From the shadows, she saw movement.

"Adam?"

"Indeed."

She squinted. Just barely could she make out his form. "I . . . I'm Belle Beiler.

Melvin's *dochder.*"

A low sound that resembled a growl came from the direction where he stood. "I know who you are." His answer surprised her. Why on earth should he know her? "What I don't know is why you are trespassing on my farm."

She took a deep breath and stepped forward, peering in his direction but unable to catch a glimpse of his face. "I . . . I've come to talk to you about my father's farm."

"You mean my farm now, *ja*?"

Swallowing, she took another step toward the dark corner his voice came from. "We have two weeks, *ja*? It's still ours until then."

"Ten days to be exact."

Was he truly so eager to see her small family displaced that he was already counting the days? "About that . . ."

Another growl.

She felt her knees shake, and she wished that she was still standing by the stall for support. But she knew that she needed to be strong, to be assertive with this stranger in order to help her family. "There must be some other way. Surely you must not have realized that you're taking our home." No response. "We will be homeless. Perhaps you didn't realize that my *daed* has three *dochders* at home. That we've lived there for

84

almost twenty years."

"Fifteen years." His rebuttal startled her almost as much as his presence.

"*Ja*, fifteen years." How had he known the exact period of time? Swallowing, she stood there in the center of the aisle and waited for him to appear. It was the proper thing for someone to do. But he remained hidden.

"What is it exactly that you want from *me*, Belle Beiler?" There was a mocking undercurrent in his deep voice.

"I . . . I wanted to talk to you about alternatives. Surely, in your heart, you don't wish to see us homeless."

This time, the noise sounded like a scornful laugh. "You think you know my heart?"

Embarrassed, Belle felt her cheeks heat up. She was glad for the darkness so that he could not see her blush.

"You know nothing about me."

"That's not true!" She pressed her lips together, searching for the right words. How could she reach this man? This isolated hermit of a man who did not interact with people? There must be something she could say to reach him. "I . . . I know that you were badly wounded. I know that you hide on your farm, concealing yourself from others. But I also know that you're a person and people *feel.* People have emotions. So I implore you to consider how we feel being chased from our only home."

"I care as much for other people's feelings as they have chosen to care for mine."

"That's not very Christian," she said too quickly, and instantly regretted her tone, which sounded as if she were scolding him. Quickly, she tried to regroup. Arguing with him would get her nowhere. "How could you want us to be homeless? Or anyone, for that matter."

"I want that farm."

She wished she had the courage to ask him the one question that lingered on her lips: *Why?* Instead, she lifted her chin. "Surely there is something else you might want. You have this farm, after all. And . . ." She looked around. Outside the stable's open door, she could see piles of garbage, trash that had accumulated over the years. Weeds grew through what appeared to have once been landscaping. She could almost imagine that, many years ago, the Hershberger farm had been perfectly manicured, tended with love. Clearly that was no longer the case. "With the exception of the stable, it seems you have more work than you can handle."

He remained silent for a long moment.

This time, Belle was determined to follow his example. She, too, refused to speak, choosing to wait for him to say something of his own accord.

A few minutes passed, the two of them standing there — Belle where he could see her, Adam where she could not see him.

"Something else that I might want?" he said at last, repeating her words as if they left a bitter taste in his mouth. "From what I understand, there is nothing else for your *daed* to give. He has a mortgage, little equity, and nothing saved. What else could your father give me that is as valuable as that farm?"

Belle shut her eyes, saying a quick prayer to God that she would say the right thing. *Please Lord, help me to know your will.* A gust of wind blew through the yard, and she heard the screen door to the house slam against the door frame. Quickly, she opened her eyes. "A housekeeper. You need a house-keeper. *Mayhaps* I . . . I might volunteer to clean your *haus* in exchange for letting us remain on the farm, where we always have lived."

The dark outline of the man appeared to toss back his head, and she heard him laugh. His reaction struck her as strange. What person could possibly enjoy living in such squalor? Clearly he understood about keeping things organized and tidy. The horse and mule stable was well maintained and clean. And while not all Amish women valued cleanliness of the home in the same way, all the Amish knew that taking care of one's property, including the home, was a tribute to God.

"Clean the *haus*?" he repeated when he finally stopped laughing. "Why on earth would *that* be something of interest to me?"

"Your *haus* is a disaster." She hadn't meant to speak her mind in such a forward manner. But as soon as the words slipped past her lips, she was glad. "A disgrace."

That noise, so low and grumbly, escaped his throat. For a moment, she feared that she had gone too far. Insulting a complete stranger was not something she had ever done before, and for a second, she considered apologizing.

But he spoke first, with a contemplative "I see." She heard him shift his weight, his feet shuffling against some scattered straw on the ground. "You're rather opinionated about my property, considering you were not invited to my farm, never mind to explore my *haus*."

She saw him move about in the shadow, as if pacing for just a few steps. When he stopped, she realized that his back was turned to her so that, even if there were light, she could not see his face.

"There is one thing I lack that your *daed* could give to me," he said at last. He turned his body just enough so that she could see his outline. She realized how tall he was, and his body appeared to be in good shape. Farmwork would do that to a man. But she wished — oh, how she wished! — that he would step closer to her. "Something far more valuable than the farm, something that would be worthy of my solving your family's financial problems."

Belle could hardly believe her ears, and immediately she brightened at Adam's sudden change of heart. Prior to that moment, she had feared that all was lost, that Adam would force her family from their home. Despite her previous dread of approaching him, she had convinced herself that, deep down, he must be a truly good man. Now she knew that she had been led by God to reach out to Adam in order to help her family. Surely God must have touched the man's cold heart. *Thank you, Lord!* she said to herself. *I knew that I should trust you.*

"What is it?" she asked Adam, eager to hear what solution he had for her. "I'm sure and certain my *daed* will oblige!"

He chuckled under his breath. "Indeed, but will *you*?"

"Oh, *ja*! Anything. Anything for the farm."

"If you are so certain," he said, "then I imagine you will readily agree."

Belle's excitement was suddenly dampened. "It's not up to me to agree on behalf of my *daed*. But I'm certain he will, *ja*."

"*Nee*, not your *daed*. It may be his possession, but it is yours to agree to actually give."

Now she was confused. "Me?" She frowned. "What is it you want from my *daed*?"

This time, he spun around and slowly extended his arm out of the shadow as he pointed his finger directly at her. "A wife."

The color drained from her face, and she felt her heart beat faster. *Surely he must be teasing,* she told herself, despite suspecting that Adam Hershberger was not the sort of man who jested with others. Yet, at the same time, she couldn't imagine that he would possibly think any woman would agree to such an arrangement.

"A wife?" she repeated. "Are . . . are you asking me to marry you?" His silence answered her question. Suddenly, she felt as if she were floating above her body, watching the scene unfold from someone else's per-

90

spective. "Why would you want a wife?" she managed to ask in a soft, frightened voice. "Why would you want to marry me?"

He wasted no time in answering her. "I need a son. Someone to leave the farm to."

Of course, she thought. He had no false notions of romance or marital partnership, just the need of a broodmare to produce an offspring. "I find your offer highly offensive," she snapped.

She could see that he shrugged his shoulders. "*Mayhaps,* but the decision is yours to make. I own the farm. If, however, you marry me, I will sign it over to your *daed* after the birth of our first son, as long as he inherits the farm."

"First son?" She almost laughed, not believing that she was engaged in such a discussion. "You almost suggest there might be a second!"

He cleared his throat.

"I would never barter myself for such an outrageous exchange!" she added. While she had not been courted by anyone yet and, unlike her sisters, had no current interest in a husband, she wanted to marry for love and to someone who would make her happy. Adam's proposal was preposterous. She would have married Gabriel if she were inclined to sacrifice herself in such a manner.

"Then we have nothing further to discuss. I win either way. Your family, however, does not."

Just as suddenly as he had appeared, Adam vanished. She saw his dark form slip through a narrow, dark doorway that she had not noticed earlier.

Left alone in the stable, Belle turned around and covered her face with her hands. How could God have led her to this? *No, she yelled to herself. It wasn't God but Satan. Surely Satan's hand was behind this, wanting her to make a deal with a man she not only didn't know but had never even clearly seen!*

And yet, something tugged inside of her. If she refused his offer, her family would have to move. Her father would have to start over again, as would the rest of them. He'd have to leave his workshop. They'd have to relocate somewhere else and, most likely, without any furniture or provisions for the winter. They'd live off of whatever money her father managed to keep from the sale of the farm after paying off his debts. She had no idea how much he owed. She only knew that paying their bills had grown increasingly difficult over the past few years. Most likely, both of her sisters would have to work in a store or hire themselves out to keep house, something neither of them was very good at doing. Without any friends or history in the new town, it would be hard for them to find husbands, and that would create more stress on the family.

Say yes, a voice whispered inside of her.

For a moment, she thought she had heard someone actually speak those words. She lowered her hands and looked around, but she was alone.

How could she say yes? Could God actually approve of such a sacrifice? Or was she making a deal with Satan? She wished she knew.

And then the wind stopped and the sun broke through the clouds. A ray of light shone through the open door of the stable and covered her in a golden light. She turned to face it and took a step so that her entire body was bathed in its warmth.

Say yes, the voice within her whispered again.

She took a deep breath. *Dear Lord,* she prayed, *please tell me if this is a sign. Is this Your will?*

From outside the door, she saw a yellow finch flying. It landed on the end of an old clothesline, or what remained of it. The wheel looked rusty, the rope long gone. Rather than flutter away, the finch opened its beak and began to sing. The sweet, sharp notes seemed to echo in her head.

"I'll do it," she whispered. The yellow finch appeared to look at her, as if it had understood her words. And then it took off, as if it had accomplished its mission. In a louder voice, Belle called out, "I'll do it! I'll agree to marry you if you let my family stay on the farm."

For a few long, drawn-out seconds, she heard nothing. If he didn't respond, she would hurry out of the stable and down the lane. She'd let her feet carry her far away from Adam Hershberger's dreadful farm, and she'd forget that all of this ever happened. But as luck would have it, he had heard her.

"Two weeks from Thursday. We'll be married then."

His words, so quick to confirm their agreement, sent a chill through her. Two weeks? How could she possibly prepare herself for marrying anyone, never-mind a man like Adam Hershberger, in just two weeks? She glanced over her shoulder in the direction from which his voice came. "It's not even wedding season yet," she said, her voice trembling.

"Two weeks." He spoke with such firmness that Belle knew there was nothing she could say to change his mind. "Otherwise, your family will be removed from my farm."

And then he was gone, this time for good.

With a heavy heart, Belle turned away. It was done. She had saved her father's farm, but at what expense? Her happiness was forfeit, that was for certain. But she had given her sisters a chance to find husbands and her father a chance to re-create his prototype. Perhaps that was all anyone ever needed, including Adam . . . a chance.

Slowly, she began to walk down the road, each step feeling as if she were approaching her doom. She had no idea how she would tell her father or what he would say. The only thing she knew was that she had given her word, and, as her father had declared before her, her word was not something she would break.

CHAPTER SEVEN

By Sunday, Belle still had not found the courage to tell her father about her arrangement with Adam. Every time she tried to gather the strength of will, she broke down in tears and left the room. She was certain that her father believed she was upset about the family having to leave. Both of her sisters behaved in a similar manner, wandering aimlessly through a house that no longer belonged to them. Only Belle, however, realized that it could still belong to them, but only as long as she married Adam Hershberger. And *that* thought would send her off to her room in another fit of tears, something she found increasingly difficult to avert.

If she had hoped she would be able to keep her secret to herself for even a few more days, she found out soon enough that she had been mistaken.

No sooner had they arrived at the Riehls'

farm for Sunday worship than she saw the bishop leaving the group of men to approach her. It was only on very rare occasions that she interacted with him, not because he was standoffish or uninterested, but merely because she simply did not have any reason to converse with him. He had been the bishop of their church district for as long as she could remember. He had even presided over her baptism two years earlier.

Now, as he asked to speak to her, she realized that he would soon be presiding over something else in her life, something second in importance only to her baptismal vows: her wedding.

"I had the strangest visitor to my *haus* just last evening," the bishop started somberly. His dark eyes stared at her from behind his small wire-framed glasses, the lenses smudged with fingerprints. There was no mistaking the intent expression on his face. "You can hardly imagine my surprise, Belle, when Adam Hershberger stood on my doorstep to inform me that I should announce his wedding banns after worship today." He reached up and tugged lightly at the end of his white beard, which hung past the first button on his shirt. That simple gesture gave Belle the impression that the bishop felt uncomfortable. "Is it true, then?"

Belle licked her lips and glanced around, nervous that her father might overhear. If the bishop announced the banns, her father was much less likely to put a stop to her betrothal to Adam. Then she would not have to face her father and tell him that she was getting married. He would learn it at the same time as the rest of the community. "*Ja,* Bishop, it's true."

The bishop blinked his eyes as he studied her face. "Adam Hershberger?"

She nodded.

"Are you sure about this?" He paused and placed his hand upon her arm. "How well do you know this man?"

Belle lifted her chin and refused to look away from the bishop. How could she possibly hide the truth from him? He had known her for most of her life. His role was to lead the church district in both earthly and divine matters. Yet what did he really know about her? How often had they interacted besides a few conversations throughout the year and biblical teachings during her instructional period, prior to her taking the kneeling vow when she officially joined the church? That was it. She cleared her throat and said, "I know him well enough that I agreed to marry him."

Slowly, the bishop shook his head. "Does

this have anything to do with your *daed* selling the farm? If it does, I don't have to announce the banns, and we can go to Adam together to discuss the matter."

But Belle remained firm. "I'd prefer that you just announce the banns, Bishop."

The bishop exhaled and gave her a sorrowful look. "I don't think you know what you're getting into, Annabelle."

"*Mayhaps* not, but I believe God has led me to this decision."

After a long, thoughtful moment, the bishop finally nodded. "Who am I to question that?" But there was no joy in his eyes.

At the end of the three-hour worship service, the bishop stood before the congregation, which was divided in the middle so that the women sat on the right and the men on the left. He took a few steps, pacing the floor in much the same manner that Adam had done when Belle spoke with him. She took a deep breath and stared straight ahead, focusing on nothing but the space on the wall behind the bishop. She heard him clear his throat and begin to speak, declaring that he had a wedding announcement. A slight murmur broke out among the congregation, but it was quickly silenced.

Belle knew what everyone was thinking:

who needed to marry so quickly outside of wedding season? It didn't happen often, and when it did, there was always speculation. Of a bad kind. Belle knew only too well that, once the bishop mentioned her name as the woman marrying Adam, the other members of the *g'may* would begin to wonder if she might be in a family way. What else they might think, Belle had no idea. But she didn't want to see any of them when they turned to look at her, surprised at the fact that not only was she marrying, but that she was marrying the one man in Echo Creek that people thought would never marry at all.

"Annabelle Beiler and . . ."

The murmur began, and Belle could feel the eyes as people turned to watch her. She forced herself to continue looking straight ahead.

". . . Adam Hershberger will be married on Thursday next."

A collective gasp came from the women around her. Belle remained stoic, even though she felt her pulse quicken and her palms begin to feel clammy. She realized that everyone was silent . . . and still staring at her. Despite focusing on the wall straight ahead, out of the corner of her eye Belle saw her two sisters leaning forward to try to catch her attention. But Belle remained composed and determined to show no emotion.

Immediately after the service ended, the men began transforming the benches used during worship into tables, carefully slipping the legs of each bench into a trestle while the younger boys collected the *Ausbund* hymnbooks to store in a crate for the next service in two weeks. Belle avoided the women as she went about her task of setting the table for the fellowship meal. But she felt the furtive glances from both the older women and her peers.

At first, no one approached her, and she thought that she might escape without having to answer questions. She noticed that Ella and Sadie stood near the kitchen, whispering to each other and looking in her direction. Belle made certain to avoid working near them. But just as she was finishing setting the plates on the table for the men, her sisters caught up to her.

"What is this news?" Verna hissed. "Adam Hershberger? Are you *ferhoodled*?"

Susie chimed in. "Belle, what have you done?"

Verna glanced around. "We'll be the laughing-stock of the church! Oh, what will Jacob think now?"

Susie elbowed her sister and shushed her.

Biting her lower lip, Belle willed herself not to succumb to the tears that threatened to trickle down her cheeks. "I'm doing what must be done," she replied, her voice soft and trembling. "It's the only way to keep the farm."

"The farm?" Verna practically spat out the two words. "You're going to become Adam's *fraa* so that we can stay on the farm?"

"Oh, Belle."

She met Susie's gaze, surprised at the concern in her sister's expression. She, too, seemed to be having difficulty controlling her tears. "It will be all right," Belle said, forcing a small smile that she knew fell far short of appearing genuine. "We all have to make sacrifices in life, I reckon."

"But . . . Adam? Adam Hershberger?" She said his full name with such disdain that Belle cringed. "Why him? Why didn't you go to Gabriel?"

Belle shook her head, wanting to lower her eyes but refusing to give anyone a reason to doubt her decision. "Gabriel didn't buy *Daed*'s farm, *Schwester*. Adam did."

She felt a hand on her arm and turned to see her father standing there. The color had drained from his face, and his eyes, wide and sad, studied her face.

"Belle," he said when he managed to find his voice. "Do you know what you are doing?"

She nodded her head, just once.

"You . . . you don't have to do this. You can change your mind."

While his words were meant to soothe her, she knew that she had to follow through with her promise to wed Adam. To go back on her word after the banns were formally announced was unheard-of, even if she was marrying Adam Hershberger. It would reflect negatively on her and her family. After all, Scripture was clear on keeping promises made: "That which is gone out of thy lips thou shalt keep and perform."

"*Nee, Daed.* I cannot, and you know that. You yourself said that going back on a pledge is akin to lying."

Melvin remained silent, his eyes filling with tears.

"We've a lot of planning to do," Belle said, hoping that her voice sounded at least a little cheerful. But even she knew that her words sounded unconvincing and lacked enthusiasm. "Only eleven days until my wedding."

Her father looked away.

Verna and Susie simply stared at her, no words forming on their lips.

"I reckon I should speak to the bishop's *fraa, ja*? She'll know what needs to be done." Belle walked away from her family, not truly eager to approach the bishop's wife but wanting to remove herself with good reason. She knew that, if she stood with her father and sisters, she would risk crying once again. And crying after her wedding was announced would add more fuel to the fire of gossip that was, undoubtedly, burning bright.

In preparation for the fellowship meal, the women were busy in the kitchen, dishing food onto plates and serving trays. It was always a simple meal: pickles, chow chow, bread, jam, cold cuts, small pretzels, and, on rare occasions, cup cheese. Dessert always consisted of two different kinds of pies. But Belle wasn't hungry.

Several of the older women caught her eye and smiled. Only the smiles lacked true joy, not like the smiles they gave to other brides. These were compassionate smiles. In fact, it was unusual for the bride to even be at the service when her wedding was announced. Usually she spent the morning with her fiancé, cooking him a meal and sharing time together alone at her parents' house. Clearly *that* was not part of Adam's plan.

Belle tried to join the women, but no one

directed her to help. So she wandered over to the tables where they would soon sit down for the meal.

Ella and Sadie made their way to her side. "What on earth, Belle?" Ella said in a soft voice so that no one could overhear.

"I had to do it," Belle whispered back. "If I marry him, he won't make my family leave the house. And after there's a son . . ."

Sadie bit her lower lip and widened her big brown eyes. "A son?"

Belle nodded. ". . . then he will give the title to the farm back to my *daed.*"

"Oh, help!" Nervously Ella scanned the room. "My *maem* will have quite a lot to say about this turn of events. I'll never hear the end of it, I'm sure and certain."

Belle didn't doubt for a minute that Ella's stepmother would corner her at some point. Linda's fascination with Adam, as well as her very vocal opinions, was well-known to Belle. "Perhaps I should leave," she said, more to herself than to her friends. But once the words were spoken, Belle saw both Ella and Sadie nod their heads.

"Let's go walk a spell," Sadie offered, putting her hand on Belle's arm. "Fresh air might do us all some good."

Quietly, they slipped through the door and made their way down the lane.

After they had put some distance between themselves and the Riehls' farmhouse, Sadie was the first to speak. "Please, Belle, you must reconsider. You don't love that man."

Ella quickly added her own thoughts. "Love him? Why, you don't even know him!"

But Belle stood her ground. "I've promised to marry him, and I cannot back out." She paused. "*Nee*, I *will not* back out."

"But he's —"

Turning to Ella, Belle frowned. "Disfigured? Is that what you thought to say?"

"Oh, Belle!" Ella's expression changed from concern to sorrow. "Would you think so little of me? *Nee*, I was going to say that he's such a recluse, and bad-tempered, too."

Embarrassed, Belle swallowed. "I'm sorry, Ella. I should've known you wouldn't say something so horrid."

Her friend acknowledged the apology with a soft smile.

"*Ja*, I know that he prefers a solitary life, but that doesn't mean he's a bad person. And bad-tempered? *Mayhaps* that's because so many people are so cruel to him." At least Belle *hoped* that was the reason. Truly no person could be as irritable and cantankerous as the community's whispered tales made Adam out to be.

Her friends, however, were not so easily convinced.

"I find this very sad," Sadie said, reaching up to brush aside a stray strand of her black hair. "Getting married for convenience, rather than love? That's not for me. Why, I can just look at my own *daed* and how he married so quickly after my *maem* passed away."

Ella concurred. "Mine, too."

Belle frowned. "But both of your *daeds* were happy when they remarried, *ja*?"

Sadie shrugged. "My *daed* isn't *un*happy. But she sure does rule the house. It's not a partnership like he had with *Maem.* And she sure is hard on me at times." Something dark passed over Sadie's face.

Partnership. That term evoked an image of a business transaction, which was a far cry from Sadie's declaration that she wanted to marry for love. In the long run, Belle thought, marriage was nothing more than a business relationship. And Belle knew that some people worked for bosses they did not especially like. Yet their professional business relationship did not necessarily suffer. While love was a fancy and fine concept, the foundation of many marriages did not rest on it. Instead, respect for the husband and faith in God were the true cornerstones to a good marriage. She knew that she had faith in God. If only she felt confident that she could learn to respect Adam as her husband, especially after experiencing his unprincipled method of obtaining a wife.

CHAPTER EIGHT

Four days went by after the banns were announced, and Belle heard nothing from Adam. At first, she didn't find that troubling. She threw herself into cleaning the house and writing letters to the people she was inviting to the wedding. But when Friday arrived, less than a week before her wedding, she knew that she needed to speak to him. It was, after all, his wedding, too. Typically, the man delivered the invitations and helped with decisions regarding the food.

But Belle was more than aware that her wedding was *not* a typical wedding.

Ever since the wedding banns were announced, her sisters had avoided speaking to her. On a few occasions, Belle caught them staring in her direction. But as soon as Belle turned around to confront them, they averted their eyes and hurried out of the room. Belle couldn't help but wonder what, exactly, they were thinking.

She suspected that Verna felt embarrassed, worried more about what other people would think, while Susie genuinely felt sorry for her. Regardless of their thoughts and feelings, Belle knew that their futures depended on her going through with this marriage.

As for her father, he walked around as if in a gray fog. Sometimes Belle thought she heard him mumbling to himself, but she couldn't make out the words. When she asked him what he was saying, he wandered away, his shoulders hunched over and his head hanging as he stared at the ground.

Belle understood how her family felt. She, too, felt as if there were a hollow pit growing inside of her chest. Most nights, she tossed and turned, frightened of leaving her family's home to live with Adam on his farm. Besides the fact that his house was a mess, Belle dreaded the isolation of living so far away from town. And with a complete stranger! If she thought about it too hard, she often began to cry and had to excuse herself, escaping to the outdoors, where she would walk down the road toward town, even though she had no intention of actually going there.

On Friday morning, her feet seemed to

have acquired a mind of their own, taking her to Ella's house. Belle found her friend in the garden, weeding between the rows of tomato plants, a basket full of ripe tomatoes at her feet. As Belle approached, Ella seemed to sense her presence and quickly looked up.

"Annabelle!" Quickly, Ella scrambled to her feet and hurried toward the fence. "Oh, Annabelle, you've been on my mind these past few days."

Belle tried to speak but couldn't. She swallowed the sob that threatened to burst from her throat and through her lips.

"*Kum*, Belle." Ella motioned toward the gate. "*Maem*'s working at the store, so we can talk. It looks like you could use an ear and shoulder."

Obediently, Belle followed her friend to the porch steps. Once they were situated on the bench near the front door, Belle turned toward Ella and began to cry. "Oh, Ella! What have I done?"

Ella wrapped her arm around Belle's shoulders. "Now, now, Belle."

But, once released, the tears wouldn't stop.

Ella rubbed Belle's shoulder and tried to soothe her. "You don't have to go through with this. You can tell the bishop that you've changed your mind. There's not a person in Echo Creek who would think twice about your backing out of this" — she hesitated as if searching for the proper word — "wedding."

"I can't," Belle whispered. She pulled back from Ella's embrace and wiped at her eyes. "You know that I have to do this. Otherwise my family . . . well, it's more than just selling the farm, Ella. If I refuse to marry Adam and he takes the farm, we'll be unable to buy another farm and quite possibly not even a house. Why, I fear we'll be homeless."

Ella gasped. With wide, shocked eyes, she stared at Belle. "Homeless? Whatever do you mean, Belle?"

Sniffling, Belle began to share the details of the story with Ella, leaving out the part about her sisters' anger that she would not marry Gabriel. Even if she might actually entertain that idea now, it was too late. "When *Daed* sold the property to Adam, he had no choice, you see. The mortgage is long overdue. *Daed* lost his horse. How can any Amish man make any living without a horse?" Belle accepted the tissue that Ella offered to her from her apron pocket. She dabbed at her eyes. "And his prototype. That's destroyed. Selling the farm must have been the last thing that *Daed* could do in order to help keep us together."

"That doesn't mean you'll be homeless, Belle. Surely your *daed* will find another place to live in another town, not that I want you moving at all. But that seems preferable to marrying that Adam Hershberger."

Belle shook her head. "*Nee,* Ella. Who knows how long we could live on whatever money *Daed* would have left from the sale of the farm? Given all of *Daed*'s bills, surely it wouldn't be much. Why, we'd just become a burden to any community that accepted us, and that's no way for an Amish family to live."

After a brief moment, as if she were dissecting Belle's words, Ella began to nod her head slowly. "I am beginning to make sense of this situation . . ."

"I didn't set out to marry Adam." Belle gushed those words as if desperate for her friend to understand. "I thought I might barter with him. I could houseclean for him, I thought. His place is a disaster. Boxes, crates, leaves, garbage. But he laughed." The sound of his laughter echoed in her mind. "He lives like an animal, Ella." She blew her nose into the damp tissue. "I tried to appeal to his better side."

Ella frowned.

"Exactly my thoughts," Belle exclaimed, reading her friend's mind. "However, I quickly learned that he simply does not have one!"

"So what happened next?"

Trying to remember, Belle stared off into the distance. In her memory, she only saw a dream, a surreal fog that masked what had truly come to pass. She had to think, to push herself to fight through the fog, to remember exactly what had happened. "He said he didn't want a housekeeper. But there was something he did want." Raising her eyes to stare at her friend, Belle felt a new round of tears threatening to fall. Somehow, she found the strength to whisper the words that she could barely believe he had uttered. "He wanted a *fraa,* someone to bear him a son."

Once again, Ella gasped.

"And I . . . I agreed."

The color drained from Ella's cheeks, and she reached out her hand to clutch Belle's. "You don't have to go through with it, Belle. You don't!"

Belle blinked her eyes as she nodded her head. But in her heart she knew that a promise made needed to be kept. Besides, to rescind her agreement to Adam's proposal, no matter how unorthodox it was, would only infuriate him further and ensure the loss of the family farm. "I do. I do have to go through with it for the sake of my family."

Ella held Belle's hands and shut her eyes. "Oh Belle. I'll pray for you. It seems that is all I can do."

"That is all I can ask for," Belle responded in a soft voice. "Prayers will be what get me through this . . . this arrangement."

The noise of an approaching buggy momentarily distracted Belle. It didn't sound like a regular buggy. Instead, it sounded heavier and with more rumbling of wheels. She looked up and squinted in the sunlight as she saw the dark, boxlike buggy nearing Ella's house. Immediately, she recognized it and gasped.

The buggy slowed down as it passed the white picket fence surrounding the Troyers' house. With the driver seated on the left side, it was hard to make out who it was. But Belle knew from the odd shape and shut doors that it was Adam.

When the buggy stopped, the black horse stomping its hooves impatiently as it tossed its neck, uncomfortable with the tight bit in its mouth, Belle turned to look at Ella. "I . . . I suppose he wants me to go to him."

Ella clung to her. "You don't have to go.

You're not married to him yet."

But Belle withdrew her hands and started to stand up. She wiped at her face in case her eyes were still damp. With a tilt of her chin and a deep breath, Belle tried to collect her wits. After the banns were read at church, she was as good as married. All that remained was the actual ceremony. "*Nee,* Ella. I must go to him. He is, after all, to be my husband."

Without another word, she turned and walked down the porch steps. Her bare feet padded against the slate walk as she headed toward the gate. She noticed that Adam made no move to open the door for her. Instead, he sat on the driver's side and waited. As she neared, she could see that he was watching her, his eyes barely visible as he peered at her from beneath his straw hat.

Rather than get into the buggy, she walked around it to his door. She stood there, trembling, as she silently prayed for God to give her strength to deal with this man, a stranger who had unexpectedly become her soon-to-be husband.

After several long, drawn-out moments, Adam slid the door back so that there was no barrier between them. "Get in," he said in a fierce voice. "I'll take you back to your *daed.*"

Obediently, Belle walked to the other side of the buggy and climbed up, pausing just a moment to slide back the door. Rather than shut it, she left it open. She needed the air to keep herself from feeling faint.

But Adam did not turn the buggy around. Instead, he continued driving toward town. Belle clung to the side of the open door, her face turned toward the road and not Adam as she tried not to bump against him in the small, confined area.

Outside the buggy, several people lingered near the Troyers' store and in front of the small post office. Echo Creek was a small town, and the center of it was the heart of the community. Not a day would pass without many of the residents walking up Main Street on the pretense of having an important errand when really they only wanted to see who else might be lingering along the sidewalks. As the buggy passed the people, each and every one of them stopped conversing and stared.

Belle was too aware that, because she had not shut the buggy door, they were all staring at her.

"I thought you were taking me to my *daed*'s," she said in a small voice.

He ignored her and continued driving the horse and buggy farther down Main Street to the small feed and grain store at the other end.

"Are . . . are you running errands, then?"

He glanced at her, but remained silent.

She licked her lower lip, too aware that her mouth was dry and her heart palpitating, the rapid beat making her chest feel tight and strained. A man on horseback rode past them, his eyes staring at her from behind round sunglasses. Belle recognized him as Jonah Miller, the young husband of Lillian, the former teacher at the Echo Creek school.

Embarrassed, Belle looked away.

"Have you changed your mind, then?"

Adam's words startled her, and she felt the color rush to her cheeks. Certainly he had seen her reaction to Jonah's inquisitive gaze. But Adam was still staring straight ahead, his face hidden beneath the wide brim of his hat. Even in such close proximity, she could not see the right side of his face. "Do you think yourself so disfigured that I would change my mind?"

A deep noise that sounded as though he were growling came from his throat. But he did not formulate a reply.

"I won't, you know." She sat back against the seat and stared out the front windshield. "Besides, our banns were announced after worship on Sunday last."

To her surprise, he responded right away. "I do know. I was there."

Upon hearing his words, Belle caught her breath. Adam had been there? Impossible. She knew everyone who had been at worship and did not see any strangers. Nor had anyone else mentioned that he was there. "You were not!"

He chuckled under his breath. "Are you sure of that, Belle?"

"Quite! I didn't see you, and others would certainly have mentioned it if you'd shown up!"

He glanced at her, just enough so that she could fully see the unmarked left side of his face. He appeared to be smiling. "I imagine they would have, wouldn't they? When the beast shows up, people talk. Adults and children alike, *ja*?"

The beast. Her mouth opened, just slightly, at the derogatory reference to himself. "You know about that, then? That they call you such things?"

Ignoring her question, Adam continued. "I was in the back of the room, where no one could see me. It wasn't the first time that I have attended worship service without being detected." Again, she thought she saw the side of his mouth twist into a smile, and she wondered if he was telling the truth. "You'd be surprised at how easy it is to live in shadows that most people don't even realize are there."

She lifted her chin. "Perhaps it's time to step out of the shadows, Adam. *Mayhaps* it's the mystery of who you are that creates the myth that entertains so many people."

"So many? Not all?"

"Not me."

"Ah!"

Belle waited, expecting him to comment further. But he did not.

Finally, she cleared her throat. "The invitations have been delivered." She paused and stared at the dark form across from her. "At least mine have, anyway. You should've been the one to deliver them, you know."

Silence.

"And . . . and I . . ."

"You what?" Another quick, stolen glance. "What vexes you?"

She pressed her lips together and wrung her hands on her lap. "I've never planned a wedding," she offered meekly. "I only know a little bit about what needs to be done."

"It's just a ceremony," he growled.

"It's supposed to be a celebration."

"Keep it small."

Once again, Belle felt the sting of tears in

her eyes. Amish weddings were normally happy occasions with well over three hundred people in attendance. When she was growing up, she had envisioned sitting at the *eck* table, the table set in the corner for the bride and groom to sit at while they greeted each of their guests during the long fellowship meal. In all of those years, not once had she dreamt of marrying a man whose face she had never seen.

"Small or not, *Daed* has no money to buy food, linens, or tableware. I'll borrow what I can, but . . ." She let her voice fade, the sentence unfinished. It wasn't unusual to borrow plates and utensils from the rest of the community. At regular-sized weddings, no family could have enough settings to accommodate the guests. Nowadays, many young couples took advantage of rental companies that would provide everything, including the cleanup. But Belle knew that her father could not afford that. He was already stretching his last bit of credit to host the wedding at their house, even if she abided by Adam's demand to keep it small.

"I see." He sounded contemplative and thoughtful, as if he were deep in thought. "Much more complicated than I expected."

Complicated? Under different circumstances, she might have laughed at the irony of his statement. But she refrained from doing so. Marriage alone was complicated. While she had few memories of her own parents' marriage, she had lived through seeing how complicated her father's life had become following his wife's death. She'd also seen how Ella Troyer and Sadie Whitaker's fathers suffered after their wives passed away. And she could see how other couples struggled. No matter how much people tried to wear a mask of serenity, the hidden undercurrents always peeked through.

But to hear Adam comment about complications? She knew that their marriage, one of convenience for him and survival for her, would prove to be the most complicated of all.

"I will take care of it," he said as he pulled the horse to a stop outside of the feed and grain store.

His vague proclamation caught her off guard. "Take care of what exactly?"

"Everything." He shifted his weight and slid open the door before he stepped down, turning his body just enough so that his right side remained out of her sight. "I will take care of everything."

For a moment, she stared at him as he stood by the open buggy door. It was her first real glimpse of the man that she knew so little about yet had promised to spend the rest of her life with, as his wife. She was surprised at how tall he was and at how broad his shoulders were. She suspected he was very strong. He wore a long-sleeved shirt, white and pressed. She wondered who did his laundry. Certainly not him! His dark hair was long and a deep mahogany brown, with loose curls hanging past his ears and neck. And she could see that his face, what she could glimpse of it, was a deep tan from having worked outside in the sun.

She sat in the buggy, watching as he walked into the store. His body filled the doorway before he passed through it. A shiver traveled down her spine and she wrapped her arms around herself. He would take care of the food? The linens? She had no idea what he meant, but she certainly did not want to push the issue. As it was, the wedding would be small. She had contemplated not even having a wedding, but she knew that the curiosity of the community needed to be quenched. Besides, as far as she knew, this would be her one and only wedding. She deserved to have something special on this day, even if she didn't feel like celebrating at all.

"Belle?"

She turned in the direction of the new

voice. "Gabriel?"

Hesitantly, he approached the buggy, his eyes staring directly into hers. "What are you doing in Hershberger's buggy?" He spoke in a hushed whisper.

His questioning caught her off guard. For a moment, she couldn't help but wonder: What *was* she doing in his buggy? And then, she realized that, in just a few short days, her place would be beside Adam for the rest of her life. "He's taking me home," she responded at last.

Gabriel, however, didn't seem to understand that she was in the buggy voluntarily. "Get down from there." He glanced over his shoulder toward the door and waved his hand. "Hurry, Belle."

"Gabriel . . ."

He reached for her hand and gently tugged. "*Kum,* Belle. Whatever is going on, I will help you."

Before she could fight back, she felt Gabriel release her hold as he fell backward onto the dry, dusty road. "Unhand her!" Adam hovered over Gabriel. His legs were spread apart and he appeared prepared to knock down Gabriel once again if he made a move in Belle's direction. She could only see Adam's back, but his muscles flexed underneath his white shirt. "You have no business speaking to my *fraa.*"

Gabriel scrambled backward, away from Adam. Belle knew that, from his vantage point, Gabriel could certainly see all of Adam's face. His expression told her that clearly enough. Getting to his feet, he glared at the man standing before him. "You . . . you . . ."

"What?" Adam took a step forward. "Monster? Beast? Say it and you'll be back on the ground."

"She's not your *fraa* yet," Gabriel spat out. He glanced in Belle's direction, pleading with her. "You cannot mean to do this!"

Belle turned her head away from Gabriel, knowing that she couldn't speak, for her words would give away her true feelings. She did not want to marry Adam Hershberger any more than she had wanted to encourage Gabriel. However, now she had no choice.

Adam waited until Gabriel had picked himself up and departed before he returned to the buggy and shut her door as if to protect her from any further altercations. Then he walked back to the driver's side door. When he climbed up and into the buggy, it jostled under his weight, and she rolled toward him, her arm brushing against him. Quickly, she scurried away, pressing her body against the door frame.

They rode away from town in silence, Belle staring at nothing as she quietly let the tears fall down her cheeks. Oh, what she would have done to turn back the hands of the clock, to have let Gabriel court her and perhaps even woo her to the altar, if that would have helped her father. But it was too late and she had made that promise. "When thou vowest a vow unto God, defer not to pay it; for he hath no pleasure in fools: pay that which thou hast vowed. Better is it that thou shouldest not vow, than that thou shouldest vow and not pay."

"You're crying."

It wasn't a question but an observation. Belle didn't turn to look at him as she nodded her head once. "*Ja*, I am."

He made a noise deep in his throat again, only this one was not rough or angry as it had been earlier. Instead, there was a hint of understanding. For the next fifteen minutes, he remained silent, until he stopped the buggy in front of her driveway.

"Go home, Belle." There was something soft about his voice when he spoke her name. He leaned forward, reaching across her lap as he slid open the door to the buggy. "Take advantage of this time to enjoy your family and friends before next Thursday." He paused. "Our wedding day."

At the mention of their wedding, she shuddered, realizing that she was not about to wake up and find that all of this was just a bad dream. Quickly, she jumped down from the buggy and steadied herself on the side of the road. She started to look up, trying to think of something to say to him, but he was already driving away, the noise of the wheels and the horse's hooves thudding on the road, too loud for him to hear any words that she might possibly have dreamed up.

She swallowed and turned toward the driveway that led to her father's house, the house that she had bought with the single commitment to marry and bear a son. Adam was right. She needed to take advantage of the little time that she had left before she became a stranger's wife in a completely new life.

CHAPTER NINE

"You don't have to do this."

Belle finished pinning her white apron over her light blue dress. She kept her expression unchanged at her sister's words. It was hard, however. Ever since the banns had been announced at church, she was growing increasingly tired of hearing those same six words. *You-don't-have-to-do-this.* From her family. From her friends. From anyone she met in the community on her increasingly infrequent trips to town. For the past few days, she had avoided leaving the house. Whenever she heard those words, she felt the urge to cry. But her tears had dried up, leaving her feeling as if she were merely walking through the motions of everyday life. She could no longer explain herself or her reasons. Instead, she adopted the typical Amish stance of silence rather than responding.

Usually that was enough to make people

stop speaking about the uncomfortable topic.

Not this time.

"Hand me my prayer *kapp*, please," she said to Verna. *"Danke."*

Carefully, Belle placed it on her head and, using a single straight pin, fastened it to the thin white hair band she wore over her hair to help keep her *kapp* from sliding off her head.

Glancing in the small mirror that hung on her bedroom wall, Belle noticed how pale her cheeks looked. She pinched them twice, hoping that they might regain some color. Her eyes were no longer red or puffy from crying. The dark circles had disappeared, even though she hadn't slept properly in almost two weeks. Despite all of this, she could hardly believe that today was her wedding day.

"I reckon I'm ready then."

"Belle . . ."

Turning to face Verna, she forced a smile. "Don't. Please."

From the open doorway, she could hear the people who were gathered downstairs. The women were in the house, while the men waited outside for the bishop and preachers to indicate that it was time to begin the service. Belle knew that she would have to join the women, to greet them with a holy kiss as they did before each church service, whether it was on a Sunday or at a wedding or a funeral.

"It's time to go downstairs, *ja?*" Belle took one quick look around the room. The next time she entered it, she would be Belle Hershberger, or, as the Amish typically referred to married women, Adam's Belle. She no longer shuddered at the thought. The days for regret were long past, even though she still felt as if she were living a bad dream.

When she walked down the stairs, she was surprised to see that the church benches were set up in the main kitchen and living area. One of the walls had been removed in order to accommodate all of the people. The women stood in the kitchen and became quiet when Belle appeared at the foot of the stairs. Ignoring the unusual silence, Belle straightened her shoulders and went about the task of greeting each woman with a simultaneous kiss and handshake. She avoided looking in their eyes as she hurried through the greeting line and assumed her place at the end. Fortunately, no one else arrived, so she did not have to greet any more women.

Slowly, the murmur of the women's voices

began to rise once again. Her nerves settled down and she tried to appear normal, if such a thing was possible. She wondered if Adam was outside with the men. She wondered if he, too, had greeted the men in the same manner she'd greeted the women. Or if he would wait to enter the house until all of the men were situated.

Ten minutes passed before the kitchen door opened and the bishop walked inside. He paused, glancing at the women until his eyes rested upon Belle. She watched as he walked along the waiting line of women, shaking each one's hand until he came to her. He held her hand in his for a moment longer than normal. She knew what he was thinking — those same six words that she despised hearing — but he said nothing, for which Belle was grateful.

The bishop and his preachers assumed their normal positions in the middle of the room, sitting on the chairs that faced the women's side. Immediately, the women began to walk single file to their places, the older ones first, followed by the younger women. This would be the last time that Belle would sit among the unmarried ones. After the wedding ceremony, she would join the younger married women, assuming her place among them as they sat upon the plain benches in order of their age.

After the women were seated, the kitchen door opened again and the men began to walk through the kitchen to sit on the benches behind the church leaders' chairs. When everyone was in their place, the men reached for their hats and removed them, placing them under their seats, the motion like a swift wave throughout the room.

Belle fought the urge to search for Adam among the unmarried men. She had never seen him at a church service, and her curiosity got the best of her. Even though she faced the front of the room, with her head turned toward the bishop, her eyes scanned the men, searching for Adam Hershberger.

He was not there.

For a moment, she wondered if he might have changed his mind. Her heart began to beat rapidly and her palms began to sweat. What would happen if he did not show up? she wondered. She had never heard of such a thing happening. Would it reflect poorly on her if he abandoned the notion of taking her as his wife? What would happen to her father's farm? She felt torn between being hopeful and discouraged. She had followed through on her part; would Adam follow through on his?

The *vorsinger,* the man assigned to lead the congregation in song, began to sing a hymn, and the rest of the congregation lifted their voices to sing with him as the church leaders stood and left the room. For the next twenty-five minutes, the congregation sang, each syllable of every word being drawn out as was the custom. By the end of the hymn, the bishop and his preachers would return. What they discussed in the back room, Belle had no idea. However, she knew they were deciding which of them would preach the two sermons during the worship service.

As luck would have it, the bishop began to preach first. He had been chosen to preach the shorter of the two sermons. Belle could hardly listen to his words as she continued peering about the room to see if Adam had arrived. She felt Ella shift her weight on the bench beside her, gently brushing her hand against Belle's knee in a soft gesture of comfort. Belle glanced at her and saw sympathy in her friend's eyes. Farther down the bench, Sadie Whitaker gave her a smile of encouragement, and Belle knew that they, too, were wondering what would happen if Adam did not show up.

After the second hymn, "Das Loblieb,"

one of the preachers stood up to preach. Belle began to fidget, knowing that, when he finished, another hymn would be sung. Typically, that was the time when the bride and groom would leave the room with the bishop for counseling. However, as far as she could tell, Adam had still not arrived. Would the bishop go through with the wedding if he did not counsel them about their upcoming married life?

By the time the preacher finished, Belle felt as if she might jump out of her skin. She knew that her hands were trembling, so she clutched them in her lap. As the hymn started, the bishop stood and walked out of the room, pausing for just a moment to indicate that Belle should follow him. Surprised, she hesitated before getting to her feet. Somehow she found the strength to make her way toward the bishop, who waited at the door for her to join him outside.

"Let's take a walk to the barn, shall we?"

Nervously, she wrung her hands before herself as she walked behind the bishop. Surely he would tell her what to expect now that Adam had not arrived. Typically, it was after the final hymn that the bishop would lead the couple back into the room and begin the wedding ceremony. That would be impossible without a groom.

She let her eyes adjust to the darkness in the barn. Three chairs were set in a circle among the hay bales. The bishop walked toward them and sat down. He gestured toward one of the chairs facing him, and Belle realized that he wanted her to sit with him.

As she took her seat, she felt a hand on her shoulder. Startled, she jumped and began to turn, but the hand tightened its pressure.

Adam.

He remained standing beside her, and the bishop began to speak.

"Marriage is for life," he said slowly. "It is not something to be entered into lightly. Like your commitment to the church when you took your kneeling vow, your commitment to each other is one that cannot be broken." He paused. "God created woman from one of man's ribs. In doing so, she became a part of him, his partner. And man holds dominion over her, committed to protect her according to God's will. Man and woman complement each other. Together they can achieve much more than they could if they were apart."

Belle's eyes began to glaze over, not from boredom but from fear. As the bishop began to talk about the permanence of marriage, she knew that he was giving her one last chance to change her mind. Would God frown upon her reasons for marrying? Despite having tried to convince herself that marriage was a business relationship, deep down Belle knew that most couples married for love. Marrying for the sake of her family's safety and homestead was a sacrifice. Nonetheless, it was one she was willing to make. Somehow, though, the magnitude of her sacrifice had not struck her until that moment.

She felt a wave of panic wash over her. Could she really do this? Could she give herself to a man she didn't even know, not just for life as his partner but also in the most intimate way?

Her mind raced and she began to think through different scenarios. No. She couldn't back out of the wedding. Yes, she would find a way to give Adam that son. But she also knew that she couldn't leave a child, not in Adam's care. It dawned on her that Adam might have known all that. She suspected that his offer of freedom after she gave him a son was one that he had made knowing full well she could never leave her child. It was an offer made with full knowledge that she would never accept. She would marry Adam and remain his wife, living at his farm, until the end of her life.

For a moment, she almost stood, contemplating speaking up and ending what she knew was nothing more than a mockery of marriage. But the firm grip on her shoulder stopped her from doing so.

The bishop had not noticed. He finished his lecture to them and then indicated that it was time to return to the house. Belle's knees felt weak, and Adam helped her to her feet. He stood on her right side, his hand on her elbow, as he guided her out of the barn and back into the sunshine. The house seemed far away, and Adam continued to lead her toward the front door. Without his help, she knew that she would have fainted. Instead, the steady pressure of his hand on her arm kept her aware that she was walking beside him and about to become his wife.

Once inside the house, the bishop led them to the front of the room. Belle stood beside Adam, staring at the wall in front of her. She could hear the collective gasps from the people seated on the right side of the room as they stared at Adam, many seeing him for the first time. Belle, however, stood on his left and, even if she were on his other side, had no desire to look at him.

The bishop cleared his throat as he began to speak.

"Adam, I will ask you first, do you confess and believe that God has ordained marriage to be a union between one man and one wife? Do you have the confidence that you are approaching marriage in accordance with the way you have been taught?" He paused, waiting for Adam to nod his head once and mumble a quick "Yes" before he asked Belle the same questions.

She, too, nodded her head.

Returning his attention to Adam, the bishop asked, "Do you also have confidence, brother, that the Lord has provided this, our sister, as a marriage partner for you?"

Adam sounded as if he sighed as he, once again, mumbled, "Yes."

"And Belle, do you also have the confidence, sister, that the Lord has provided this, our brother, as a marriage partner for you?"

The bishop waited for her to respond. For the briefest of seconds, she hesitated. How could she answer that question? she wondered. Was it, indeed, the Lord who wanted her to marry this man? This complete stranger? She struggled with her thoughts, asking herself if God truly wanted her to be Adam's marriage partner. If not God, she finally told herself, then who?

She took a deep breath and responded at last with a soft "Yes."

There was a rustling noise from the side of the room where the women sat. Belle glanced over in time to see Ella and Sadie, their faces pale as they grasped each other's hands. When she started to turn back, the bishop was asking Adam the next question in the wedding ceremony.

"Do you also promise your wife that if she should in bodily weakness, sickness, or any similar circumstances need your help, that you will care for her as is fitting for a Christian husband?"

This time, Adam spoke with more confidence, affirming that he would. Surprised, Belle let her eyes fall on him and was even more astonished to see that he was staring at her. She saw his face, the puckered skin over his cheek and the slight hooding over his eye. It was the first time that she had seen him head-on, and to her amazement, she realized that he was a handsome man, except for the scarring. What she had imagined was far worse than what she now saw.

"And Belle," the bishop continued, "do you promise your husband the same thing, that if he should in bodily weakness, sickness, or any similar circumstances need your help, that you will care for him as is fitting for a Christian wife?"

With her eyes still on his face, Belle gave a quick nod of her head. "Yes, I do."

The vows ended with the bishop addressing them both with one last question: "Do you both promise together that you will with love, forbearance, and patience live with each other, and not part from each other until God will separate you in death?"

In unison both Adam and Belle managed to agree that they would, although Belle wondered if it would be possible to live with love in Adam's house. But she knew that, once the word "Yes" slipped through her lips, she had committed to God that she would try. And try she would.

With the vows finished, Belle sat down at the front of the room, Adam taking a seat next to her. The *vorsinger* began singing the final hymn. At first, Belle couldn't sing, however. Her nerves had made her forget the words, even though the congregation sang in unison. She noticed that Adam merely stared straight ahead, not even attempting to join the others in song.

The wedding over, Belle stood beside Adam, her hands shaking as she watched the room transform. The men began to convert the plain benches into tables while the women busied themselves with carrying plates of food to the tables as these were assembled. Belle stared at the platters of chicken and beef, the bowls of corn and beans, the baskets of bread and buns. Where had all of this food come from?

She glanced up at Adam, not surprised to see that he was turned so that the right side of his face was hidden from view. "Did you do all of this?" she asked. "The food?"

He did not respond to her question, but she understood from his silence that he had.

"Danke," she whispered.

He cleared his throat. "Enjoy your wedding feast, Belle."

She started to reply to him, but her father approached both of them. He reached out and shook Adam's hand, offering his congratulations in a flat, emotionless voice. Then he embraced Belle, his hold lingering longer than she expected.

"It won't be the same around this *haus* without you, Belle," he said when he pulled away.

But at least you still have the haus, she thought. She started to say something, wanting to tell her father that she would return frequently, probably more often than most brides returned home. She stumbled over her words, not wanting to offend Adam. When she glanced to her side, she realized that he was gone. Quickly, she began to search the room, wondering where he might have disappeared. But she couldn't locate him.

"Where did Adam go?" she asked her father.

"Why, I don't know. He was just here a moment ago." Her father appeared as perplexed as she was.

"Has he left?" She did not wait for an answer. Instead, she hurried through the gathered people and made her way to the door. As she stepped outside, she saw Adam's buggy pulling away, heading in the direction of his farm.

Her father stood behind her.

Belle glanced over her shoulder. She felt the threat of tears welling in her eyes.

"Don't fret, Belle. *Mayhaps* it's best that he left."

She nodded, even though she wasn't certain if she felt relief or embarrassment. After all, it was her wedding . . . *their* wedding. How would it look that the groom had disappeared, leaving the bride alone? Certainly people would talk — even more than they already were. She lifted her chin and forced herself to follow her father back into the house. With Adam gone, the least she could do was enjoy the bountiful feast that he had provided for the gathering.

CHAPTER TEN

So perplexed was she by Adam's strange behavior after the wedding, Belle hardly slept at all. The one night that she had dreaded ever since she'd agreed to marry him had turned out far different from what she had imagined. In the morning, she awoke before anyone else, including her father. After dressing, Belle hurried downstairs, carrying a kerosene lamp to light the way. Most of the room appeared in order. The previous evening, all of the tables had been packed away into the church wagon. Someone had folded all of the table linens, and all of the dishes had been washed.

Belle took it upon herself to pack away the rented items that Adam had arranged for the wedding. It helped calm her nerves as she carefully stored the dishes, glasses, and utensils in the different containers. She couldn't help but wonder why Adam had left so abruptly. Typically, the groom spent that first evening with the bride, and they would return to their new home, together, in the morning. In the increasingly rare cases where the groom had not purchased a home yet, the bride might stay with her parents for a few months, the groom visiting on the weekends. But that was a much more old-fashioned way.

Perhaps it had been the way she looked at him when, for the first time, he stood before her and she saw the scar tissue that covered the right side of his face, from his temple to his lower jaw. His eyes, so piercing and blue, had stared at her as if anticipating a reaction. But she had given him none. And yet he still fled.

She paused as she shut the last box, which contained the dessert plates. For a moment, she stared at the empty wall next to the staircase. Was she supposed to stay with her father, or perhaps Adam expected her to walk to his farm? She had no idea what he wanted her to do, and in that moment, she realized the enormity of the mistake she had made.

Shutting her eyes, she whispered a prayer to God. "Please, dear Lord, show me your will. I am trying to do what you have shown me as your path for me, but I fear that it is too much for me to bear. I need you now more than ever."

The kitchen door opened, and Belle turned around to see Adam walk through it. He wore a straw hat, tilted in a way that covered part of the scars on his face. He wore the same clothing that he had worn the day before: black trousers and his white long-sleeved shirt. Had he slept in those clothes?

"You left last night."

"I did."

"Why?" she asked.

"It wasn't a place I wanted to be."

She supposed she could understand that. After all, she had heard many of those same people comment about Adam being ugly and disfigured. Despite preaching grace and kindness, many members of the church district clearly did not practice it. Of course, it was also clear that neither did Adam.

"But it was our wedding."

He arched his eyebrow over his left eye, the only eye that she could see. But rather than respond to her comment, he merely said, "I have come to fetch you."

Her heart skipped a beat when she heard his words. Would he bring her to his home so early in the morning that she would not have a chance to say goodbye to her father and sisters? Dare she mention that she wanted to see her family before leaving? She started to speak, but stopped before the first word could slip past her lips. It would be harder to leave if she had to say goodbye. Perhaps Adam's early arrival was more fortunate than she thought.

"I'll . . . I'll get my things."

She hurried up the stairs and grabbed her clothes, quickly folding them and placing them into her satchel, an old canvas bag with rope handles. She only had a few dresses: three for working, one for church, and her wedding dress. Packing her things took just a few minutes. Leaving the room, however, seemed to take a lifetime. So many memories were woven into the corners and walls of the bedroom, as well as the rest of the house. At least she had managed to save the rest of her family from the same fate of having to say farewell to their home.

Carrying the bag in one hand, she held on to the railing with the other as she descended the stairs. Outside the windows, she could see that the dark sky was beginning to shift to a deep gray. Soon it would become blue, and then a light gray as the sun began to approach the horizon from the east. By that time, she would be at Adam's farm and beginning her first day as his wife.

"That's all you have?"

Belle looked from him to the bag in her hand. "*Ja,* that's it. I have some books, but I've read them all."

"Books?"

She nodded. "Novels."

"What kind of novels?"

She blushed. How could she confess that she liked romances when her own love life had taken such an unromantic turn?

When he stared at her, his one eye seeming to study her reaction, she wondered if he had read her mind. "Never mind." He reached out for the bag and lifted it as if it weighed nothing. "Come along, then."

Obediently, but with a heavy heart, she followed him as he turned to leave the house. He held the door for her, a gesture which surprised her, but he spoke no more as he walked ahead of her toward his strange buggy. She watched as he tossed her bag through the open door. It plopped onto the floor behind the front seat. Without any effort, he flipped the back of the seat up and moved aside, waiting for her to step up and into the buggy.

Their ride back to Adam's farm was silent. Neither spoke. Belle stared out the window, the feeling of emptiness filling her stomach with each jostle of the buggy that forced her arm to brush against his. She tried to shift herself so that she sat as far from him as possible, but the small seat gave her no room to escape him. Being so close to him, she noticed that his work clothes smelled. Or maybe it was just him. She wasn't certain. It was a musky, earthy scent, one that spoke of hard work and sweat. While it was not entirely unpleasant, she wasn't used to it and found herself feeling nauseous. When the buggy wheels ran through a particularly rough patch of road, her stomach twisted, and she knew that she was going to be ill.

"Could you pull over?" she whispered, knowing that she needed a moment outside, away from him and the future that faced her.

He didn't ask why as he pulled back on the reins, a soft "whoa" escaping his lips.

Once the buggy stopped, she slid back the door and hurried to the ground. Embarrassed, she walked off the side of the road, hopefully out of his sight, and bent over as she got sick. *I can't do this. Please, Lord. Please make me wake up and have this just be some sort of nightmare.* A gentle wind blew through the trees, the leaves moving enough so that raindrops fell onto her head. While cooling her neck and face, the drops also confirmed what she knew to be true: it wasn't a nightmare — not the kind that she would wake up from.

"Belle?"

She didn't turn around when she heard him call her name. Instead, she lifted her hand and motioned for him to keep driving. "Let me walk," she said. "I'm not feeling well."

"Get back into the buggy. It will be quicker."

Quicker for what? she wanted to ask. But she knew better than to argue. Less than twenty-four hours ago, she had vowed before her family, her community, and God that she would claim this man as her husband. And God wanted wives to obey their husbands. Taking a few last gulps of fresh air, she wiped her mouth with her hand and slowly walked back to the buggy.

Less than fifteen minutes later, the buggy stopped once again. This time, when she exited the buggy, it was only to stand before the dark house that she knew was to be her new home.

It looked no more inviting to her than it had when she had first been there, almost three weeks ago.

Adam unhitched the horse from the buggy and led it to the stable, leaving Belle alone as she stood there, staring at the house. She hadn't moved when he returned, her bag in his hand. For a moment, he stood beside her and seemed to contemplate what she saw. She wanted to look at him, but she was afraid to. Instead, she lowered her eyes and fought the urge to cry.

"Best get started, then," he said at last.

"Started"? His choice of words frightened her. What exactly did he mean? Started with their marriage? Their new life? Or simply started with the chores ahead of her?

He walked to the front door and opened it. The hinges were rusty, and they squeaked, something she hadn't noticed the other day. Once again, he held it open and waited for her to take that first step into the house.

She remembered it as being dark and dirty with a great feeling of oppressiveness, but it seemed twice as bad now that she realized she was going to be living there. She stood inside the doorway, looking around at the collection of crates and wood, dirt and cobwebs. Adam did not wait for her as he ascended the staircase that ran along the wall farthest from the hallway leading to the kitchen. He was gone for only a few seconds when she heard a thump on the ceiling above her head. She jumped at the noise and only calmed down when she realized that Adam must have dropped her bag on the floor of the bedroom.

Their bedroom.

She shuddered and crossed her arms over her chest, her hands rubbing her arms as if to warm her flesh from a chill.

When he returned downstairs, he paused only to say, "I'll leave you to your chores," and then he headed toward the kitchen. A few seconds later, she heard the back door slam shut, and she shut her eyes, exhaling in relief that he was gone.

If God leads you to it, she thought, *God will lead you through it.*

With Adam gone from the house, curiosity got the best of her, and she slowly approached the staircase. With a trembling hand, she reached out and touched the banister, not surprised that she felt the sticky residue of dust under her fingers. Slowly, she began to take each step, listening to the creaks and groans of the old wood beneath her shoes. She hadn't noticed those noises when Adam took her bag upstairs.

The second story was dark; there were no windows in the hallway. Instead, there were five doors, two on each side and one at the far end. She opened the first two doors, one on the left at the top of the staircase and one on the right. Both rooms were empty.

She left the doors open so that the light from the dirty windows could brighten the second floor. As she walked down the hall, she noticed that the walls were wood and had never been painted. That, too, surprised her. No wonder the hallway was so dark and ominous-looking.

The second door on the right was locked, but when she tried the fourth door at the end of the hallway, it opened to a surprisingly large bedroom. There was a double bed against the back wall, with two nightstands underneath the windows. Her bag was on the floor, and she realized that this bedroom faced the front of the property. While it wasn't necessarily clean, someone had made an attempt to make it orderly. A small, narrow dresser was against the wall by the door, and there was a ladder-back chair on the other side of it. Empty pegs lined the one wall, waiting for clothing to be hung. Clearly, no one lived in the room, and she couldn't help but wonder where Adam's clothes were. Besides an old quilt and two pillows on the bed, there was no sign that anyone inhabited this room.

But her bag at the foot of the bed clearly indicated that it was to be her room, and that meant it would be *their* room.

She shuddered.

Trying to keep her eyes away from the bed and her thoughts focused on the present, not the nighttime, when she would be forced to recognize her wedding vows, she began to unpack her bag. Her clothing was limited to her three work dresses, one of which she wore, her Sunday dress, and her wedding dress. Quickly, she hung them on the wall and put the rest of her undergarments in the empty drawers of the dresser. She folded her empty bag and stored it under the bed.

Her exploration took her to the last door on the second floor, and she was surprised to find that the room was set up almost identically to her own bedroom. There were dresses hanging on the wall, as well as a pair of suspendered pants. But the cobwebs in the corners and the dust on the clothing led Belle to believe that no one had lived in that room for many years.

After shutting the door, she made her way back downstairs, trying to avoid looking at the boxes and dirt, dried leaves and cobwebs, that awaited her. She wrapped her arms around herself again and stepped over a pile of sticks as she walked down the hallway toward the kitchen. If she had hoped that Adam might have made an attempt at cleaning that room, she was sorely disappointed.

With a sigh, she stood in the doorway and assessed the chaos that greeted her. She wasn't even certain how to start addressing the disaster. There was an old farmer's table near the back door, littered with papers at one end. A bench was knocked over, and she saw some garbage behind it, as if Adam might have simply tossed old papers on the floor.

She walked toward the table and bent down to right the bench.

There, she thought. *One thing done.*

She walked over to a door on the other side of the table. When she opened it, she saw a pantry with empty shelves and a ratty-looking broom in the back. She retrieved the broom and set about sweeping the dirt and debris on the floor into piles. She couldn't find a dustpan, so she searched for some cardboard or anything she could use to lift the dirt and toss it outside. Finding nothing, she decided to just push the piles toward the door and sweep them onto the porch.

It took her almost an hour to clear the floor.

For the rest of the morning, she moved garbage and boxes onto the back porch, deciding that removing things from the house before she started cleaning the floors was wise. They would need to be scrubbed, and probably more than once or twice. From the looks of the brown linoleum, it hadn't been cleaned in years.

By the time she heard footsteps on the porch steps, it was noon.

The door opened, and Adam stepped into the kitchen.

"What's all of that stuff out there?" He didn't sound happy.

Belle stood by the kitchen counter, thankful that she had a buffer between herself and Adam. She noticed the sweat stains on his shirt and how the back of his hair was wet. Still, he didn't change into a short-sleeved shirt, and he kept his hat on his head, despite the heat. "Garbage, I presume."

He turned, looking around the room. "Where are all of my papers? How am I supposed to find anything?" he said angrily. "And why isn't there any food ready for dinner?"

Belle pressed her lips together and frowned. She didn't like the way he had just raised his voice to her. Not once had her father ever used such a tone with her. She might be Adam's wife, but she would not permit him to disrespect her. "I don't know how you found anything to begin with," she retorted sharply. "And I certainly cannot cook food in such a pigpen. Besides, I don't see much in the way of food to cook!"

Adam spun around and glared at her. "I am your husband. You will respect me."

She lifted her chin. "I will respect you when you have earned it. So far, that has not happened."

He crossed the room in three long strides, a noise that almost resembled a growl escaping his lips. Belle shrank back, frightened that he might strike her. But Adam merely slammed his hand on the counter and glowered at her. When she stood her ground, Adam huffed and, without another word, left the kitchen, retreating back the way he had come.

She breathed a sigh of relief and leaned against the dirty refrigerator. How on earth would she ever get through the rest of the day? The thought of having to spend the night with him made her feel nauseous once again. She couldn't be a true wife to him. She simply could not. And yet, she had made him that promise . . . to bear him a son. Fulfilling that part of her marital obligation was something she simply could not — and would not! — think about.

Returning her attention to the kitchen,

she continued cleaning the counter, washing dishes, and organizing cabinets. Slowly, the room began to be transformed from a disastrous mess to a satisfactory condition that, while not up to her personal standards, was certainly livable.

By three o'clock, Belle needed a break from working inside. She hadn't tackled any other room in the house, and her back ached from scrubbing the floor. The kitchen was finished for the day.

Outside, the air was cooler than it had been in previous days. She wandered over to the overgrown garden, trying to assess if there was anything edible growing there. To her surprise, she found a few tomato plants that had somehow managed to grow, as well as a vine of not-quite-ripe pumpkins. While it was too late in the season to gather many tomatoes, she did hold out hope that she might harvest some pumpkins in just a few weeks. Further tugging at weeds in the back of the garden revealed that wild onions and peppermint plants had taken over there. While she knew that the wild onions had clearly already flowered and were probably not good for harvesting, she felt hopeful that she'd have a bumper crop the next spring. And, although the peppermint was done for the year, with only a few stalks worth plucking for tea, she also knew that cutting back the plants would help cultivate a much healthier batch for the next year.

At least I can make some meadow tea. She wiped her hands on her apron and stood up, pressing her hands into the lower part of her back to stop the aching. She returned to the kitchen. As she did, she looked around the room, surprised by how much she had achieved in one short day. *God works miracles.*

The door opened again. This time Adam walked in carrying a large box, which he dropped onto the counter. He stepped back and stared at her. The dim light of the room cast a shadow on his face, and she could almost make out the scarring that she had seen the previous day during their wedding. The puckered skin glistened, just a little, from sweat. His right eye looked at her piercingly through the folded skin that partially hid it.

"There. See what you can do with that for some food."

Cautiously, Belle peeked into the box. Potatoes. Onions. Celery. And a half-empty bag of flour. "What's this?" She reached inside and withdrew the celery. It was wilted and hung from her hand. She raised her eyes to stare at him. "This is all that you have?"

Once again, he huffed at her. "It'll do. It has for me."

Belle swallowed. "I see."

Had he truly been living off such limited supplies? She had found some old containers with sugar, salt, and what appeared to be packages of yeast. She might be able to make some bread; she wasn't certain. But she could try to make potato soup, which at least would stop the rumbling in her stomach.

"Perhaps there is some milk?"

He motioned with his head toward the door. "Go fetch it yourself."

Belle frowned. He had wanted this arrangement. This marriage of convenience to bear progeny. Yet he seemed as unhappy with the prospect as she was. Their future was uncertain and their relationship was nonexistent, but that didn't mean that their interactions needed to be coarse and unkind. "This is our first day together, Adam," she said in a soft voice. "I would think that, given the trepidation you know that I am feeling being in a strange place —"

"You mean a pigpen," he interrupted.

She ignored his angry comment. "— that you would attempt to make my first day here less inhospitable. That is, after all, the Christian thing to do."

He laughed. Just once.

"So I am going to ask you again if there is milk, and this time, perhaps you might be gentlemanly enough to respond that you will fetch it for me. Or at least take me to show me where you store it."

His good eye widened at her gentle reprimand.

"Danke."

She didn't wait for him to reply as she began to empty the box onto the counter. She sorted through the potatoes, putting the usable ones aside from those that looked too old. Not once did she look at him again. Instead, she began to hum a hymn, hoping that he would get the hint and leave the room.

He did. But not without slamming the door behind himself. Moments later, he returned with a plain steel bucket of milk, which he slammed onto the counter, white liquid spilling over the edge. She refused to address him, focusing her attention on cutting the potatoes and dumping the pieces into a pot of water that she already had on the stove. She continued humming, losing herself in the melody and unaware that he watched her for a few long moments before snatching the empty box and storming back outside.

By the time Adam returned, the aroma of freshly baked biscuits filled the kitchen, and Belle had set the table with two place settings. She glanced at him and forced a nervous smile. "If you wash up, we can have supper."

Rather than walk to the sink, Adam took his place at the head of the table. Clearly good hygiene was not part of his eating ritual. It was a battle Belle decided not to fight this day. Instead, she carried a basket of biscuits and set it down in between their places. Then she returned to carry over the large pot of soup.

She took her place on the bench to his left. When she lowered her head to pray, Adam reached out for a biscuit.

"Adam!"

He looked at her.

She gave him a fierce look of disapproval and lowered her head once again. When he did not follow her example, she gave in and said her own silent prayer of gratitude to God for the food that they were about to eat. It was hard to concentrate with Adam already serving himself, ignoring her moment of reflection and prayer.

When she finished, she reached for the

ladle to serve herself. "You don't pray?"

He ignored the question and continued to eat, slurping the soup from the spoon.

"And I suppose manners are out of the question, too?"

Her question was met with silence.

"I suppose you have your reasons, Adam," she said quietly. "It would, however, be helpful if we could talk about our expectations. I am quite certain that we both are feeling similar apprehensions about this . . ."

She paused. What was this? A marriage, yes. But not the way she had envisioned it.

". . . this arrangement."

He reached out for another biscuit and began dipping it into his soup.

"We will both have to make sacrifices. That is part of two lives joining together." She sipped her soup and, to her surprise, was satisfied with the taste. Though she suspected that it would leave her as unfulfilled as her marriage to Adam Hershberger, she knew that it would suffice for the evening. "And I would like to know more about you."

The spoon dropped from his hand and clattered against the bowl. "There is nothing to know. I am a beast, *ja*?"

"A beast?"

"I am a beast," he repeated. "That is what

they say in town, those Amish folk who claim to be good Christians."

Belle stared into her bowl of soup. How would he know what people said in town? What games the children played in the school yard? And yet, despite the truth behind his words, he needed to accept some of the responsibility for that label. Any person who lived such an isolated and dark life needed to realize the consequences included an aura of mystery that might damage his reputation.

"Not all of them speak of you in such a way," she said in a soft voice.

Slowly, he turned his head so that his entire face was in her line of sight. "Their silence does not mean they hold a different opinion."

"Nor does it mean they hold the same opinion. Perhaps if they knew you."

He waved his hand at her in a dismissive manner. "There is nothing to know about me. I live here alone —"

"Not anymore."

"— and I don't want people in my business. And that includes you."

"Me? But I am your wife."

He returned his attention to the food. Without any attempt at good manners, he began slurping at it again. "You're to bear me a son, Belle. That's all you need to do. Then you can return to your family."

Belle felt her heart race.

Adam hadn't really discussed that part of the deal — at least not in detail. On the one hand, the idea that she did not have to live the rest of her life with him gave her hope for the future. Yet she knew the stigma that would be attached to her as a wife cast out by her husband. And what about the child? Would Adam expect her to simply walk away from what would, undoubtedly, be her only child? What if she didn't bear him a son but daughters? If she did bear him a son and left — something she couldn't possibly imagine doing! — unless Adam died, she would never be able to marry again and live the life she had always imagined. A life that included a loving husband and large family. And while she knew that she could never love a man like Adam, she had *hoped* that they could at least develop a relationship that was tolerable enough to provide some degree of happiness.

Clearly that was not what he had in mind.

"So I am to merely be a broodmare?" she asked when she found her voice.

He stared at her, his one eye so crystal clear and bright, while the other was shadowed by scars. For a long, silent moment, he seemed to consider her question, and then he lowered his voice and responded with his own. "Do you love me?"

Belle blinked in surprise. "What?"

"It's a simple question. Do you love me, Belle?"

She could hardly believe that she had heard him correctly the first time. But when he repeated it the second time, she was stunned. How could he possibly ask her that? She knew nothing about this man outside of whispered gossip. Her own, limited interactions with him had been strenuous and tense. And yet he asked her if she loved him.

"Adam, I . . . I don't even know you," she managed to say.

He shoved the empty bowl away and reached out for the remaining biscuits. "What is there to know?" Glaring at her, he stood up. "I told you, Belle, I am nothing more than a beast." He pushed back the chair so roughly that it fell over. Without making any move to pick it up, he stomped to the door and passed through it, this time leaving it open. Belle watched as he headed toward the stable and disappeared.

To her relief, he did not return again that evening.

CHAPTER ELEVEN

When she awoke in the morning, it was to the sound of Adam's deep voice talking outside of her partially opened window. Her eyes opened, and for a moment, she was confused. Where was she? Why did the room look so strange? As she blinked her eyes, she tried to place where, exactly, she was. And then it dawned on her: Adam's house. She rolled over in the bed and peered out of the window. Adam was walking in the bluish light of dawn toward the barn, a small dog at his feet.

Funny. She hadn't known that he had a dog on the property. Not once had she heard it bark or make a noise.

She watched as Adam talked to the scrappy-looking brown mutt. He reached for a stick and threw it for the dog to retrieve. The dog ran after the stick, its tail wagging happily when it returned to Adam's side with the stick in its mouth. Adam bent down, rubbed its head, and pulled the stick from its mouth so that he could throw it once more.

It was the closest expression to joy that Belle had seen on Adam's face.

Sinking back into the pillows, Belle stared at the ceiling. She didn't understand Adam. He acted so gruff and mean, yet what she had just witnessed was a tender display between a man and a dog. While she knew that many *Englischers* treated their pets as family, Amish men did not.

Perhaps there was more to Adam than met the eye.

She sighed and tossed back her covers, reluctantly swinging her legs over the side of the bed. At once, she noticed that the bedroom door was slightly ajar, and she quickly looked around the room. Nothing seemed out of place. But she had definitely shut the door the previous night. Had Adam come into the room while she slept?

That was when it dawned upon her that, for the first time in the three weeks since she had agreed to marry Adam, she had actually slept through the night.

While she wouldn't say she felt refreshed, she certainly felt less tired than she had been of late. When she had gone to bed at eight o'clock the previous night, Adam had not yet returned from the barn. She'd been sure she'd never fall asleep, but exhausted from the hard physical labor of the day, as well as the emotions of the last several weeks, she had quickly nodded off and slept the night away.

And he had not disturbed her. Why?

In the darkness of her room, she trembled as she dressed and fixed her hair. If Adam had come into the room, he had most certainly not slept there. And while she was more than relieved about *that,* she felt vulnerable and unguarded nonetheless. Even though Adam was her husband and intimacy was part of marriage, Belle wasn't in a hurry to experience the carnal needs of a man, even if she was married to him.

Once dressed, Belle hurried downstairs and out the kitchen door. At her father's house, she would have been up already and finished with the morning milking. Today, however, she was late, having overslept just as her sisters usually did. She wondered if either Susie or Verna had arisen to help their father with the milking. And who would make breakfast? Immediately, she felt a pang of homesickness and had to swallow the lump that was forming in her throat.

The morning dew felt wet on her bare feet as she crossed the yard to the barn. With each step, she felt nervous and frightened. What would Adam say to her? Would he mention the fact that she had fallen asleep so early? An overwhelming sense of dread seemed to course through her veins, and she tried to ignore the feeling.

Instead, she focused on the crisp predawn air, knowing that with cooler mornings, the season would begin to change soon enough. Hopefully not too rapidly, for she always enjoyed autumn the most of all seasons. It seemed to present the most marked contrast, with cold mornings and hot afternoons. And she loved when the trees began to change colors. That was how she felt, like a tree in autumn, the beautiful green leaves slowly dying and falling to the ground. Belle's only hope was that, like a tree in the springtime, she might see a rebirth once again.

She stopped in the entrance of the barn. It was dark inside, and she let her eyes adjust. When they did, she saw that Adam stood before her, facing her directly. However, this time, he did not turn away. Instead, he lifted a small kerosene lantern and took one step toward her. The orange glow from the flame flickered, casting dancing shadows around him, but it was just enough light for Belle to study his scars. She knew he had been burned, but she didn't know how it had happened, and she wished she could ask him about it. One day, she thought. Perhaps she might find out more about the tragic fire that had left him with such an obvious and permanent injury.

"What are you doing here?" he asked at last.

The color rose to her cheeks. "I . . . I was coming to help with morning chores."

"Women work inside the house. Men work outside."

She tried to smile. "Don't be silly. I always helped my *daed* with the barn chores."

"You are not with your *daed* anymore."

Standing there, she felt her shoulders droop, disheartened by his harsh tone. "Are you saying you don't want my help?"

"I don't need your help, *nee,*" he snapped.

Without warning, she felt tears stinging her eyes, and she quickly covered her face with her hands. She didn't want him to see her cry, didn't want to feel rejected, yet again, by this man who had wanted to marry her yet did not appear to want a wife. How could she possibly honor her commitment to God to live in love with this impossible man? She turned and ran back toward the house, embarrassed that she had let him

171

see her cry and angry with herself for even caring.

In the kitchen, she wiped her face with the bottom of her black apron. She knew that it would take time to adjust to a new home and new routine. Regardless of the couple, newlyweds faced change. Adam would have to get used to having someone else living in the house, and Belle would have to get used to . . . well . . . everything. She sighed and bent over, letting her forehead rest on the counter. Shutting her eyes, she said a quick prayer to God, praying for the strength to get through the long day that undoubtedly lay before her.

If Adam was assigning her the inside of the house, then she knew that she needed to get into her own routine. She searched for a pad of paper and a pen before she sat down at the table and began to make lists. She would follow the same schedule as she had at her father's house: wash on Mondays and Fridays, cheese making on Tuesdays and Thursdays, and a complete house cleaning on Wednesdays. She'd do all her baking in the mornings and weed the garden in the evenings. While she no longer lived close enough to town to walk there every afternoon, she decided that she would try to reserve Saturdays for that. She would want to visit her family and her friends as often as possible.

Determined to do something productive, Belle made a long list of things that she needed from the store. The previous day, she had inventoried the sparse pantry and knew that Adam had next to nothing in the house. When she finished, she gathered her cleaning supplies — a scrub brush and a bucket of warm, soapy water — and headed toward the hallway. If she tackled one room a day, the house would be neat and tidy within a week. While she had no idea how to create a livable marriage, at least she could work on making a livable home.

This time, rather than dumping all of the boxes and garbage on the back porch, she dragged it out the front door. She piled everything into a heap, realizing that she'd have to burn it in order to get rid of everything. It was simply too much to take to the local garbage collection place in town. When the hallway was empty, she got down on her hands and knees, focusing all of her energy on scrubbing the wide plank floor. Three buckets of water later, she sat back on her heels and assessed her progress.

"What are you doing?"

She heard him before she saw him storm over to the door and look outside at the pile of garbage.

"I'm cleaning," she replied as she stated the obvious.

He pressed his lips together and put his hand against the wall. For a moment, he stood there like that, his back to her as he gazed out the open doorway. Finally, he lowered his arm and took a deep breath. "I suppose it was time," he mumbled.

"I should say so." Belle managed to get to her feet, her knees sore from having been on them for so long. "When was the last time this house was cleaned?"

Adam turned around. "Twenty years ago."

If anyone else had said that to her, she would have thought it was a joke. But, despite knowing so little about him, Belle did know one thing: he wasn't the type of person who teased. She glanced at the walls, the cobwebs still clinging to the corners of the ceiling and dust covering the woodwork. Even though the floor was clean, she still had a lot of work to do. And Adam had probably come inside for the noon meal.

"I reckon you're hungry," she said as she wiped her hands on the front of her apron and began to walk to the kitchen. "I didn't make anything, but I can put out some biscuits, butter, and leftover potatoes from yesterday."

He grunted.

"And I made a list." She pointed to the yellow pad of paper. "The second page. *Mayhaps* I could go into town this afternoon?"

He glanced down at the list and frowned.

"Without a garden, I cannot can anything." She pulled out the biscuits and began to slice them in half. "And I don't see any chickens running around. Might be a good idea to have a small flock for fresh eggs, *ja?*"

Another grunt.

She opened the refrigerator and pulled out a container with butter and a bowl of leftover potatoes. "I made this butter yesterday," she said as she carried it to the table and set it down. "I just need some mesophilic culture and I could make Colby cheese. I do so love Colby cheese, don't you?"

"Enough!" Adam covered his ears with his hands. "Stop prattling so!"

Belle's eyes widened at the intensity of his voice. "It's not prattling," she said sharply. "It's called conversing. That's what a husband and wife are supposed to do. Converse with each other."

Under his breath, he growled as he sat down and reached for a biscuit.

"Adam!"

He rolled his eyes at her and waited until she sat down and prayed. Once she finished, he began to cover the biscuit with her fresh butter.

"So, do you think I might go into town then?"

"Give me the list," he grumbled. "I'll go."

"*Mayhaps* we could go together?"

He scowled and shook his head. "*Nee*! I already have a headache from your 'conversing.'"

She pursed her lips in disapproval of his remark but made no further attempts to talk with him. Instead, she ate two biscuits in silence, the only noise the sound of birds chirping outside the kitchen door. When she finished eating, she stood up and carried her plate to the sink. Her list, written in neat, cursive handwriting, lay on the counter. She glanced over it before picking it up and carrying it to him.

"There," she said. "Your list."

She watched as he read through the different items, the furrows in his forehead deepening. She could tell that he was displeased with the length of the list, and she waited for his rebuke.

But none came.

Instead, he pushed back his plate and

grabbed the piece of paper before he stood up and stomped out of the kitchen. Belle was still sitting there, staring out the window at nothing, when, fifteen minutes later, she heard his horse and buggy heading down the long lane toward the main road.

She was disappointed that he had not permitted her to go to town. She had hoped to see her friends, even if only for a few minutes. She felt alone on this strange farm that she was, somehow, supposed to consider home. But home was where the heart resided, and her heart most certainly did not reside anywhere that Adam Hershberger did.

Leaving his plate at the table, Belle decided to spend some time outdoors, hoping that the sunshine and fresh air might help improve her mood. She had seen the remnants of a garden on the first day she visited Adam, a day that felt a lifetime ago. So much had changed since then. *She* had changed since then. But she had made her vows to God to be a wife to Adam, and that was what she intended to do.

And part of being a good Amish wife was taking care of the house and garden. Even though it was too late in the season for the garden to bear any produce, she could at least start cleaning it for the next season. If nothing else, working outside would get her away from the house and the disaster that awaited her in the other rooms that she had yet to clean.

As she had already seen, the garden was mostly a mass of weeds with a few rogue plants that had somehow managed to survive what Belle presumed was years of neglect. Certainly nothing had been planted in it for years. Belle suspected Adam wasn't one to garden at all.

However, the fencing remained good, even if it needed a fresh coat of paint, and she could tell that the soil was rich. In her mind, she could envision the large plot of ground cleared of debris and organized properly with rows of corn, tomatoes, root vegetables, and cucumbers. She'd grow carrots and beets, as well as trellises of green beans, to make chow chow. And of course the back part would be filled with juicy, sweet onions and tall mint for tea.

As she stood there assessing the garden, it dawned on her that, by the time she had grown anything worthy of cooking or canning, it would be almost a year living with Adam.

The thought seemed impossible to comprehend.

How would she survive a year? How

would she survive bearing him a child? And she had yet to approach him about what he really meant when he said she could return to her family if she gave him a son.

She felt a wave of panic in her chest, and in order to calm herself, she took a few deep breaths, standing in the middle of the weedy garden and refusing to let out the sob that rose in her throat.

What on earth had she done? How could she have thrown away her life?

And yet, as soon as she asked herself those questions, she felt a sudden sense of calmness wash over her. *For I know the plans I have for you,* a voice whispered inside her head.

Ah, she thought, that feeling of peace spreading throughout her body. So it was true that God had led her to Adam. Belle didn't understand why, but she knew that he had a plan. She knew better than to question her faith in God's decisions for her life. One day, something would make sense about this arrangement . . . if that was God's will. In the meantime, he had led her outside to the garden, and Belle knew that, for now, he wanted her to get on her knees and pull weeds, to prepare the soil for next year's planting. In order for anything to grow, time needed to be spent on preparing the foundation of the garden. The more she invested in preparing the soil, no matter how distasteful the task seemed due to the years of neglect, the more likely she would have a bountiful harvest.

She was still working outside when, almost two hours later, Adam returned to the farm. She heard the sound of the buggy wheels and the horse's hooves on the dry, dirt road long before she could see him. Rather than look up when he pulled up to the barn, she remained on her knees, tugging at weeds and tossing them onto the other side of the fence. Already she had cleared half of the garden, and despite knowing that she had at least another two hours of work ahead of her, she felt a sense of accomplishment.

"Why are you tossing the weeds outside of the fence?"

She glanced over her shoulder and saw Adam standing near the gate. Sitting back on her bare feet, Belle lifted her arm and wiped the sweat from her brow. "I reckoned it would be easier to rake them up afterward rather than to keep carrying buckets of weeds to a compost pile," she said, before adding, "or wherever you put weeds." Although, after working outside for so long in the weedy garden, she highly doubted that this was a problem Adam had faced in recent years.

"I'll rake the weeds," he said, "after I unload the buggy."

Belle got to her feet, wiping her dirty hands on her apron. She pushed open the gate and followed Adam to the buggy to help carry the boxes filled with flour and sugar, coffee and yeast, eggs and butchered meat, and all of the other items that she had put onto her list. He had even purchased two boxes of fresh produce. Belle almost felt excited at the thought of making some real food for supper that evening.

"*Danke,* Adam." She began unpacking the boxes, setting each item onto the counter so that she could better assess what he had purchased and then organize the pantry.

He plopped the last box onto the floor near her feet. It was filled with fresh apples and a large bottle of corn syrup. She hadn't asked for the apples, and she looked up in surprise. But Adam was already retreating from the house.

Perhaps a nice apple pie would help break through his rough exterior, she thought, surprised to realize that she actually wanted to break through it. A lifetime was a long time to live with someone whom she knew nothing about. And, regardless of their arrangement, in order for her to return to her father's farm, she had to bear Adam a son, and that son would link them together forever.

She worked in the kitchen for the rest of the afternoon, determined to make a decent supper for herself and Adam. By the time he returned to the house, the kitchen smelled of fresh bread, baking chicken, and cooked vegetables, with a hint of onion in the air. Belle watched for a reaction from Adam as he went to the sink and began washing his hands. He splashed water on the back of his neck, apparently not noticing (or caring) that he was spilling water on the floor and the front of his shirt.

"I . . . I hope you are hungry," she said in a forced, cheerful voice.

He turned around, a damp cloth in his hands that he used to rub against his cheeks. She noticed that he avoided touching his right side, focusing most of his attention on his undamaged skin.

"Does that hurt?" she asked.

"What hurt?"

Hesitantly, she reached for the towel and made a move to dab at his right cheek. "Here. Does this hurt?"

Adam recoiled from her, shoving her hand away. "Never do that."

She pressed her lips together and lowered

her eyes. "I'm sorry, Adam. I'm just —"

He glared at her as he finished her sentence. "— curious. *Ja,* I know. So is everyone." He offered her no more insight into the cause of the scarred skin that covered the side of his face. "And *nee,* I am not."

Belle looked up, uncertain what he meant. "Not what?"

"Hungry." He threw the towel onto the floor and brushed past her as he retreated, once again, to the outside.

This time, however, Belle was not about to let him escape her so easily. She hurried after him. "Adam! I have made a *wunderbarr* meal. I know you barely ate any breakfast, and you barely ate any dinner either. You simply must *kum* inside and eat. Please."

He stopped and turned to face her. For one brief moment, Belle thought that he would return with her to the house. Instead, he tilted his face and simply repeated his question from the previous evening. "Do you love me?"

Belle winced at the question. "Adam, please. Why do you keep asking me that?"

His left eye narrowed, a stern look on his face. "Do not follow me into the dairy, Belle. That is my domain, not yours. Go back to the house and enjoy your *wunder-*

barr meal. I told you that I am not hungry." He spun away from her and slipped through the door into the darkness of the barn, leaving Belle standing alone in the barnyard, the sun beginning its descent behind the building, covering her in the golden blue of dusk.

With a sigh, Belle returned to the house, pausing only to glance at the garden. All of her work, work that she had hoped might impress Adam, seemed for naught. But as she climbed the steps to the back porch, she noticed that, true to his word, Adam had cleared away the weeds that she had tossed outside of the garden. Perhaps, she thought, there was more to Adam than met the eye. If only he would give her a chance to discover it.

CHAPTER TWELVE

Long before the sun arose, Belle stood in the kitchen, sipping some weak coffee from a chipped cup. She wore her black dress and apron, ready for the drive to the worship service. It was Sunday, and she looked forward to seeing her family and her friends. It would feel strange not to sit with the other unmarried women. Now that she was married, she would sit among other married women. While she would miss sitting next to Ella, Belle rejoiced in the fact that she could visit with Ella and Sadie after the worship service and during the fellowship hour.

Just as she had the previous morning, Belle felt refreshed. She had, once again, slept well. The fact that Adam had disappeared after supper and never returned to the house certainly contributed to her ability to sleep without fear of his joining her. But when she awoke, she noticed that the bedroom door was open. Again. She knew that she had shut the door, just as she had on the first evening. Since she had never been a heavy sleeper, she knew that if Adam had come into the bedroom, she would have heard him. Wouldn't she?

She set down the coffee cup and looked around the kitchen. The walls were still bare, which gave the kitchen a cold, unloved look. But the woodwork shone from her cleaning. And the walls, while in great need of painting, no longer had cobwebs and dust clinging to the corners. On the table, she had a ceramic pitcher filled with wildflowers that she had managed to find along the driveway. It lacked the warmth of her father's home, but it was a definite improvement over the disastrous mess that had greeted her on Friday.

In two short days, she had transformed it into a livable room. Belle felt pleased with her efforts, even if she wasn't pleased with the living arrangement.

Her thoughts were interrupted when the door opened and Adam stomped into the kitchen. He was wet, his hair matted to his head and his white shirt clinging to his chest.

Belle leaned forward and gazed out the window. She looked into the sky. It was gray and ugly. "Oh, help! Such rain!"

Adam shook his head, droplets of water sprinkling the counter.

"Let me get you some coffee!" She didn't wait for a response as she reached for another cup and poured the warm coffee into it. "It's not very good, I'm afraid. I suspect that coffee is rather old."

He stared at her outstretched hand offering the cup, and, hesitating, he reached for it. Slowly, he raised it to his lips and sipped. "That's terrible!" He glared at her. "You didn't have coffee on that shopping list!"

Belle frowned as she sipped her own cup. "We had some already. I didn't realize that it wasn't good. At least we'll get some nice coffee after worship."

"Worship?" Adam winced, giving up on the coffee and setting his cup onto the counter. He didn't seem to notice, or care, that the liquid spilled out. But Belle saw it and quickly wiped it up with a grungy towel that had been hanging over the edge of the stainless steel sink.

"Today is worship Sunday, Adam. Have you forgotten?"

From the look that he gave her, she almost second-guessed herself. Wasn't it Sunday? She counted backward and, after reassuring herself that she was correct, she nodded.

187

But Adam shook his head. "I have work to do."

Belle gasped, horrified at the mere mention of such a thing. "You can't work on the Lord's day!"

"I can and I will!"

"We *have* to go to church service!"

Adam placed his hands on the counter and leaned forward, his face fully exposed. "As the head of this household," he said in a calm, even voice, "I don't *have* to do anything."

"Adam!"

She knew that he didn't usually attend worship service. Despite his claim to have attended service, watching undetected from the shadows, Belle couldn't recall ever having seen him on the alternating Sundays when the Amish community gathered at the different farms and houses in Echo Creek. She remembered hearing one of the Troyers comment that the bishop and preachers visited Adam at home, permitting him to skip worship in town. Whether it was because his farm was so far away or because he preferred to avoid contact with others, she didn't know. But surely he hadn't expected that she, too, would miss gathering with the others to worship God.

The realization that, perhaps, he had no

intention of going — or even taking her! — caused her to panic. How could she survive if she was forced into the same isolation that had created such an insulated world for Adam?

"I . . . I need to go to worship," she managed to say. What she wanted to add was that she needed to see other people, to have four hours of real life, in order to survive the next week living with Adam Hershberger.

But Adam did not seem to care. He glanced toward the window and snickered, a reaction that Belle found more than inappropriate; it was unsettling. "I will not stop you from attending." He stared at her, his face turned askew. "Enjoy your long walk to town or wherever your worship service is being held."

Her mouth fell open and she put her hands on her hips, flustered. Surely he didn't expect her to walk all the way to town in such weather! "You'd have me walk? In this weather?"

"If that makes you happy . . ."

"What would make me happy is if my *husband*" — she emphasized the word — "accompanied me to church." What would people think if she showed up alone? It was bad enough that he had disappeared from her father's house after their wedding ceremony.

For a long minute, he stared at her. From his expression, she knew that he was irritated with her demand. She felt conflicted knowing that, just three short days after their wedding, she was disobeying him. Yet she could not fathom the idea of not attending worship. Not only did she feel isolated and lonely, but she wanted to properly worship God, to thank him for his many blessings, even if she wasn't certain that she saw too many of them at the current moment.

And then he raised his fist and brought it down on the counter, knocking over his cup of coffee, which immediately spilled onto the floor. Belle jumped, startled at his reaction. She moved backward until her back was pressed against the refrigerator as she cowered from the rage in his eyes.

" 'Let a woman learn quietly with all submissiveness,' " he quoted, holding up one finger and slowly pointing it at her. " 'I do not permit a woman to teach or to exercise authority over a man; rather, she is to remain quiet.' "

Belle trembled under his steady, repressive stare. His quickness to anger over something as righteous as worship frightened her. How could a man who felt compelled to stand before the congregation to declare his marriage vows refuse to honor God with worship? How could he confess his willingness to be a good Christian husband while rejecting worship service? And yet Adam quoted Scripture to her, which only added to her confusion.

Adam lowered his hand and turned, hastily making his way out of the kitchen and forgetting to shut the door behind him.

Taking a few seconds to catch her breath, Belle shut her eyes and leaned her head against the refrigerator. Clearly she was not going to attend worship on this Sunday that was set aside for God. And while that was disappointing enough, even more troublesome was that she would now be stuck in this house . . . this dreadful house with that dreadful man. She pressed her lips together as she walked across the floor to shut the door, pausing to peer outside in time to see Adam disappear into the barn.

To both her relief and her dismay, he did not emerge for the rest of the day.

The rainy weather brought a cold dampness that, by late afternoon, had chilled Belle to the bone. She had fixed a soup for dinner, but Adam had not returned to the house to take a meal. Belle left the soup on the stove, figuring she could reheat it if he decided to appear for supper. In the mean-time, she wandered into the sitting room and made an attempt to start a fire in the fireplace. She crumpled some old news-paper pages and placed them under pieces of broken up crates that she had found in one of the rooms. It took her a few tries for the fire to catch, but when it did, the comforting smell of burning wood filled the room. Belle sank down into the rocking chair with her Bible on her lap.

If she could not attend worship, she could still spend time with God's Word.

But even when she tried to focus on read-ing her Bible, her eyes wandered to the mess that surrounded her in the room. Like the kitchen, it appeared that no one had used the room for years. A broken windowpane let in more dampness than the fire could warm. The green shades that covered the top half of the window were torn in differ-ent places. Garbage littered the corners. With a sigh, Belle put down her book and stood up. It wasn't really working if she threw some of the litter onto the fire, was it? She didn't answer her own question. Instead, she gathered some of the papers and tossed them into the fireplace. Near the window were leaves that must have blown in over the years. She knelt down and swept them into her arms. When she tossed them onto the fire, they began to burn at once.

She had so much to do around this house. While the task was daunting, she appreciated the diversion. Without it, she would be lost in her new life with a husband who did not honor his vows, either in marriage or in baptism. She walked over to a corner curio cabinet and looked inside at the items on the shelves. A few figurines. A pretty plate. A framed cross-stitch with the Lord's Prayer. Clearly someone had loved this house at one point in time. Someone had tried to make it feel like home. But that person was long gone, leaving only a trace of hope amidst the years of dust, dirt, and decay.

After she had burned as much of the garbage and litter as she could find in the room, Belle returned to the rocking chair. The room felt warmer; not a lot, but just enough. She picked up her Bible once again and focused on reading Romans. Her feet gently pushed against the floor, the rocking chair making a soft squeaking noise whenever it rolled backward.

"For I consider that the sufferings of this present time are not worthy to be compared with the glory which shall be revealed in us." Belle paused at this verse, putting her hand inside the Bible and shutting the cover. She closed her eyes and thought about the words. Despite her suffering, she had to keep faith that God would reveal a glory in her future, even if it was not on earth but in heaven. What was suffering, she tried to tell herself, when heaven awaited the righteous?

She must have fallen asleep, for when she opened her eyes again, the Bible was on the floor by her feet and the fire had gone out. Yet she wasn't cold. She yawned, wondering how long she had slept, for the room was dark. As she started to get up, she realized that someone had covered her with a quilt. It was old and torn in a few spots, obviously having been used frequently in the past. But now it was wrapped around her, and there was only one person who could have done that: Adam.

She stood up, holding the blanket against her chest. This one small act of kindness, so simple and thoughtful, surprised her. Perhaps it was his way of apologizing for not taking her to church. Or perhaps it was his way of extending an olive branch, an attempt to show the softer side that Belle had to believe was there.

Carrying the blanket into the kitchen, she noticed that there was a dirty bowl and spoon on the counter. For some reason, the realization that Adam had come back to the house, had chosen not to disturb her sleep, and had helped himself to the soup pleased her. There was hope, she told herself as she neatly folded the blanket and placed it on the table so that, if he returned to the house, Adam would see that she appreciated his gesture.

She returned to the sitting room to collect her Bible before wandering upstairs to retire for the night, wondering if Adam would, once again, visit her bedroom while she slept.

Chapter Thirteen

After Adam's kindness on Sunday evening, Belle had hoped the week might progress in a more productive manner. Unfortunately, she quickly realized that hopes and dreams were the same thing: great to have but with no guarantees.

The rain continued until Tuesday evening. With the gray skies and the starkness of the house, which lacked any sort of warmth, or any feeling of its being a home — never mind *her* home — Belle felt as blue as the sky hidden behind the thick clouds. She spent the days cleaning the house, scrubbing walls and floors, washing windows and woodwork. But the house still felt cold and unsettled.

On Wednesday morning, she had ventured down the narrow wooden stairs to the basement, and, with a kerosene lantern in her hand, she had searched the boxes and crates, most of them covered with cobwebs.

That was when she made the discovery of an old dresser filled to the brim with yarn.

A sigh of relief escaped her lips. Yarn meant that she could crochet. Even if it wasn't autumn or winter yet, the seasons when she usually crocheted, at least she would have something to occupy her time. She dug through the different drawers, each one cleverly sorted by color, and picked out various skeins in shades of brown, cream, and tan. With her newfound treasure tucked under her arm, she hurried back upstairs to the kitchen.

After retrieving her crochet hooks from her bedroom, Belle settled onto the bench at the kitchen table and started a new blanket. She chose the arch column afghan pattern. Using each of the three colors to crochet a thick two-block row, she would use the tan to edge it. Maybe, she thought, with little items like a homemade blanket tossed over the rocking chair in the sitting room, the house might begin to feel like a home.

The thought of home gave her a moment's pause. She wondered what her father was doing. She glanced outside and, after seeing that it was still raining, decided he was probably in the barn trying to rebuild his grill, the one that would set him on the path to riches. Well, not riches, but financial freedom.

"What are you doing?"

Belle jumped when she heard Adam's voice. His words were asked not as a question, but more as an angry statement. She regained her composure and set down the four rows of crocheting that she had finished. With as much self-control as she could muster, she looked at him and replied, "I'm making an afghan."

He stood in the doorway, his large frame filling it. The look of displeasure on his face was more than apparent. "I can see that!"

Surprised by his response, Belle raised her eyebrows. "Then why did you ask?"

He raised his hand and pointed at the yarn on the table. "I meant that yarn! Where did you get that?"

Confused, Belle reached for one of the skeins. "This? Why, I found it in the basement."

He stormed across the room and snatched it from her hand. "That is not yours!"

Belle frowned, pursing her lips together. "Adam. It does no one any good in a cabinet, does it now? Besides, who else would be using it?"

"It was my mother's!" he practically growled at her.

But, this time, Belle was not intimidated. She stood up and faced him, squaring her shoulders and meeting his eyes. Reaching out, she snatched back the skein and held it against her chest. "Regardless of whose it might have been, from the looks of the basement, no one has been down there for years. I may not know much about you or your family, but I can guess your mother would not want the yarn going to waste. Especially since her new daughter — your chosen *fraa*, might I remind you? — is using it!"

Adam glared at her.

When he did not respond, Belle presumed that she had made her point. Carefully, she laid her crocheting onto the table and stood up. She clasped her hands before her waist as she faced him. "Now, since it is almost noon, I'll happily prepare you some dinner."

He glanced around the kitchen.

"*Nee,* Adam, I've yet to start cooking. You didn't come to the *haus* for dinner for the last three days. I thought it better to wait to cook for you, rather than waste food. It won't take me but a few minutes to prepare it, though. Perhaps you might wash up in the meantime."

He grunted, but, to her surprise, he followed her suggestion.

For some reason that Belle could not understand, his acquiescence made her heart race. Why had he decided to come into the house today? She hadn't seen him at dinner since Saturday, although the previous few evenings he had come in for supper. Always for supper, it seemed.

She busied herself with heating up leftovers from the previous day. She had made fried chicken and mashed potatoes, and while they were warming in the oven, she sliced some fresh bread to set upon the table, along with some homemade butter and a jar of store-bought jam.

When she finally joined Adam at the table, the kitchen had taken on the scents of a home, and the table was covered with enough food to restore his energy for an afternoon of work.

She lowered her head for the silent prayer, thanking God for the bounty of the food that she was about to eat (and adding a quick prayer that Adam might soften his harsh tone with her). When she looked up, she noticed that Adam had waited for her to finish. *Small miracles,* she thought.

"You have been busy these past few days," she said as a way to ease into conversation.

He dished the food onto his plate, heaping a pile of potatoes alongside two big pieces of fried chicken. Belle watched, amused at first, and then horrified when he took three pieces of bread and began spreading butter over them with such force that the bread crumbled.

"Oh, help!"

"What?" he asked before taking a large bite of the bread.

"I imagine you must be rather hungry, then," she commented, not hiding the disapproval in her voice. "You are eating like a starved horse!"

He glanced down at his plate and then back at her. "That is the point of the noon meal, *ja*? Eating?"

"Well, one might slow down to enjoy it a bit." As if to prove her point, she began to dish regular-sized portions onto her plate. "And the other point of meals is fellowship." Setting down the bowl of potatoes, she looked at him and forced a small smile. "It hasn't been a whole week, Adam, and I know even less about you than before our . . ." She hesitated before she added the word "wedding."

"That isn't possible." He shoved the rest of the bread into his mouth.

Belle winced. "Perhaps we could start now. Perhaps we could talk a bit."

"About what?"

"Well, for starters, about proper table manners." She picked up her fork, took a small portion of potatoes and held it up for him to see before placing it into her mouth.

Adam leaned his elbow on the table and stared at her, an amused look upon his face.

Belle set down her fork. "See? It's much more pleasant to enjoy your meal, not inhale it."

With a sigh, Adam glanced toward the ceiling and then followed Belle's example. He exaggerated as he scooped up some potatoes and delicately placed them into his mouth.

She smiled, genuinely amused by his dramatic imitation. "Much more civilized!" she said. "Now we can talk."

Another sigh.

"You have been busy outside, Adam," she started again. "May I inquire as to what you are working so hard at?"

"You may. In fact, you just did."

Belle did not appreciate the sarcasm in his response, but she remained focused on trying to break through to this man who sat at the head of the table. "And . . . ? Your response?"

"I didn't say that I would answer."

Belle pressed her lips together and frowned at him. He was being difficult. That much was clear. She crossed her arms over her chest and stared at him, anticipating his response.

After a few long, drawn-out moments of silence, he gave in. Setting down his fork, he looked at her. "But since you are so curious —"

"I am," she interrupted.

"— I've been working in the back fields, cutting corn and shocking it. I've many animals to feed in the cold season, and I need to fill the silo. Whatever is left, I sell to smaller farmers, like your *daed*."

Belle had seen the field of corn behind the house. But it certainly was not so large that he could make enough feed for others. And, on the few occasions that she had been outside when he was working, she had not once seen him in that field. In fact, she thought she remembered that the cornstalks in that field still stood.

"And, of course, there is tobacco," he continued. "Now that the weather has cleared, I must cut the leaves and hang them in the barn to dry."

"Tobacco!" Now she was genuinely confused. She had not seen any fields with tobacco crops. "Do you have a magical farm that can produce so much when I've seen none of these things?"

For a moment, she thought Adam might laugh. The look in his eyes changed from denigration to amusement.

"Magical? There is nothing magical about hard work."

The color flooded to her cheeks. "God does want us to labor. 'And whatever you do, do it heartily, as to the Lord and not to men.' Perhaps it is his hand that guides yours."

"I don't do it for the Lord. I do it to survive."

Belle shook her head. His words alarmed her. "*Nee,* Adam. You shouldn't say such things."

"And why not?" His voice rose, and his words sounded angry.

"You are baptized, Adam. You committed to God that you accepted Jesus as your Savior and that you would honor God. You must seek God's favor in everything you do."

He shoved his plate away from himself. It knocked against one of the bowls and made a loud clinking noise that startled Belle. "Look at me! How has God favored me?" He gestured to his face and neck. "I am scorned by everyone! Children see my disfigurement and run the other way! Adults mock me! The hand of friendship has never been extended my way."

"And has yours?"

He stopped ranting and stared at her as if trying to understand her question.

"Have you, Adam, ever extended your hand of friendship? Have you reached out to the community? Attended barn raisings? Or have you hidden away from the people, the community, even the church?" She paused, letting her words sink in. "The Bible tells us to 'rejoice in our sufferings, knowing that suffering produces endurance.' But it appears that you have wallowed in self-pity, Adam. If only you would reach out to God and lay your faith at his feet, acknowledge what Job learned, that God can do everything, and no thought can be withheld from him. Perhaps it is time that you, like Job, finally *see* God . . . truly see him . . . and repent in dust and ashes for having doubted his plan."

"You don't know what you are saying." His voice was low, barely audible, and for the first time since she had met him, she sensed emotion. Had she uncovered the root of Adam's self-imposed isolation?

"I don't know what happened to you, Adam. Perhaps one day you might trust me enough to confide in me." She watched him as he sat there, his expression stoic but his eyes telling Belle that he was listening. "What I do know is that you have a purpose. Disfigured or not, you are one of God's children. Release your anger over your injury and *mayhaps* others will see beyond the scars, too."

He turned his head and met her gaze. There was tension around his lips, and his eyes narrowed. "And you. What about you, Belle?" He raised his left eyebrow as he asked, "Are you able to see beyond the injuries? To love a man who looks like this?"

She hesitated. His question had caught her off guard. How could she answer that? Ever since her agreement to marry him, hadn't she proven that she was willing to try? If only he would recognize her effort . . .

In the brief silence, Adam nodded his head. There was a severe look on his face. "That's what I thought." He stood up, shoving the chair backward. "Like all of the others."

As he walked toward the door, Belle got up and hurried after him. "Wait, Adam. That's not true . . ."

He held up his hand as if to stop her while he continued walking toward the barn. "Silence speaks a truth far greater than words."

Belle leaned against the porch column and watched as Adam headed toward the stable. Her heart throbbed, and she felt a wave of sorrow wash over her. She had been close to a breakthrough with Adam, a chance to enter his life and finally learn about the man hidden behind the anger. But with just one hesitation to a question that, in truth, she didn't know how to answer, she had ruined everything.

CHAPTER FOURTEEN

By the time Saturday arrived, Belle felt as if she were walking on pins and needles. With Adam refusing to take her to worship service on the previous Sunday, she had spent the entire week at the farm with no human interaction except the few times a day Adam came inside to eat a meal. And while she wasn't particularly looking for more opportunities to be around him, she *was* starving for conversation with someone . . . anyone! . . . other than him.

After she had cleaned the breakfast dishes and prepared a casserole for dinner, she hurried to change her apron and wash her face. Eagerly, she slipped out the front door and began the long walk to town. She knew that the road would take her past her father's house, and she intended to visit with her father and sisters on her way home. But as much as she missed them, she was even more anxious to visit with Ella and Sadie.

By nine o'clock, she found herself at Ella's house, knocking at the kitchen door in the hopes that her friend was home.

No one answered.

Sighing, she walked farther down the road to Sadie's house. But she, too, was not home.

Despondent, Belle sat down on a nearby bench under a tall oak tree. She didn't want to head back, not just yet. But she also did not want to sit there, alone, until she needed to return to Adam's farm. *Our* farm, she corrected herself. She wondered if she would ever truly consider it her farm, too.

With a sigh, Belle stood up and headed into the center of town. Even if she couldn't see her friends, she could at least visit the stores in town. She needed to purchase some items that Adam had neglected to buy.

The bell over the Troyers' shop door jingled when she opened it. She tried to smile as she entered, and Linda greeted her with a pleasant hello. But there was something odd about Linda's expression, which appeared strained with curiosity. Belle tried to appear nonchalant, but she felt the tension in the air.

"New books came in last week," Linda said. "Thought we might see you on Thursday."

It was more of an unspoken question than a statement. "Adam came to town already this week." Belle suspected that Linda already knew that. Certainly if Linda and her daughters were aware that Adam only came to town twice a year, their tongues would have been wagging that he had come three times more often during this particular summer.

Belle wandered to the book section and began to peruse the titles. She found a book that she hadn't read before and began to leaf through the pages. So engrossed with the book was she, Belle didn't hear the bell tinkle once again as another customer entered Troyers' store.

"Morning, Linda," the man said.

Belle looked up and noticed John Grimm and his young children, Hannah and Gideon. She rarely saw them, except at worship services. His older daughter, Anna Rose, had been a schoolmate of Belle's. While her cousin Elizabeth Grimm was the same age as Sadie, Ella, and Belle, but had run with an older group of girls, Anna Rose was two years younger, and Belle didn't know her very well. What she did know was that John and his wife, Naomi, had seemed just as surprised as the rest of the community when they learned they were expecting twins just seven years earlier. There was a ten-year gap between Anna Rose and the twins. With all of their older children married, except Anna Rose, the suspicion was that Hannah and Gideon had not been planned, a double surprise that had not been met with the usual joy accompanying the birth of children into an Amish home.

And it showed in their behavior.

Gideon was the first to notice Belle. Immediately, he leaned over and whispered to his sister, Hannah, and she began to giggle, blatantly staring at Belle. She thought she overheard Hannah say the word "monster" and saw John glare at them. He followed their gaze to where Belle stood, and he frowned.

Belle lifted her chin and tried to appear undisturbed by the children's rude behavior. She half expected that John would reprimand them. When he didn't, Belle realized that the children had most likely overheard such a description of Adam from their parents.

Determined to face the situation head-on, Belle took her book to the counter and slid it toward Linda. "Good day, John. It's nice to see you out with your *kinner.*"

He did not reply.

"How much, Linda?" Belle asked, opening up the small purse that she kept tucked in her apron pocket. She extracted a twenty-dollar bill and gave it to Linda. "And please give my regards to Ella. I had hoped to see her today, but she wasn't at home when I stopped there."

Quickly, Linda gave her change. "She's off with Sadie to a youth picnic at the lake." The way Linda said that, Belle got the impression that she wasn't happy about it.

"That's nice. A right *gut* day for it."

John continued to stare at her, and his son began to giggle.

Belle turned toward the boy, who was no more than seven years old. "And what, Gideon, is so funny? I love to laugh and would enjoy joining you if it is something comical."

He pointed at her and scrunched up his face, a poor imitation of Adam.

Hannah hid her face behind her hands, laughing. This time, John shot Gideon a stern look.

Belle felt angry that John did not reprimand his son for being so disrespectful and, frankly, unchristian. "Ah, you are making fun of my husband, is that it?" Belle leaned down and stared at Gideon, her face inches from his. "I'm surprised that you think it funny to laugh at someone who is disfigured.

Perhaps I shall start laughing at you for being so ill-mannered." She paused. "But no, I shall not. And do you know why?" Another pause. She continued to stare at him, her close proximity to him making him shuffle his feet as if uncomfortable. "Because I know that God is watching, and God loves all of his children — those that are disfigured due to no fault of their own, and those who are rude and badly behaved due to the fault of their parents." She stood up, facing John Grimm as her words sank in. Then she reached for her book and said a pleasant goodbye to Linda before walking toward the door.

To her surprise, John walked out behind her. He called her name, and she turned.

"You have no right speaking to my son that way," he said, the anger on his face mirrored by the rage in his voice. "I'll be speaking to the bishop about this!"

"I'm certain the bishop would find it rather concerning, indeed." Belle maintained her composure. "After all, it is not the Amish way to mock others. If a parent does not raise his son, or daughter, to respect the differences among people, it reflects as poorly on the parents as it does on the children."

"How dare you!" He took a step toward

her, but Belle did not cower. "You married that . . . that abomination of a man. What do you expect? People to suddenly embrace him? A man who isolates himself from the rest of the community?"

Belle maintained her eye contact with John, a cool expression on her face. "I expect that we will practice love and acceptance, the way that God's Son taught us. Clearly the bishop will have his work cut out for him, teaching you and your children the proper way to love one another. It's a lesson you must have forgotten!" She did not wait for him to respond before she turned and started to walk away from the store. But she had only taken a few steps before she stopped, startled to see Adam standing beside his buggy, his arms crossed over his chest as he observed the exchange between Belle and John Grimm.

"Is there a problem here, Belle?" he asked, his one good eye staring directly at John.

"*Nee,* Adam. Everything is fine." But it wasn't fine. Her heart beat rapidly, embarrassed for Adam that he had witnessed John's terrible behavior. For a moment, she felt pain for all of the years that Adam must have encountered similar prejudice because of his physical appearance. No wonder, she thought, that he isolated himself.

"Then get in the buggy, and I shall take you home." He made no move to shield his face from John Grimm, nor did he stop staring at the man.

As Belle neared the buggy, Adam stepped aside and put out his hand, palm side up, for Belle to take. This gesture caused her to hesitate. He had never done that before. Without thinking, she placed her hand in his, her heart beating even faster, but this time not out of embarrassment. She couldn't explain what she felt as Adam helped her step up and into the buggy. After a week of silence and avoidance, Adam had made his first attempt at being a caring husband. As soon as she realized this, she immediately wondered why.

"Do you have any other errands?" he asked as he got into the buggy beside her.

"Nee."

"You did not tell me you were leaving."

The buggy jostled, and her arm brushed against his. "I'm sorry. You were working, and I know how you don't like to be disturbed. I wanted to visit with my friends and family, but my friends are at a youth gathering."

"And your family?"

She thought about it. She hadn't stopped there on the way to Echo Creek. Now, however, she suddenly did not feel like stopping there on the way home. "I can visit with them another day."

He held the reins in his hands, guiding the horse down the road. As Belle watched, she realized that he had not shut the buggy door. Instead, a nice breeze blew through the opening.

"What did you buy?"

She showed him the book, and, for a brief second, she thought she saw his mouth twitch as if he were trying not to smile. At the same time, she noticed the hint of a beard growing along his cheeks and chin. Why hadn't she seen that before? The realization that Adam was growing the customary beard of a newly married man startled her. She wasn't certain why. Perhaps it was the fact that she didn't *feel* like his wife, didn't *feel* as if they were truly married. And yet, clearly, Adam did.

While the thought surprised her, even more surprising was the realization that it did not entirely displease her.

For most of the drive, they sat in silence. Only this time, for some odd reason, Belle felt less uncomfortable than the last two times they were in the buggy together. She leaned back against the seat, not caring that she sat closer to Adam than before. When her arm brushed his or her leg touched his, she didn't cringe or feel threatened. Instead, she felt as if butterflies were in her stomach.

Over the past week, he had avoided her and made no move toward any intimacy. Her fear of him had been replaced by the gentle peace of a simple routine that involved little to no interaction. Yet today, when he had stood there and spoke to her in a kind voice, she had felt something stirring inside. An emotion that she had never thought she'd feel: tenderness toward the man who was still a stranger but had finally acted like a husband toward her.

"You were in town," she stated as they neared the farm. "I hadn't known you were going there."

He exhaled. "You wouldn't have known, for I didn't know, until I discovered you were gone."

"Oh." It came out soft, like a small poof of air.

"I thought you'd left."

Her eyes widened. "Left?"

"To return home."

"So you came looking for me?"

"You are my *fraa*." He glanced at her, his gaze lingering for a moment longer than usual. "But you were not at Melvin's."

"You went to my *daed*'s?"

He nodded. "So I realized you must have gone to town."

"So you came looking for me? To drag me back to your farm?"

This time, he did smile, even if he tried to hide it. "*Nee,* Belle. I came to give you a ride home. It's too warm for such a long walk."

She let his words sink in. He cared. That was what she heard: he cared about her. Those pesky butterflies fluttered once more, and she felt shy in his presence.

"You heard what John said."

He nodded.

"I'm terribly sorry."

He chuckled softly under his breath. "I'm not."

"Oh? I would think you would despise him for such horrible words."

"*Nee,* Belle. I am used to hearing those horrible words. What I am not used to hearing," he said, staring straight ahead, "is someone like you chastising people like John Grimm." He paused before he added, "So I am quite glad that I overheard it."

She knew that her cheeks flushed at the strange compliment. She didn't know how to respond, so she didn't, choosing to remain silent for the rest of their journey.

But something had changed. Something

was different between them.

When they arrived at the farm, Adam helped her get out of the buggy. This time, when her hand held his, he paused, waiting for her to look up at him. While he didn't smile, she saw that he had a calm expression on his face. No more hostility lingered in his eyes. Instead, she thought she recognized admiration there.

"*Danke,* Adam. It was thoughtful of you to fetch me," she whispered, too aware that he still held her hand.

He nodded once and gestured toward the house. "Go on and enjoy your book."

Reluctantly, she withdrew her hand. He stepped away from her, grabbing the horse's bridle and leading it toward the stable. She didn't wait to watch him unharness the horse. Instead, she hurried into the house, and, after shutting the door behind herself, she leaned against it, the book clutched against her chest.

Was it possible? she wondered. Could she ever have feelings toward Adam like a wife should toward a husband? And could Adam ever feel something toward her? A week ago, she would never have believed such a thing was possible. But today, she had hope that something . . . even if just friendship . . . could develop between them. If something as simple as Belle standing up for him could change him, perhaps time would add a deeper affection to their relationship.

CHAPTER FIFTEEN

The rain hadn't been forecast, and it caught Belle off guard. She had planned to work outside, weeding the garden and painting the fence that surrounded it. When she awoke and saw the gray skies, she sighed and hurried to get dressed. But by the time she had finished cooking breakfast, the rain was already pouring down the kitchen windowpanes.

"Oh, help!" she muttered as she stood at the sink and gazed outside.

"What's the matter?"

Startled, she spun around and placed her hand upon her chest. "Adam! You frightened me."

He gave her a look as if trying to interpret exactly how she meant that.

"I didn't know you were there," she said gently. "And look at you! You're soaking wet!" Quickly she hurried to take his hat and coat, mindful not to slip on the puddles of water that he had tracked into the house. "Sit down and let me get you some hot coffee."

She hung up his hat and coat on two pegs in the wall near the door. Water dripped down and collected on the floor. She'd have to dry that before it left marks on the wooden floor, but first she wanted to make certain that he warmed up.

After giving him a mug of steaming coffee, she went to the fireplace and threw in another log. "Did you know that it was to rain today?" she asked him.

"Only God knows what the weather will do."

She frowned as she stood up from the fireplace. He was in a sullen mood, that was for sure and certain. Perhaps it was just the weather. For the past few days, he had been more quiet than usual, if that was even possible. Belle did her best to walk wide circles around him as she went about her daily chores. "It was such nice weather yesterday," Belle commented as she hurried back to the kitchen stove to dish up his breakfast. "I had hoped to work in the garden a bit. Reckon that won't happen today, *ja*?"

"Reckon not."

She set down the plate before him. "This should warm you up right quick."

He made a noise deep in his throat but said nothing else as he waited for her to join him at the table.

Bowing her head, she gave thanks to God for the blessings of the day, including the rain, before she began to eat. The silence in the kitchen began to feel overwhelming, especially since she had been looking forward to working outside.

Even though it hadn't yet been two weeks, her long days of solitude were beginning to wear on her nerves. She missed being around her sisters and father. With Adam being so sullen and usually outside anyway, she was spending far too much time alone in the house. She missed conversations during meal times and playing games in the late evenings. Even the housework was dull, for ever since she had finished cleaning the house, it rarely got dirty, since Adam only came in for meals.

With a big sigh, Belle set down her fork and reached for her glass of water. "I should have picked up some apples while I was in town the other day. I could've canned applesauce today."

He didn't say anything as he continued shoveling food into his mouth.

"And I've already finished my book."

The sound of her voice in the room

sounded empty and hollow. If only she knew how to reach Adam and help him soften the harsh edges of his personality. Whether or not she loved him — and she most certainly did not! — she had committed to being his wife. Was it possible that he might, one day, treat her as such? Instead, he continued to treat her like a stranger in his home and life.

"I reckon I'll clean that back room, then," she said, mostly to herself, since she expected no answer from him. "I saw a china cabinet in there. I imagine nothing's been cleaned in it for years."

He grunted.

She made a face and sighed. Then, without waiting for him to finish, she stood up and carried her plate full of uneaten food to the sink. She was just about to throw it out when she had another idea. "Where's Shep?" She directed the question to Adam, who, for once, looked up and acknowledged that she had spoken. "You know, Shep? Your dog?"

"What for?"

She held up the plate. "No sense wasting the food." Carrying the plate to the door, she opened it and called out for the dog.

"That's not his name."

The irritation in his voice surprised her.

Why should he get so offended by her calling the dog the wrong name? "Well, I had to call him something," she countered. "And you never call him anything but 'dog.'"

"That's his name."

She almost laughed. "Dog? You named your dog Dog?" Despite trying not to, she couldn't help herself and finally laughed. "Why, I should think calling him Shep is quite an improvement over just calling him Dog."

At the sound of her laughter, he glared at her and shoved his plate away from him. "His name is Dog!" He stood up and stomped to the door, pausing to snatch the plate from her hand before he pushed the door open and stormed away.

Belle couldn't keep herself from laughing. She hadn't meant to upset him, but the ridiculousness of a man living without any other companion besides a dog with no name struck her as humorous. Adam seemed to genuinely care for the dog, but to never have named it?

While she cleaned up the breakfast dishes, she continued shaking her head and smiling over the farcical situation.

An hour later, with all of the other chores completed, Belle made her way into the large room across from the sitting room. Earlier that week, she had swept and washed the floor. Twice. But she hadn't tackled cleaning any of the furniture. There wasn't much in the room — just a large sideboard and the china cabinet. The size of the room would have been perfect for hosting worship services, but it appeared that there was currently no use for the room at all.

Sitting on the hardwood floor before the china cabinet, she opened the lower doors and peeked inside. She caught her breath at the sight of beautiful, stacked china dishes. Carefully, she reached for one, withdrawing it and holding it up to the dim light that shone through the windows in the front.

It was white china with pretty, rose-colored flowers around the rim. Painted gold trimmed the edges. From the looks of it, there were twenty-four place settings. A set like this often started as a wedding gift, with pieces and place settings added to it over the years. Belle had never seen such a beautiful set of dishes, and she longed to know their history.

She opened another cabinet door and found serving bowls and platters, teapots and teacups. With as much care as possible, she removed each piece and set it upon the floor. By the time she finished, she realized what a hidden treasure she had just found.

Rather than carry all of the pieces to the kitchen for washing, she decided it was safer to wash them in that very room. After fetching one tub full of soapy water for washing and another full of plain water for rinsing, she set about the task of wiping away the years of neglect and abandonment. It was a task that took time and patience, for she did not want to chip even one of the pieces.

As she dried them, she wondered how many family meals had been served on these plates. Surely Adam's mother must have come from a large family, for no one would need such a tremendous set unless there were plenty of children and grandchildren. And yet, why would his mother have been the recipient of such an heirloom? Shouldn't the gift have passed to another, perhaps a sibling who had more children and could actually use the china?

That was when an idea occurred to her: she would set the dinner table with the china and prepare a wonderful meal for Adam. Perhaps that would encourage him to open up to her at last!

After cleaning the cabinet, including the glass doors on top, she carefully returned all of the pieces except for two place settings and serving dishes, enough to set the dinner table.

By the time Adam returned to the house, with the empty plate from breakfast in his hand, the kitchen smelled of pan-fried ham, mashed potatoes, fresh bread, and steamed vegetables that she had purchased in town. And the table looked beautiful, the food perfectly arranged on the china platter and bowls, set before the two place settings.

"What is this?" He looked genuinely curious as he walked to the table and picked up one of the plates. "Where did you find these?"

She smiled at him, her hands clasped behind her back. "In that big empty room. They were in the china cabinet."

The curious expression on his face darkened, changing into a scowl. "Then these are my *maem*'s." He set the plate back onto the table. "Who said you could use them?"

Belle's mouth opened into a small O at the harshness of his voice. "Who said that I could not?" she countered sharply. "What good does the china do sitting there? Unused? That's wasteful, Adam. Just like the yarn that was downstairs in the dusty old basement!"

"These things are not yours."

She pressed her lips together. "You didn't even know the china was there! Why, how long has it been since you even stepped into that room? How long has it been since she died?"

From the way the muscles twitched in his jaw, Belle could tell that he was agitated. She didn't fancy an argument with her husband, for she knew that the Bible said "stirring up anger produces strife." She tried to take a deep breath and calm herself, hoping that Adam was capable of doing the same.

"I don't mean to pry, Adam," she said in a soft voice. "I'm sure that it was not easy, living here alone for so long." Cautiously, she took a step toward him. "Surely your *maem* would want her china used for delicious meals. She'd want her yarn used to make warm blankets and winter hats. Simply boxing away her things and pushing them into the corners of the house does not make them go away. Nor does it lessen the pain of her passing." She took another step toward him. "Mourning your loss is one thing. Refusing to live your life . . . well, that's quite another."

He lifted his chin defiantly, his one good eye staring at her.

"Clearly you want to live," she continued in that same soft voice. "You want a son. That's what you told me. Do you want your son to live like you did when she was alive, or would you prefer he live the way you do now, isolated and alone?" Slowly, she reached out her hand as if to touch his cheek. But he grabbed her wrist and leaned backward. Belle remained determined to try to reach him. "It's as if Satan has your heart locked up in a little box. But don't you know that you hold the key, Adam? You can unlock that box and live again, Adam."

For a moment, he closed his eyes. There was a pained look on his face, and Belle waited, hoping that her words might have triggered something — anything! — to break through the self-constructed barrier that surrounded him. But then he shook his head, mumbling, "No, no, no." Gently, he pushed her away from him and stepped backward. "No."

"Why 'no'?"

He kept shaking his head. "You don't know what it is like. Being abandoned. Being unloved." His voice trembled, and he refused to look at her. "Being a beast to everyone who sees you."

"I don't think you are a beast," she said.

He snapped his gaze to meet hers. "Don't you?"

"I most certainly do not."

"Do you love me?"

And, once again, Belle hesitated too long.

That same dark expression crossed his face, his eyes turning icy as he pressed his lips together. "That's what I thought." He spun around and stormed out through the kitchen door, letting it slam shut behind himself.

Belle started to run after him, stepping outside and dashing down the porch steps. She stood in the rain, her bare feet in a mud puddle. Adam was already entering the barn, Shep barking and dancing around his legs in happy circles.

"Adam!" she shouted. "How can I learn to love you if you won't show me who you are?"

But her words were drowned out by a rumble of thunder.

CHAPTER SIXTEEN

It was a warm day, even for late September. Belle wiped the perspiration from her brow with the back of her hand. All that morning she had made applesauce with the carton of apples that Adam had picked up for her the day before. The windows were open, but even the occasional breeze did nothing to cool the kitchen.

She leaned down and glanced out the window. The sun was still high in the sky, and Belle wondered how Adam was making out in the fields. At breakfast, he had commented that he would be cutting hay. Belle had frowned, wondering about all of the crops he said he was managing. But she didn't ask. Now, with the applesauce canned, Belle decided she would bring Adam some fresh meadow tea (for there was plenty of mint growing around the gardens) and see for herself.

With a plastic cup and a pitcher in hand,

Belle headed toward the barn. She wandered behind the dairy and noticed a dirt path that ran between the large paddock for the cows and the cornfield behind the horse stable. She followed the path to the tree line just beyond the two fields. To her surprise, the path continued into the woods, winding to the left. It was cooler under the cover of the trees, and she found herself lost in the noises of nature. Birds singing. Leaves rustling.

But the woods were not very large. The path ended at the edge of the trees. For a moment, Belle stood there, staring in amazement at a large field that merged into another and another. Her mouth dropped as she realized that all of the land she was staring at belonged to Adam. If she had wondered about where all of his "magical" crops were, she now knew: here.

In the distance, she saw Adam on the hay cutter, driving his team of four Belgian draft horses across the field of grass. He was far enough away that he didn't see her, so she began to walk along the edge of the hay field toward him. She watched him as he worked, realizing that it was the first time she'd had an opportunity to see him in the midst of his farm duties. He wore black trousers that had a tear over the knee and a long-sleeved white shirt that clung to his back with sweat. The straw hat shielded his face from the sun, but even from this distance, she could see the moisture on his brow.

When he guided the horses to turn, she lifted her arm and waved to him.

"Whoa!" He leaned back as he pulled on the reins to stop the horses. *"Wie gehts?"*

She held up the pitcher. "I thought you might be thirsty working outside."

He squinted as he glanced at the sun overhead. "*Ja,* I am."

As she poured him a cup of the iced tea, she couldn't resist inquiring about the fields. "I didn't realize that your farm went all the way back." Handing him the cup, she met his eyes. "I've never been over here. And from the house, I never suspected the farm was so large."

Adam lifted the cup to his lips and drank down the liquid in one long, slow gulp. "It used to be larger," he said as he handed her the cup to refill.

"Larger?" Nothing he said could have surprised her more. "Why! It's already the largest farm in Echo Creek! Who on earth can farm all of this land?"

"It's been in the Hershberger family for generations, Belle. Passed down from father to son."

She thought she caught a sad tone in his words. Usually the Amish passed down their farms to one of the younger sons. With smaller families, however, older sons might inherit the farm. "Do you have any siblings?"

He shook his head and looked away. "Seems like you now know the truth about the magical crops," he said, changing the subject away from his family. He returned his attention to her. "The only magic is a man who works from before sunup and long after sundown."

"That's a lot of work for one man." She hesitated before adding, "It would be easier with the help of another, don't you think?"

His expression softened, and he lowered his tone as he said, "Women don't belong in the fields."

"That's nonsense, Adam Hershberger," she scolded. "It's also nonsense that you are too proud to ask for help. Why, I see women helping their husbands in the fields quite frequently in Echo Creek!"

He exhaled sharply. "*Nee,* Belle. Not my woman."

"Pride is a sin."

"It isn't pride, Belle."

"Then what is it?"

But he wouldn't answer her question.

His silence infuriated her. Just when she thought they were beginning to have a breakthrough, he shut down and retreated into himself. How could she ever learn to feel something for a man who constantly hid behind invisible barriers? "Well, Adam," she said in a pithy tone, "*mayhaps* one day you will see fit to confide in me. To open up and share so that I can understand. In the meantime" — she took the empty cup from his hand — "I'll just busy myself in the house." She started to walk away, but stopped and added, "Like a good *fraa, ja?*"

Angrily, she retraced her steps quickly to put as much distance as she could between herself and Adam. Once she reached the path in the woods, Belle stopped and shut her eyes. Her shoulders felt heavy and her chest tight. Before she could stop herself, she began to cry. The tears rolled down her cheeks, and she wiped at them with her free hand.

She knew that God had a purpose for her. At the moment, however, she could not begin to imagine what it was. While she knew better than to complain about her current situation, for others bore much heavier crosses, she was beginning to feel that her shoulders were simply not strong enough to carry her particular cross.

When she emerged from the woods and began walking down the path toward the house, her thoughts of self-pity were interrupted by voices coming from the distance. Eager for a distraction (and any interaction with another person!), she quickened her pace. It was only when she was almost clear of the cornfield on her right that she saw two women standing near the back door of the house.

"Ella! Sadie!" She practically ran toward them, her eagerness for female companionship overtaking her sense of propriety. As she neared them, she dropped the pitcher and cup so that she could embrace her two friends.

"Oh, Belle!" Ella was the first to extract herself from Belle's hold. "You've been crying!"

Sadie shook her head and clicked her tongue. "Crying," she exclaimed as she reached into her pocket for a handkerchief. "New brides should not cry."

Belle took the neatly folded hanky and dabbed at her eyes. She almost laughed as she looked at her two dearest friends. "I think I'm crying now for joy at seeing the two of you."

Ella kept her arm around Belle's shoulders and guided her toward the house. "Take us

237

inside, Belle, and let's visit a spell. I'm sorry we didn't come earlier, but we thought you might want some privacy. When *Maem* mentioned that you stopped at the store last Saturday, I was sorry to have missed you."

Once inside the kitchen, Belle gave them a brief tour through the house. She tried to explain the condition in which she had found the place two weeks ago when Adam had brought her to live there. But words could not describe the lack of care over the years. When they went upstairs, Belle showed them her bedroom. From the clothing that hung on the wall, it was clear that only she occupied the room.

Sadie gave her a look but made no comment.

"*Kum* now, Belle," Ella said, reaching for her hand. "Let's sit in the kitchen and catch up. I'm sure you have much to tell us."

Only when they were seated at the table, some freshly baked bread and butter set out for her friends, did Belle begin to open up.

"He's as much a stranger to me now as he was when I said I would marry him," she confessed. She wrapped her hands around the glass of water before her.

"A stranger?" Sadie bit her lower lip. "Have you no interactions with him, then?"

"*Nee,* not many. He spends most of his

time working outside. Sometimes he doesn't even come in for meals."

"Well, that's not because of your cooking," Sadie quipped. "That's for sure and certain!"

Ella laughed and even Belle smiled.

"He refused to take me to church. My heart simply broke. I couldn't believe that I wouldn't see you or my family."

"But that was just a few days after your wedding. *Mayhaps* he wanted to avoid prying eyes," Ella said. "Will you be coming tomorrow?"

"I hope so!" She tried to appear nonchalant and quickly changed the subject. "Tell me, then. Tell me about what has been happening in Echo Creek. It's so isolated out here that I feel lost and rather out of touch with reality."

Ella glanced at Sadie, a silent and secret communication exchanged between them.

"What? What is it?" Belle reached up her hand to cover her heart. "Has something happened to my *daed*?"

"*Nee, nee,*" Sadie quickly reassured her. "Nothing bad has happened at all."

"Then what are you afraid to tell me?"

Ella swallowed, and only after Sadie nodded her head did she begin to talk. "It seems that your *daed* is suddenly doing rather well, Belle. The entire town is talking about it. He drove a new horse and buggy into town just two evenings ago. And your *schwesters* . . . they both have new dresses that they wore to a youth gathering on Saturday evening."

"New dresses?" Belle stared at Ella in amazement. "But . . . my *daed* cannot afford those things."

Sadie leaned forward. "There's more," she whispered. "When we walked past your *daed*'s farm, there were cows. Lots of cows."

Stunned, Belle leaned back in disbelief. "How is that possible?"

"Linda told me that she overheard a customer talking about someone investing in your *daed*'s latest invention. That grill. The entire town is talking about it."

"Tongues are wagging along the Amish grapevine," Sadie confirmed.

Belle frowned. If someone had invested in her father's grill, then her marriage to Adam had been unnecessary. She had tried to save her family from being destitute and homeless. Now, however, they were doing better than ever, and just weeks after she had sacrificed her own future for theirs. Her shoulders sagged and she felt deflated, devoid of any emotion beyond defeat.

"And that's not all." Ella reached up to

push back a strand of her blond hair that had fallen from beneath her prayer *kapp.* "Adam . . ."

Belle looked up. "What about Adam?"

"Why, he's come to town more often in the past two, three weeks than he normally does in that many years!" Ella glanced at Sadie, who nodded her head in agreement. "No one can believe how frequently he rides to town."

Belle couldn't help but wonder what, exactly, he was doing. She knew that he had driven in twice, once to shop for her and another time to fetch her. But she didn't always pay attention to what he was doing throughout the day. "Such strange happenings," she muttered under her breath. "I know so little about this man that I must spend the rest of my life with."

Sadie reached out and covered Belle's hands with her own. "Certainly he cannot be that intolerable."

"Intolerable"? The word struck Belle, and she made a face. *"Nee,* that's not it at all. Why, I hardly notice the scars, Sadie. And, every so often, I find that there is some tenderness beneath that gruff exterior. On Sunday night, I fell asleep reading the Bible, and he must have covered me with an old quilt that he found. And when I arrived at

the house on Friday after the wedding" —
how strange that word sounded on her lips!
— "he had fixed up my bedroom upstairs,
even if the rest of the house was in shambles.
There are some very thoughtful qualities
about Adam. But he shares nothing with
me and refuses to let me assist with the
outside chores."

At this statement, both Ella and Sadie
frowned.

"*Ja,* it's true," Belle continued. "I thought
it was pride, that he wants to do it all
himself as if he must prove something to
others. He says it's not. I just don't understand why he will not accept my help in the
fields or the dairy — especially the dairy.
He's quite adamant about that."

"That does seem rather odd." Ella glanced
at Sadie. "Do you know anything about
him? I was too young when his *maem* died."

Sadie raised an eyebrow. "You and I are
the same age," she said. "Why should I
know any more than you?"

"Perhaps your *daed* told you about him?"

But Sadie merely shook her head. "*Nee,* I
only know the same school yard stories as
the rest of the town."

They talked for another thirty minutes
before Sadie mentioned that they should
get started on the long way home. Besides,

Ella pointed out, Belle probably needed to start preparing supper for her husband. Belle couldn't believe that their visit was over. Time had flown far too quickly.

Belle sighed. "If he decides to take his meal with me. If only he would see my efforts and make his own to open up to me."

Ella gave her a soft smile. "In due time, Belle. I'm sure he'll come around in due time."

As Ella and Sadie turned toward the door, Belle started when she saw Adam leaning against the door frame. "Adam!"

His arms were crossed over his chest, and, despite the scowl on his face, he appeared relaxed. She wondered how long he had been standing there.

"My friends . . ." she stammered. "Ella and Sadie . . . they've come visiting."

"I see that." His deep voice filled the room, and for a moment, Belle panicked. Would he be angry that her friends had come without being invited? Would all of the progress they had made over the past two weeks disappear? The way he stood there without entering the room was intimidating enough, never mind that there was such an aura of mystery about him among the Amish community in town.

"We were just leaving, actually." Ella gave

him a warm, genuine smile. "It'll be supper time by the time we reach town."

Adam glanced at the clock on the wall. "I'll harness the horse —"

"Nee, nee!" Sadie held up her hands to stop him. "That's kind of you, Adam. But I'm looking forward to the long walk." When she said this, Ella nodded in agreement. There was no malice or judgment in word or action.

"Suit yourselves, then." Adam shifted his gaze toward Belle, his eyes holding hers for just a few seconds, but long enough to cause her to wonder if he was trying to secretly communicate with her. If so, she did not understand. Their marriage lacked the years of bonding that permitted couples to communicate with silent conversation, spoken only with their eyes.

"Mayhaps we'll see you in church on Sunday, *ja?"* Ella said as she readied herself to depart for the long walk to Echo Creek.

"I hope so." Belle walked her two friends to the front door, repeating her goodbyes before they left.

For a long moment, she stood in the open doorway, watching them walk down the lane until they disappeared around a bend, the trees blocking them from her view.

CHAPTER SEVENTEEN

Once again, when Sunday came around, Adam was nowhere to be found. Belle had arisen early in order to dress for church and prepare a light meal so that they wouldn't be too hungry during the worship service. But as the sun began to rise over the roof-line of the barn, all Belle could hear was the distant barking of Adam's dog and the morning song of the birds in the trees.

Sighing, she covered a plate of food for him and left it on the table. If he wasn't going to attend church, that was his business. But she'd have to start walking in order to get there on time.

As she headed down the lane toward the main road, she kept looking into the paddocks that lined the driveway. The cows grazed under the warm autumn morning sun. Clearly he had already milked them. *So where is he hiding?* she wondered.

With each step that took her farther away

from the farm, Belle began to gain a new sense of freedom. She couldn't wait to sing with the rest of the congregation and to enjoy fellowship with her friends afterward. Perhaps she would stop to visit with her family before she returned home to make a modest supper for herself and Adam.

Even though the weather was beautiful, Belle was glad that church was being held at one of the homes neighboring her father's farm and not one of the houses on the south side of town. *Adam's farm,* Belle corrected herself as she approached her old home. As she neared the farm, she noticed that the new buggy was already gone. One glance up at the sky told her that she needed to hurry if she wanted time to visit with her friends before the worship service began. But her legs were increasingly tired from the long walk to town.

"Belle!"

She heard the voice just as she was turning into the driveway at the farm where church was being held. It was Anna Rose Grimm, standing with Sadie under the shade of a tall tree. Smiling, Belle jogged a little to meet up with them.

"You haven't entered yet, then?"

Anna Rose shook her head. "We were waiting for Ella to join us." And then, with a big smile, she asked, "I haven't seen you since the wedding. How *is* married life, anyway?"

If only I had the answer to that, Belle thought. *"Gut.* Right *gut,"* she heard herself say, and she hoped her voice was believable. She suspected that it was not. "And how are you doing, Anna Rose? I saw your *daed* just the other week in town."

Whether from the change in subject or the subject itself, Anna Rose laughed. In her pink dress and with her shiny blond hair just poking out from beneath the front of her prayer *kapp,* Anna Rose was a pretty young woman who, as far as Belle knew, never had an unkind word to say about anyone. So she was surprised to hear Anna Rose say, "Oh, I heard all about your meeting with *Daed.*"

Belle's mouth opened just a little.

Waving her hand, Anna Rose indicated that everything was fine. *"Nee,* Belle. Don't worry none. Those two little ones are a bit unruly, don't you think?"

Her cheeks flamed hot pink. "I'm so sorry, Anna Rose. It's just . . ." How could she possibly excuse the fact that she'd spoken so sharply to Anna Rose's father? She didn't know the young woman well enough to explain exactly what had happened, and she could only imagine what John Grimm had shared with his family in regard to Belle's confronting him. ". . . I reckon I shouldn't have scolded your *bruder.*"

"Someone has to." Anna Rose's eyes twinkled with mischief. "It's a known fact that those twins could use a bit more of the rod behind the woodshed."

Sadie glanced over Belle's shoulder. "Oh, now. Here comes Ella. We can walk in together then, *ja?*"

Talk of the incident with John Grimm having been put to rest, the four young women walked down the rest of the driveway and entered the barn where church service was being held. It felt odd to walk into the barn, her first time as a married woman and without her husband beside her. Belle wasn't certain which made her feel more uncomfortable. Many people glanced in her direction when she started making her way through the line of women, shaking their hands and greeting them with a kiss. But Belle held her head high and hurried to take her place at the end.

She looked around and was surprised not to see her father or sisters. If the buggy wasn't at the farm, where on earth could they be?

"You're looking for your *daed* and

schwesters, ja?"

Belle glanced over at Ella. "I am."

Ella shook her head. "They won't be here today. Your *daed* had business out of town yesterday, and I heard that your *schwesters* went with him. A hired boy is tending to the cows in their absence."

For a moment, Belle felt overcome with disappointment. How was it possible that her entire family had simply moved on with *their* lives without any consideration for *hers*? No letters, no visits. While she hadn't anticipated accolades for the sacrifice she had made, she certainly hadn't expected her family to sever all ties with her. She felt as if she didn't exist anymore, at least not as a Beiler. Perhaps that was what they thought — that Belle was Adam's family now, not a part of theirs.

Or was it something more?

As the youngest sister of the three daughters, it was highly uncommon that she should wed when the older daughters had not. Perhaps there was some jealousy on the part of her sisters? Perhaps they didn't want to see her because it was a reminder that Belle, not either one of them, had married first. And her father . . . surely he felt some shame that his inability to properly provide for his children had resulted in Belle having to marry Adam. Now that he was actually becoming successful — at last! — the weight of guilt must be tremendous.

With these new thoughts, Belle's disappointment changed to compassion. As she sat on the hard bench, only half listening to the sermon, she made a mental note to write them a short letter and drop it in the mailbox the next time she went to town. Perhaps that might encourage them to reach out to her.

After the service, as the women began to prepare the food and the men prepared the tables, Belle was surprised to see the bishop heading toward her. His long white beard touched the second button on his black vest, making him look older and wiser than she had remembered.

"It's right *gut* to see you, Belle," he said when he stood before her.

"*Danke,* Bishop. I'm glad to be here."

The bishop looked around as if to seek someone else. "No Adam then?"

"*Nee.*"

If Belle thought that the bishop might scold her for Adam's absence, he did not. Instead, he nodded his head and sighed. "In due time, I'm sure. He'll come around."

His words stunned her. Wasn't that what Ella had said the previous day? And while

Belle would have liked to understand what exactly that meant, she did not. " 'Come around,' Bishop?"

The old man smiled, just slightly. His eyes looked tired as he stared at her, studying her face. "Sometimes, Belle," he said in a slow, deliberate voice, "things are not what they seem. It takes a truly righteous person to realize that."

To Belle, this was just one more riddle to add to the puzzle. Was he referring to Adam? What was it that Adam might be seeing in such a different light that, until he removed his blinders, would keep him from being a truly righteous man? She wanted to ask the bishop to explain, but she didn't want to insinuate that there was anything wrong between her and Adam. The problems between a husband and wife were not to be aired to others.

"I'll be certain to pray about that" was all that she could think to say.

He reached out and patted her arm. It was a reassuring gesture, one that she had never seen the bishop make to anyone. "*Mayhaps* I was surprised to learn you agreed to marry Adam, but now I see God's wisdom behind the choice."

Wisdom? Choice? Belle frowned, unhappy with this exchange. She didn't see any wisdom behind her decision to marry Adam, and she certainly didn't feel as if she'd had any choice. No, her decision had been based strictly on desperation to save her family from being homeless. And yet the bishop seemed genuinely pleased. It was clear that he truly believed what he had said. Perhaps the bishop was becoming addle-brained. His words seemed intended to confound her, as if he wanted to leave her with something to ponder. But she had no time to ask him any further questions.

The bishop's eyes shifted over her shoulder toward the door. There was something in his expression, the way it changed, that made Belle curious. It was almost as if he were hiding a smile, and his eyes suddenly looked less tired. Almost simultaneously, a hush fell over the gathering, and from where Belle stood, she could see that the others in the room were also staring in the same direction as the bishop.

Belle turned around to see what had caught their attention.

A tall figure stood in the doorway. Adam. His black felt hat was planted firmly on his head, his face tilted in such a way that the scars on it were hidden from view. His eyes moved across the room until he spotted Belle.

Before he had a chance to approach her, the bishop hurried to greet him.

"Adam, it's right *gut* to see you."

Adam nodded. *"Danke."* Belle could hear the trepidation in his voice. He was nervous about being there. And yet, he had come. She felt a presence beside her and noticed that her friends were standing next to her, as if surrounding her with support rather than leaving her to stand there all alone.

"Had you come a few hours earlier," the bishop said in a half-teasing, half-serious tone, "you might have caught the sermon."

Belle saw several other people watching the exchange, their curiosity greater than their manners.

While Belle watched, Adam glanced around the room, clearly too aware that everyone was watching him. "My apologies, Bishop," he managed to say. "Perhaps next service." His eyes caught hers, and he hesitated, just long enough for her to feel the heat rise to her cheeks. "If you'll excuse me," he said to the bishop in a soft voice, his eyes still watching Belle, "I've come to fetch my *fraa.*"

"Reckon I must go now," she said to her friends.

Ella leaned forward and whispered, "See? In due time . . ."

Belle blushed and tipped her head down. "I'm rather pleased that he came for me, I admit it."

With an encouraging smile, Ella started to step away from her. "It is rather romantic, isn't it?"

Sadie hid a smile, and Anna Rose's eyes widened. "Romantic? Oh, help."

Belle hoped that her cheeks were not as red as they felt. She hurried over to where Adam waited for her, just inside the doorway. He took a step aside to let her pass him. "You bring anything with you?" he asked.

"*Nee*. Too far to carry anything anyway."

As they walked across the porch and down the steps, two children ran across the walkway, laughing. One of them tripped and fell on the walkway. Immediately, Adam bent down to assist him. But the boy looked up and, upon looking into Adam's face, recoiled. His tears of pain turned into those of fear as he scrambled to his feet and ran toward the house.

Belle placed her hand on Adam's arm. "The more you are around people, the less they will react like that."

Even though her gentle words were meant to soothe him, she could tell that he was hurt by the boy's reaction. He said nothing as he walked farther away from the house. Belle followed, her heart hurting for the pain that he surely felt. She couldn't imagine how anyone could go through life with people rejecting them as soon as they walked into a room. Adam's confidence must have disappeared years ago. No wonder he seemed so bitter.

When he helped her into the buggy, she looked directly into his eyes. "*Danke,* Adam."

The muscle between his eyes twitched. "For . . . ?"

"Fetching me. While walking is nice, especially in such weather, so is riding in the buggy."

He made a noise deep in his throat acknowledging her words of appreciation. For a few moments, he focused on backing up the horse and buggy before turning the horse to head down the driveway and toward the road. Only then did he speak again. "Did you see your family, then?"

Even though he was looking straight ahead, she shook her head. "*Nee,* they weren't there."

He made another noise, almost a scoffing sound.

"Funny thing is . . ." she began cautiously, "I heard that many *wunderbarr gut* things are happening for them these days. That *Daed* is doing quite well. Apparently people are ordering his new grill. In just the two weeks since we've married, things are starting to look up for my *daed*."

He glanced at her, a concerned expression on his face. "What are you saying, Belle?"

She lifted her shoulders in a simple shrug. "Just that it's interesting how everything improved for them so quickly."

His eyebrows dipped together as he frowned. "Would you go back on your word now?"

That hadn't been what she meant. Still, his reaction amused her. She laughed. "We're married, Adam! Whether I would or would not, the answer is that I couldn't."

"You could, Belle. You know that." He paused, and she could see the tension in his face. "We are married, but we are not" — he pressed his lips together — "husband and wife."

Belle realized what he was insinuating. A marriage that was not consummated was not really a marriage at all. "I don't think God looks at it that way, Adam."

He remained silent.

"Adam, we vowed to God that we would be husband and wife. If for whatever reason you do not wish to act upon that, so be it.

But I will never go back on my promises to God." She reached out and placed her hand upon his. It surprised her when he jumped at her touch. "Nor to you. It doesn't matter how we came together. What matters is that we *are* together."

Something seemed to relax in his shoulders.

Swallowing, Belle decided to take advantage of being in the buggy with him. There was no way for him to simply walk away if he didn't like what she said. "And part of being together is being truthful with each other.

"Please, Adam. You need to talk to me. I can take almost anything, but not your propensity to keep silent when you don't like the conversation."

His hands tightened on the reins. But once again, he kept silent.

Would she ever be able to break through his walls?

Chapter Eighteen

"Belle Hershberger!"

Belle almost did not turn at the sound of her name. After three weeks of marriage, it still sounded unfamiliar to her ears. But soon she realized that someone was calling to her. It was Elizabeth Grimm, Anna Rose's cousin. With her blond hair and bright green dress, she stood out among the dark shelves of Troyers' store.

"I didn't see you there," Belle said, putting aside the book that she had been reading. Linda had told her that Ella was busy in the back storeroom, but would soon be out to say hello. Belle had been passing the time by browsing the books.

"You were quite engrossed in that book." Elizabeth laughed, the sound cheerful and kind. She was older than Belle but had always been good to her. "I had hoped to visit with you after church on Sunday, but I was told that you left early. I wanted to tell you I was sorry to have missed your wedding the other week."

At the mention of the wedding, Belle paused. A lot of the community had not been at the wedding, mostly because it had been held outside of the normal marriage season. Yet, in hindsight, Belle could hardly remember who had or had not attended. The day had been a blur, and the memory of it seemed two lifetimes ago. So much had changed in her life over the past few weeks, especially since she had married Adam.

"How have you been?" Elizabeth smiled politely.

"*Gut,* right *gut,*" Belle responded, hoping that her voice did not catch and betray the truth. "And you?"

"Oh, just fine enough. Been a bit tired recently," Elizabeth admitted. "Change of seasons and all, I reckon. It's tough with teaching, too."

Belle had forgotten that Elizabeth was the schoolteacher. "That would just about make anyone tired, I'm sure."

For a few more minutes, they exchanged pleasantries before Elizabeth said goodbye, leaving the store with her package under her arm.

Belle sighed and reached for the book that she had been reading. She flipped through the pages, trying to find the spot where she had left off. But she knew that she should not spend Adam's money on a book. She had come to town to purchase some vegetables. Right before she had left, Adam had harnessed the horse and hitched it to the buggy, asking her yet again if she wanted him to drive her. But Belle knew that he needed to bale the hay that he had cut three days before. Rain was forecast for the following afternoon, and wet hay could not be baled. So she had declined his offer and drove herself into town.

However, Adam still had one more surprise for her. Just as she had been ready to leave, he slipped some money into her hand, his fingers lingering a second or two longer than necessary, and told her to treat herself to something nice.

Her first thought had been to purchase a book. She spent her evenings alone, her only companions the characters in the stories. While she wasn't necessarily complaining, she was feeling a void in her life, one that could not be filled by her imagination alone.

But now, as she stared at the shelves lined with all sorts of literature — inspirational, romance, spiritual — she knew that it would be selfish of her to use his money for that. After all, she had just bought a book recently, and she needed to be more practical, even if Adam had wanted her to buy something special.

As Belle wandered through the Troyers' store, her eyes fell upon the fabric section. Perhaps, she thought, I'll buy some cloth for a new work dress. Certainly Adam would approve — or at least not *disapprove* — of that acquisition.

She hurried over to the shelves and let her fingers gently touch the edge of each bolt. So many beautiful colors: blues, purples, greens, pinks, and even a few reds, a new and exciting color that the church leaders must have just recently approved for their congregation. But, as for Belle, she still favored bright, sunflower yellow.

"Belle?"

She looked up, glad to see Ella, laden with a large cardboard box, walking through the door from the back storeroom.

Ella set down the box that she was carrying and slapped her hands together to shake off the dust. She smiled at Belle as she walked over to her, her bare feet barely making any noise on the hardwood floor.

"So what brings you to town on a Wednesday? Besides books, that is," Ella teased gently.

"Just picking up some vegetables." She

didn't mention that she was also hoping to see her family on the way back. Given what Ella and Sadie had shared with her on Saturday, Belle felt particularly hurt by their neglect, but she didn't want to go into that with Ella. "And thinking I might buy some fabric," she added, her hand lingering on one of the bolts.

"Making some new shirts for Adam, then?"

Belle made a face. "For Adam?"

Ella nodded and pointed to the fabric beneath Belle's hand. "That's a particularly good one for work shirts."

"Yellow?"

"*Nee,* the white one that you have your hand on, goose."

Belle turned to look and saw that, indeed, she had touched not the yellow bolt of fabric but the one next to it, which was a heavier white polyester/cotton blend. There was the slightest hint of a pattern to the fabric, and Belle could tell that Ella was correct: it would wear well. Still, she hadn't wanted to make a shirt for Adam, but a dress for herself. For a moment, she stood there and fingered the white material. Perhaps Ella was onto something, she thought. When was the last time someone had made Adam anything? And he was always wearing those long-sleeved shirts. It was hot working outside, and his two shirts looked almost threadbare. If she bought enough material, she could make him a nice, short-sleeved work shirt to carry him through the Indian summer and then make him a long-sleeved one for the winter.

"Why, that's a splendid idea!" She pulled the fabric from the shelf and set it down on the cutting table behind her. "May I have four yards of fabric, please?"

Ella nodded as she took the fabric from Belle. "Let me give you five yards, just in case. Adam seems rather tall and broad in the shoulders."

While Ella cut the fabric, she talked to Belle about the recent happenings in town. Mary Esh had a new baby. John Paul Stoltzfus was courting Rachel Mast. And Elizabeth Grimm had sent her own cousin, Gideon Grimm, home from school after he put a tack on some girl's chair — something Elizabeth had neglected to mention to Belle during their earlier conversation.

To Belle, it sounded as if life was continuing as normal for the townspeople's lives — babies, courtship, even though she felt as if everything had become stagnant in hers.

When she had finished the rest of her shopping, Belle drove the horse and buggy away from Echo Creek and toward her father's farm. She was anxious to see what, exactly, was happening with her family. It took her several minutes to remind herself to release her disappointment in their lack of concern for her well-being. While she would have thought they might have visited her, she couldn't fault them for not doing so. After all, they had responsibilities at the farm, especially now that it appeared her father was doing so well.

When she pulled into the driveway to her father's farm, she stopped the buggy midway between the main road and the house. Her mouth fell open, and she could hardly believe what she saw. The fencing along the first paddock was completely new. A herd of black-and-white Holsteins grazed in the grass, which, because of the cows' presence, was no longer overgrown. The barn door was open, not because the hinge was broken, but because it had been repaired and propped open by a rock. And the once-broken windowpane in the side of the barn had been replaced.

The house itself appeared the same until she managed to move beyond her surprise and urge the horse farther down the driveway. Before she exited the buggy, she noticed that the sagging porch was now straight and the clothesline hung taut. Even more surprising was the fact that dresses hung from the line, waving in the warm afternoon breeze. Six dresses, to be exact, and in new, bright colors that had never adorned that clothesline when Belle had been living there: lilac, deep purple, hunter green, and even those pretty reds.

"Oh, help . . ." Belle whispered as she scrambled down from the buggy.

The porch door opened (no creak), and her sister Susie came running out, a big smile on her face. "Belle!" She met her sister at the edge of the grass and embraced her. It was a greeting that caught Belle off guard. "Oh! It's just right *gut* to see you, *Schwester*!"

Belle waited until Susie released her. "It appears much has changed since I left."

Susie laughed, clearly delighted to see Belle but also with a jovial enthusiasm that was foreign to Belle. "*Kum* in and sit a spell. I have so much to tell you!"

"And *Daed*? Verna?"

"*Daed*'s in Liberty Village with Verna."

At first, Belle thought she hadn't heard her sister properly. "Liberty Village? Whatever for?"

Glancing over her shoulder at Belle, Susie's mouth opened, and she made a small gasping noise. "Why, that's just th' thing! You won't believe what has happened around here since your wedding!"

Inside the house, the kitchen appeared much the same as when Belle had left — which surprised Belle almost as much as what she had seen outside. Neither Susie nor Verna had ever been much for house chores — or any chores, for that matter. Yet the kitchen was near spotless. It was as if Belle had cleaned it and walked away, and not one person had used it since. The smell of baking bread, however, let Belle know that someone was indeed using the kitchen. Baking, in fact. But who?

"Cows? Fencing? Fresh wash drying on the line? And bread baking?" Belle gave Susie an incredulous look as she sank into a chair at the kitchen table. "What on earth . . . ?"

Sitting across from her, Susie clapped her hands and laughed once again. "Isn't it *wunderbarr*? Why, just after your wedding, everything happened at once! A letter came to *Daed* with a certified check. An attorney in Liberty Village has a client who wants to invest in selling *Daed*'s grills. Can you believe it?"

Belle felt as if her heart would jump into her throat. Ella and Sadie had mentioned that someone wanted to invest in her father's grill, but they hadn't mentioned a certified check from an investor! That sounded like nothing except trouble as far as Belle was concerned. Her father had *never* been good at managing money properly. "Please, Susie, don't tell me that *Daed* bought the cows, the new horse and the new buggy and made all of these repairs with that money?" She felt ill at ease even suggesting such a thing. If her father had squandered that money, what legal problems lurked in his future?

"Well, *nee,* not at all!" Susie leaned forward, putting her elbows onto the table and lowering her voice as if she wanted to share a big secret. "That's just the thing. You see, everything else around here . . . why, it was done by your husband!"

"Adam?" Belle almost choked on the word. "Adam fixed the fence and barn door and porch and —"

Susie nodded. "*Ja,* he most certainly did. Came around early in the morning and late at night to do it, too. Scared Verna half to death when she heard him banging on the barn door with that hammer one morning before sunrise!"

This time, Belle let her mouth hang agape.

"At first, we reckoned he figured it's his

property, so he might as well take care of it," Susie said in a soft voice. "But then he spoke with *Daed* about keeping some of his herd here. He even hired a boy in town to come out for the early morning and evening milkings! Why, we don't have to do a thing; the boy even tends to *our* cows."

Now it began to make sense. With so much work on his own farm, it was practical for him to keep some cows at her father's farm, which was closer to town and, therefore, easier to hire someone to help care for them.

"And the horse? Buggy?"

Susie could hardly contain her joy. "Why, another miracle! The bishop came around with them. Said that the community had pooled their resources to buy them for *Daed*. Like Amish Aid when someone's sick, *ja*?"

For a moment, Belle sat there and simply tried to digest all of this information. It was incredible, this story that Susie was telling her. How could so much good fortune befall her family just shy of three weeks after her wedding? If all of this had happened even four weeks ago, what a different future Belle might have had.

"Who's been taking care of the *haus*?" Belle asked, almost afraid to hear the answer. With all of the recent changes, she half expected Susie to tell her that they had a hired girl helping with the housework.

But Susie's answer surprised her. "Oh Belle," she said in a teasing way. "Did you really think that we'd let the *haus* fall into disarray after you left? That we were incapable of taking care of things?"

Stunned, Belle's mouth opened.

Susie laughed at her sister's reaction. "We never helped out because you made it too easy *not* to help."

"*You've* been tending to the housework?"

But Susie nodded, appearing quite pleased. "*Ja,* Verna and I have been cooking, baking, and cleaning. It's not that hard, I reckon, as long as you stay on top of it."

Belle could hardly believe it. "And you said that Verna's with *Daed*?"

"She is, *ja*. In fact, she's been helping him in Liberty Village. Third trip she's made there." Susie's eyes sparkled as she added, "I believe she's rather smitten with a young man who works at the hardware store."

A hardware store? "Certainly she can't know him well enough to be smitten."

Susie reached out her hand and touched Belle's arm. "He's been here twice, once to take her to the singing in Echo Creek and once for a long walk by the lake." And then, after a brief hesitation, Susie added, "And

Gabriel has been stopping by to check on me when they go to Liberty Village." The color rose to her cheeks. "He even offered to bring me home from worship service on Sunday, but of course I wasn't there to take him up on his offer. You know we were in Liberty Village. We just came home on Monday, but *Daed* had to turn around and go back there again today."

"I . . . I don't know what to say," Belle managed to whisper. "It's unbelievable, all of these remarkable things that have happened to you." Even as she spoke the words, she felt the far-too-familiar constriction in her chest. "No wonder no one has been to visit me . . ."

The look on Susie's face startled Belle. It was one of confusion, not offense. "Been to visit you? Why, Adam told us not to."

The outer periphery of her vision seemed to blur as she stared at Susie. Belle wondered if she had truly just heard her sister confess that Adam had told her family to stay away from the farm. If so, why on earth would he have said such a thing? Was he truly intent on keeping her isolated and away from the outside community? To learn this just when she was beginning to warm to the idea of their friendship was shattering to her trust in the man.

"I have to go," she whispered and stood up. She made her way to the door, barely hearing Susie urging her to stay.

The rest of the ride home felt as if she were in a foggy dream. Everyone else's life seemed to be headed into a bright, happy future, while hers was increasingly mired in isolation and despair. Had Adam thought that she wouldn't have discovered his deceit? That she wouldn't have learned that he'd told her family to stay away? And yet, if that was true, why would he have gone to the trouble to repair not just the fencing but also the other things? The porch, the clothesline, the broken window, the un-hinged door . . . not one of those things impacted the care of his cow herd.

Something didn't make sense, but there was only one person who could answer the questions that rattled through her head: Adam. If only she had the nerve to ask him.

CHAPTER NINETEEN

Immediately after cleaning the breakfast dishes Thursday morning, Belle began working on the shirt for Adam. It wasn't likely that she would be interrupted. Adam had hitched the Belgian drafts to the baler and driven them toward the back of the property. With a cup of warm coffee next to her, Belle focused on cutting the fabric, using one of his other shirts as a guide.

She had always loved sewing, almost as much as she loved reading. There was something exciting about creating something from scratch. And the quiet that filled the room gave her a strong sense of peace. Just the birds chirping outside the open windows and the soft noise of the scissors cutting the fabric. She knew that it wouldn't take long to piece and sew the shirt, but she was surprised at how quickly it came together. Perhaps she could wrap it and give it to him as a present later today. True, the finishing touches were not yet in place — the bottom still needed to be hemmed.

As she busied herself peeling potatoes for dinner, she thought again of the previous day's events. By the time she had returned home, the initial shock of Susie's revelation had subsided, and rather than confronting Adam with how he had kept her from her family, she decided to focus on the kindness he had shown to them. After all, wasn't that more important?

So at supper, she told him she had stopped at her family's farm, and she sincerely thanked him for all he had done: the repairs on the fence and the porch and the barn, the hired help for the cows. Knowing he didn't like her to go on and on, Belle kept her thanks simple and to the point. To her surprise, her words seemed to hit home. Although he said nothing, his face softened, and he lingered a bit after supper, helping to clear the table before he disappeared once again into the barn.

When Belle heard the horses on the driveway, dinner was still cooking. Glancing out the window, she noticed that the anticipated rain was not yet falling. So why was Adam back so early? Quickly, she set the table. Just as she was setting down a water glass by his plate, the sound of his heavy footsteps stomping up the porch steps carried into the kitchen. She turned and greeted him with a smile.

"Dinner's not quite ready yet."

He nodded his head in acknowledgment and walked over to the sink. She watched as he washed his hands.

"Did you finish raking the hay, then?" She held a towel out for him.

He glanced at the towel, almost as if surprised that she had offered it, before he took it.

"*Ja,* I did." Adam wiped his hands on the towel and handed it back to her. For a moment, he stared at her intently before clearing his throat. "*Mayhaps* I could use your help baling this afternoon."

Stunned, Belle's mouth opened. Had she heard him correctly? Had he just asked her to lend a hand in the fields? "I'd like that very much."

"*Gut.*" He walked around her and sat down at the table.

With a newfound energy, Belle hurried to finish preparing the meal. She felt as if her insides must be glowing. She set the white bowl of applesauce next to him and stood there for a moment, staring down at him as her thoughts raced. Was it possible that he was beginning to warm up to her? To see her as a wife and partner, not just an unpaid housekeeper? Adam must have sensed her presence. He glanced up, and Belle blushed. She felt flustered and scurried to the oven, but not before seeing that he raised an eyebrow, a hint of amusement in his expression.

When she finished putting the food on the table, she sat beside Adam and lowered her head to give thanks in silent prayer. Adam remained still, and she thought she saw that he had also bowed his head. She wasn't certain, however, and when she opened her eyes again, he was watching her.

"Something amiss?"

He took a moment to respond, his eyes studying her face. She waited for what felt like an eternity for him to answer her question.

"*Nee,* Belle. Nothing is amiss."

"You appeared to have something on your mind." She reached for the bowl of steaming vegetables.

But he merely shook his head and turned his attention to the food as he mumbled, "Helping me in the fields is enough for one day."

For the rest of the meal, they ate in silence because, as usual, there wasn't much to discuss. Still, Belle felt something different

275

in the air. A growing tension. And while tension usually made her emotions feel strained, there was something different this time. Almost as if butterflies tickled her insides. She stole a peek at Adam, pleased that he was enjoying the meal that she had prepared for him. And that surprised her. She had never felt joy — truly intense joy! — over such little things. The cleanliness of the house. The pristine garden beds. The mouth-watering aroma in the kitchen.

With a newfound warmth in her heart, she bent her head and tried to focus on her food, even though she no longer had an appetite.

Thirty minutes later, with the dishes only partially cleaned from their meal, Belle found herself driving the Belgian horses, who pulled the baler while Adam stacked the hay bales as each one emerged from the bale chute. With the sun high and the air not necessarily cool, it was hard work, and Belle wished that she had thought to bring out a thermos of water for him. By the time the wagon was full of bales, her own arms ached from holding the reins as she guided the horses along the long rows of dried hay. Sweat dripped down her back, and she knew that the back of her neck was sunburned.

She felt his hand on her shoulder. His

touch made her jump. "Best take this load in," he said. "You can take a break while I stack it."

"I can help stack," she heard herself say. "But I'll fetch us some water first."

If she thought that he might argue with her, she was pleasantly surprised. He did not.

For the rest of the afternoon, they worked together. While they rarely spoke, Belle felt a sense of calm just being in his presence. Occasionally, she would look over her shoulder to make certain that she wasn't driving the horses too fast. When she saw him working, his white shirt clinging to his chest and arms, the sweat glistening on his cheeks, she felt those same butterflies inside of her. He was so strong and independent when he worked. She couldn't even imagine how he had ever baled hay without someone's help in the past. However, if any man could do it alone, she knew that it was Adam.

The sun had begun to dip toward the horizon when he approached her once again. She sensed him before he laid his hand on her shoulder, just as he had done earlier. "Reckon we can call it a day." Only this time he did not remove it. While she guided the horses back toward the farm,

Adam stood on the baler behind her, his body almost pressed against her back. Occasionally the swaying of the baler and wagon caused him to brush against her. Each time, his hand would tighten, just a little, on her shoulder, and she felt as if a bolt of energy coursed through her veins.

"What is it?" he asked.

Embarrassed that he must have sensed her reaction, Belle stammered a quick response. "You . . . you startled me. That's all."

Did she imagine it, or had he gently squeezed her one last time before removing his hand? She glanced up at him and saw that he was staring straight ahead. Perhaps it was where she was sitting on the baler, or maybe it was the way the light shone on him, casting a slight shadow from the brim of his hat, but Belle realized that she could barely see the scarring on his face. In fact, she almost had to search in order to see the burned skin. It was as if it had evaporated, simply disappeared. She blinked and looked harder. Only then did it appear, and she wondered if her mind was playing tricks on her.

Once in the barnyard, Belle stopped the team near the hayloft. Adam jumped down from the wagon and, rather than hurry to unhitch the horses, he turned toward her, lifting up his hand to help her get down. She placed her hand in his, surprised at how warm his skin felt against hers. Her eyes fluttered upward, looking into his face once again. Only this time, he stared back at her. She jumped down from the wagon and stood before him, her hand still inside his. She was close enough to him that she could smell the musky scent of a hard day's labor mixed with the fresh smell of hay.

"*Danke* for letting me help you," she said.

He frowned. "You thank me? It should be the other way, *ja*?"

Belle laughed. "*Mayhaps,* but I'm truly grateful."

"As am I." He took a step backward and leaned against the wagon. "Certainly made it easier, having your help."

"How on earth did you ever do all of that baling without help?"

He gave her a slight smile, and there was a mischievous twinkle in his eyes. "Angels help me."

"Angels?" She put her hand on her hip and pursed her lips. "Really, Adam."

"You don't believe me?" He reached out and tugged at the white ribbon that hung from her prayer *kapp.* "One helped me today, *ja*?"

The gesture surprised her as much as his

words. She knew that her cheeks reddened at the compliment. "Such flattery. I only did what any good wife would and should do." She reached up and touched the string that he had just touched. "And now this wife needs to prepare supper for her husband."

She hurried into the house while Adam unhitched and unharnessed the horses. For a moment, she stood at the window and watched as he worked, her fingers still caressing the ribbon. She didn't understand her conflicting emotions. She wanted so much to feel like a wife, but she did not. Not truly. And yet she did not know why.

Slowly Adam was shedding the wall that protected him from the outside world. The fact that he had reached out for her help with the fieldwork proved that he was willing to adapt. Certainly she, too, had changed, but was it enough?

It was only after they had finished the meal — a meal they ate in silence — that Belle had the courage to speak up. She had already cleared the table, and, to her relief, Adam had remained seated, reading an old newspaper under the light from the kerosene lantern. Nervously, she stood next to him with her hands holding the wrapped package behind her back.

"I . . . I have something for you."

Adam looked up, surprise in his eyes. "Something for me?"

She nodded her head and waited until he put down the paper, the pages crinkling in the silence of the room. He turned his chair so that he faced her, not the table, and raised an eyebrow.

"Close your eyes."

"Belle . . ."

She gave him a stern look. "Please, Adam. I want to surprise you."

He grumbled but did as she said.

"Now hold out your hands."

He started to argue, but she silenced him with a quick *shh.*

Another grumble escaped his lips as he held his hands out before him.

Carefully, she placed the package in his hand. She didn't have any real wrapping paper, so she had cut up an old brown paper bag that she had found in the basement. Since she hadn't found any tape, either, she had tied it with twine from a bale of hay.

"What's this?"

"A surprise!" Joy radiated from her face and she rocked on her feet, anticipating the moment when he would see the gift she had made.

"I . . . I don't understand."

"Open it, silly."

He glanced at her, his forehead furrowed in confusion, but did as she instructed. He untied the twine and pushed back the brown paper. Inside was the white shirt that she had made for him that morning. The confused look on his face did not go away as he lifted the shirt and held it in the air before him. "A shirt?"

She nodded. "*Ja,* I made it for you this morning."

"I don't need a shirt."

She gave him a stern look. "Usually people say 'thank you' when they receive a gift, Adam."

He blinked his eyes.

"And it's a short-sleeved shirt." She slipped her hand into one of the sleeves. "See? When you are working outside and get hot, you won't sweat so much."

In silence, he stared at the shirt. He swallowed and let his fingers move to the shortened sleeves. Something changed in his face and he scowled. Abruptly, he stood up, clutching the shirt in his hand. "I don't wear short-sleeved shirts."

"I . . . I know that all of your shirts are long sleeved, Adam. And I can guess the reason why. But surely you don't have to suffer when it's warm out. Even October can be hot, especially when we get an Indian summer."

The scowl on his face darkened as a wave of rage shadowed his expression. "I don't wear short-sleeved shirts!" he bellowed, throwing the shirt onto the floor before he stormed out of the kitchen.

"Adam!" She knelt down to pick up the shirt and ran after him.

This time she followed him into the barn. When he realized that she was following him, he spun around. "The dairy barn is no place for you!"

She held out the shirt. "I made this for you. You have no right to speak to me in such a manner, Adam. I am not the enemy!"

He took a step forward, anger still in his eyes. "I didn't ask for that shirt. I didn't ask for you to make it. And I won't wear it."

Putting her hands on her hips, she stared him down. "Why? Because you have scars on your face? On your arms?" She clicked her tongue and shook her head. "Oh, Adam. You don't have to hide your scars from me."

He lifted his chin and looked at her defiantly. "I don't hide them from you."

"Then who?"

Taking two steps, he stood before her, leaning down so that he not only towered over her but stared directly into her eyes.

"From me. I hide my scars from me!" he hissed, and then, snatching the shirt from her hand, he started to walk away. "Leave me alone, Belle! I mean it!"

She stood in the entrance of the barn, watching as Adam disappeared down the aisle where the cows stood, chewing their nightly ration of hay. Shep ran after him, his tail wagging, oblivious to the heated exchange that had just occurred.

Frustrated, Belle stomped her foot and turned around, crossing her arms over her chest. How could he continue to isolate himself from everyone, including himself? If only he would open up to her and try. While nothing about their marriage was ideal, at least Belle was willing to make an attempt at serving Adam as a wife should. What, if anything, was he doing for *her*?

CHAPTER TWENTY

The lengthy walk to Echo Creek was exactly what she needed after another long, restless night. She had tossed and turned, wondering what she could do to make Adam understand that it was up to him to open up in order for his life to change. She wasn't certain of the exact time when she heard her bedroom door open, the hinges creaking just enough to announce his presence, but surely it was after midnight.

Belle lay in bed, motionless, as she listened to the sound of Adam's footsteps approaching the side of the bed. She kept her eyes closed, even though the room was too dark to see anything. He must have stayed there for ten . . . maybe fifteen . . . minutes. And then, just as quietly, he left, making certain to close the door behind him.

Because her door was often ajar in the morning, she had guessed that Adam often peeked in, but this was the first time she'd been awake enough to realize he actually came into the room. In fact, for weeks now, every night she left a small piece of thread on the doorknob. Just in case, she told herself, she was dreaming. Every morning, the thread lay on the hardwood floor, and she'd know again that he'd come to her room.

But he never woke her; never attempted to touch her.

On her first morning at Adam's farm, she had felt scared and apprehensive when she'd realized that Adam had come into the bedroom. She worried that he would blame her for having gone to sleep. Now, weeks later, Belle found that her fear had turned to frustration. How could they possibly be husband and wife if he never once addressed the physical aspect of marriage? And yet, there was something protective and romantic about Adam coming upstairs and watching her while she slept — as if he felt the need to check on her at night, even if he never once spoke about the fact that he did it!

It was just one more mystery revolving around the man she called her husband.

She had set out for town before he came to the house for his breakfast. After leaving his plate of food on the table, Belle hurried out the front door, eager to get away from the farm. She needed time to think, to be alone . . . something she found ironic, since she spent most of her days alone and thinking.

When she rounded the curve in the road near her father's farm, she was surprised to see that the barn had been painted. With the overgrown bushes cleared and the fencing fixed, the farm was looking especially prosperous. She felt a pang of resentment, knowing that her family was finally living the life that they always should have. But as soon as she identified that feeling, she shook her head and prayed for forgiveness. Hadn't that been the reason she'd agreed to marry Adam? So her family could stay in Echo Creek? The last thing she should feel was resentment. Instead, she should feel joy that her sacrifice had proven exactly what her father needed to turn things around.

The bell over the door to Troyers' store jingled as Belle stepped inside. She had a basket slung over her arm in anticipation of her purchases: flour, sugar, yeast, and a few other dry goods. And, of course, a book.

"Belle Hershberger!"

She looked up at the sound of her name being called out from the back of the store. Ella was working there and greeted her with a smile. *"Gut morgan,"* she said as Ella hurried around the front counter. They embraced each other. "How are you, Ella?"

"Fine, all things considering. And you?"

Belle shrugged. She wasn't about to attempt to hide her heartache over the previous evening. "As well as can be expected, I reckon."

Ella gave her an empathetic look. "I'm sorry, Belle. I wish things would get better for you and Adam."

Exhaling, Belle changed the subject. "How are things in Echo Creek? I feel so out of it, living way outside town."

Ella glanced over her shoulder as if looking for someone, and when she saw no one, she grabbed Belle's hand and led her down an aisle far away from the front counter. "Oh, Belle. The craziest thing has happened!"

"What is it?"

"Sadie. She's gone missing."

Belle gasped and covered her mouth with her hand. "Oh, help!"

Solemnly, Ella nodded her head. *"Ja,* missing. No one knows where she is. Her *daed*'s distraught as all get-out."

"I imagine so!"

And then Ella narrowed her eyes as she leaned closer so that she could whisper into

Belle's ear. "Sadie had told me that her stepmother was up to something. I think Sadie has run away."

Another gasp. Belle's hand went to the base of her throat. *Run away?* While she knew that Sadie's stepmother had never been fond of her stepdaughter, what could possibly have happened to make Sadie run away? "I will pray for her."

Ella nodded. "That's all we can do, I fear. Pray."

"And what about you?"

Ella shrugged in a noncommittal way. "There's a big youth gathering next spring. At the lake. My *schwesters* are saving every dime to attend, but *Maem* says I cannot go."

That wasn't surprising. Linda Troyer never let Ella do any of the fun things that she let her own daughters do. "Well, you have time, don't you think? *Mayhaps* she'll change her mind."

But Ella didn't look too convinced.

"I wonder if Verna and Susie will go."

At the mention of Belle's sisters, Ella stiffened.

"What is it, Ella? Tell me."

Ella made a face. "Hasn't Susie told you? I hear that Gabriel intends to ask the bishop to announce his engagement to her."

Belle rolled her eyes. Why didn't *that*

surprise her? Apparently one Beiler sister was just as good as another, in Gabriel's eyes. "I wish them all the best." She tried to sound happy, but it was forced. "How everything seems to change," Belle lamented. "I'm not certain I like being a grown-up after all. Life was so much easier when I was still a child."

At this, Ella gave a soft sigh. "Oh, Belle, how sad. True, but sad. It was easier when my *daed* and *maem* were alive. But we can't stay children, can we? Besides, Belle, you don't know what plans God has in store for you."

Belle saw the truth in what her friend had said. Agreeing with Ella, she nodded her head. "Enough about such things." Forcing a weak smile, she glanced over her shoulder at the bookshelves. "Now, show me the new books that have come in. Surely Linda can't fault you for spending time with me if you're helping me to shop!"

Thirty minutes later, Belle selected two books and placed them in her basket. As she walked next to Ella toward the front of the store, her eyes caught sight of the fabric table. There were new bolts of fabric set on display, and one of them caught her attention.

"Oh, *ja,* isn't that a pretty color?" Ella ran

her hand over the beautiful bolt of yellow fabric. Unlike the pale yellow that was usually used by Amish women, this bolt was so brilliant and beautiful that Belle had only seen that color in one other place: the sunflowers in Ella's garden. "I don't know how the bishop will react to that bright color," Ella said, "but I'm sure he'll have something to say."

"It's breathtaking."

The bell over the door jingled, and Ella sighed. "You keep looking while I see if that customer needs help. And I can fetch that list of dry goods you need." Ella started to walk away. "No hurry on your part."

Belle pulled out the bolt of yellow cloth and ran her hand over it. It was soft, a polyester and cotton blend. And there was a pattern to it, hardly visible to the eye. Stripes that were just a shade lighter than the brilliant yellow, which made it look as if the sun were hitting it. Oh, how she would have loved to wear a dress made of that fabric. She glanced at the price written on the cardboard. Almost ten dollars a yard! Immediately, Belle put back the bolt of fabric and stepped away from the table. That was far too dear for her budget, that was for sure and certain.

With one last longing glance at the fabric,

Belle took a deep breath and turned around, startled to bump into someone. "Oh!" She dropped her basket and knelt down to retrieve it. "I'm so sorry. I didn't see . . ." But she stopped in midsentence as she recognized the boots standing before her. "Adam?"

Quickly she stood, her basket once again tucked onto her arm.

He stood there, his hat in his hand as he stared down at her.

"What are you doing here?" Belle asked.

His face was pale, and she thought his eyes looked bloodshot.

"Are you unwell?" She started to reach up and touch his forehead, but he took her wrist in his hand.

"*Nee,* Belle, I'm not unwell." He paused, glancing into her basket. "Not now, anyway."

She tilted her head. It was still early in the morning. She knew his chore schedule kept him busy with the cows until well after ten o'clock. "Why are you here, then?"

He shifted his weight and softened his grip on her wrist. "I . . . I thought you had left."

"I did leave. To come to town."

"But your clothes . . ."

She pursed her lips. Had he gone into her bedroom and noticed that her clothes were not hanging from the hooks in the wall? Had he thought she had left him? Over their argument the night before? "They are hanging to dry in the basement, Adam. Truly you are *ferhoodled* if you think I ran back to my *daed*."

"Ferhoodled." He nodded his head. *"Ja, mayhaps* I am *ferhoodled."*

She remembered the last time that he had thought she left him. He had come to town and found her during that altercation she had with John Grimm. Why was he so convinced that she would leave him? Hadn't she proven her commitment to their arrangement? "Ella is fetching my things. I best go pay for them."

He nodded, but his eyes never left her as she hurried to the front of the store to pay.

Ella raised an eyebrow, obviously aware that Adam had entered the store. "Everything all right, then?" she whispered.

"Ja, I reckon so."

After paying, Belle gave her friend a smile. "Let me know when you hear anything about Sadie."

"Of course. I'll come out to the farm right away."

Belle took her purchases and placed them into her basket. At least she wouldn't have to walk home carrying the weight of the items she had bought.

Outside, Adam was waiting near the buggy. He paid no attention to the people who passed by and stared. Neither did Belle. While she would probably never get used to it, she knew she could simply ignore the inquisitive gazes of people who were less accepting of the way Adam looked.

Taking the basket from her, Adam helped her into the buggy and then climbed in beside her. He leaned over the seat, setting the basket on the back floor. And then he urged the horse to back up so that he could turn around.

As soon as they were on the road leading away from town, Adam cleared his throat. "I thought about what you said, Belle. Not just last night, but last week. When it was raining out."

It took her a moment to remember. She had followed him to the barn, and he had stormed inside, forbidding her to follow him. Standing in the rain, listening to the thunder, Belle had shouted out that she could never learn to love him if he didn't show her who he was. She hadn't even known that he had heard her.

"And I apologize."

"Oh, Adam . . ."

He held up one hand. "*Nee,* let me finish."

Even though he wasn't looking at her, she nodded. "All right, then. Go ahead."

He licked his lower lip and remained silent for a long moment. Another buggy passed them, and to her surprise, Adam lifted his hand to wave at the other driver, who looked equally as surprised as she was.

"And I'm willing to try."

She felt her heart beat faster. "Try what, Adam?"

He gave her a quick glance. "Try to let you know who I am."

"Oh!" It came out in a breathless whoosh. "Adam!" She reached out and wrapped her hand under his arm. "What glorious news!"

She felt him stiffen. "It won't be easy for me, Belle. You don't know what it's like to be me. To be abandoned and teased. To live alone with no hope."

"There's always hope, Adam. The Bible tells us so."

He shook his head. "Even Job felt that God had abandoned him."

"But when God spoke to Job about his mighty acts of creation, Job was humbled and realized that, despite all of the bad things that happened to him, God was still in control."

Adam seemed to contemplate that, and after reflecting upon her words, he nodded his head. "*Ja,* I reckon so."

Silence befell them once again.

Belle leaned against the seat back and watched the farms along the sides of the roads. Drying cornstalks would be cut and shocked soon. Most farmers had cut their last batch of hay. It was the end of one harvest, but that only meant a period of dormancy before a new one was planted. Perhaps this was the moment of Adam's new harvest.

The buggy grew warm, and Belle struggled to open the window in her door. But it was stuck. Adam reached over and easily slid it back.

And then, to her surprise, he started to remove his black coat. He slid his arms out and pushed his coat onto the back seat. When he took the reins in both hands again, Belle caught her breath. He was wearing the new shirt — both of his arms were exposed, and on the right side, so were his scars.

She must have been staring, because he cleared his throat once again. When she looked up, his eyes were not on the road but on her.

"*Danke* for my new shirt, Belle," he said

in a soft voice. "It was right *gut* of you to think of me."

The color rose to her cheeks, and she felt warm inside. "You are most welcome, Adam."

"And I hope to wear it next Monday at the horse auction. Gets awfully warm in there with all those men."

"Oh, I wouldn't know. I've never been." She had heard about the horse auctions in Liberty Village, but she had never attended, for her father never had any money to bid on horses or buggies or farm equipment.

Adam returned his attention to the road. "*Mayhaps* you might accompany me, then."

Clapping her hands together, she drew in her breath. "Really, Adam? Oh, how I would enjoy that!"

She thought she heard him chuckle at her reaction. "Then consider it a . . . date."

A date, she thought. A real date with her husband. She shut her eyes and gave a prayer of thanks to God for having helped her somehow break through to Adam. If he was willing to take her on a date, certainly things could only get better.

CHAPTER TWENTY-ONE

The large auction house was filled by men seated on the benches, most wearing tattered straw hats and a few with a young child seated next to them. A few women were gathered at the back of the room, talking among themselves, as they clearly had no interest in the actual auction. Belle, however, was fascinated.

The benches were tiered and surrounded an open sand arena where a young Amish man ran beside a horse. Two other Amish men stood on either side of the arena, staring into the crowd as another man, the auctioneer, spoke rapidly into a microphone. Belle could hardly understand what the man was saying, for he spoke so fast in a singsong manner that not one word seemed intelligible to her.

"What's happening?" she whispered to Adam.

He motioned to two empty seats in the

second row. "I'll explain it when we sit down."

She nodded and followed him, too aware that people were doing double takes as Adam passed before them.

The auction house was outside Liberty Village, and most of the faces were those of strangers. She recognized only one or two people, and even with those she could not place their names, for they were not from Echo Creek. How Adam could ignore the intrusive stares was beyond her. She felt her pulse quicken and her palms sweat, wishing fervently that she might have the strength to say something to them.

But she didn't.

Once they were seated, Belle sat as close to Adam as possible, not wanting to have to talk to any of those other people. She even reached out to touch his arm as if silently signaling to any curious onlookers that she was, indeed, his wife. "So tell me now. Please."

He glanced down at her, and she thought she saw him hiding a smile. "So curious."

Unable to contain her excitement, she practically bounced in her seat as she clung to his arm. "I am! Explain everything to me!"

He almost laughed, and even though he

did not, she liked the way his eyes lit up at her enthusiasm. "Now, Belle," he started and just those two words sent a warm feeling throughout her body. "It's very simple." He pointed to the area where the horse was being paraded before the onlookers. "That horse is up for auction. See the number in white on its rump?"

She hadn't noticed that before Adam pointed it out.

"And anyone in the audience who would like to bid on the horse raises the white card with the bidders' assigned number." He showed Belle the card that was tucked into the white document that listed all of the horses that were to be auctioned that day. "Most people have already walked through the back where the horses are kept so that they can see which horses suit their fancy and can ask questions prior to the horse being auctioned."

Belle glanced toward the one end of the arena and saw two other horses with Amish handlers waiting for their turn. "Back there?" She pointed in that direction.

He nodded. "*Ja*, that's right."

"Well, how do the men know what they are bidding?"

Adam chuckled and gave a little shake of his head, clearly amused. "The auctioneer," he said and pointed to the rapidly speaking man with the microphone, "is requesting bids in increments. He starts high, perhaps a hundred dollars, and then when his voice slows, he lowers the number to, say, fifty or twenty-five."

She gasped and looked at the auctioneer. "People can actually understand him?"

Smiling, Adam covered her hand, which was still tucked near his elbow, with his. "Ah, Belle, you're rather charming," he said lightly. "*Ja,* people can understand him, and you will, too, if you listen hard enough. Those other two men monitor the crowds to see who raises their card." He waited until one of the men pointed to a man in the audience. "See? That man just bid on the horse, so the monitor pointed to him."

Everything happened so fast that Belle could hardly follow the card raising, the pointing, and the rambling of the auctioneer. She sat back, staring at everything and watching, enjoying the entire experience. One horse was "sold to 186" and was walked out of the arena as another horse was walked in.

For the next half hour, Belle was transfixed, watching the activity. She almost forgot that, besides her and Adam, other people were there. By the time the seventh horse had been auctioned, Adam shifted his weight and leaned over. "Reckon I could use some water. Would you like something to drink?"

She nodded, and when he stood up, she followed him.

They made their way to the refreshment stand at the back of the building. A few people stared at Adam, but Belle was beginning to find it easier to simply ignore the curious onlookers. However, as they stood in line, waiting for their turn, one man stopped beside Adam.

"Hershberger, right?"

Adam moved his head so that the brim of his hat shielded his face. *"Ja?"*

"John Eck. 'Member me?" The man reached out his hand for Adam to shake. Belle noticed that Adam eyed the man suspiciously, clearly not remembering who he was, but eventually accepting the handshake. "So how's that horse and buggy you bought the other week?"

Adam stiffened and withdrew his hand as Belle looked at him questioningly.

"That was you, *ja?*" John said, obviously recognizing Adam's face. "That bay Standardbred? And the new buggy? That was a great deal. Why, you practically stole those from me!" But the man laughed good-

302

naturedly. "Hope that horse is serving you well."

Seeing that Adam looked discomfited, Belle spoke up. *"Ja,* indeed. The horse is *wunderbarr."* She smiled at the man. "My husband purchased them for my *daed,* who recently lost both his horse and buggy." Her statement was a guess — a stab in the dark, since she'd never seen the new horse and buggy — but someone had to say something. And Adam clearly was not in the mood.

John raised an eyebrow. "You don't say? Ach, I'm sure he was most appreciative."

With the smile still on her face, Belle nodded. "For sure and certain."

After the man parted from their company, Belle did not look at Adam. Instead, she stood by his side and stared straight ahead. What was the meaning of this? she wondered. Why would Adam take such a pointed interest in bestowing gifts upon her father when he had only just begun to show any type of husbandly interest in *her*? And why had the bishop agreed to such a thing? It was unlike him to bestow such a gift on her father, claiming it was from the community when, in fact, it was from Adam.

Her thoughts seemed to run in different directions. The community. Yes, she should have known right away when her sister informed her that the bishop had taken a collection from the community. The people in Echo Creek were not that philanthropic. These were the same people who laughed at her father's inventions. Even the shopkeepers in town wouldn't help him promote his new grill. So why had she so easily believed that they would pool enough money to purchase something as grand as a new (and beautiful!) horse and buggy for him?

It wasn't until they sat back down in a new section of the arena that Adam spoke.

"I hadn't wanted anyone to know."

"Obviously," Belle replied. She toyed with the water bottle in her hands. "However, what is not obvious is why." She turned her face and looked at him, her eyes searching his. It took her a minute to realize that, as she looked at him, she saw none of his scars. Instead, she saw only the beauty of his heart shining through every ounce of his being. For the first time, she realized that Adam was a beautiful man, more handsome than any other she had ever met. "Why would you hide something like that?"

"It's complicated . . ."

Belle shook her head. "*Nee,* it's not complicated. It's humble, and I find that very attractive, Adam." She graced him with a soft, compassionate smile. "Still, why you would let the entire community think that they contributed?"

He sighed and stared straight ahead as though he were watching the current horse being auctioned. "The bishop. He did take up a collection. Only . . ." He paused and pressed his lips together. She thought she saw tension in his jawline. "No one contributed."

Belle gasped. "No one?"

"Not one person." He said each word in a short, clipped manner.

Immediately, Belle felt a wave of dismay at the magnitude of what Adam was saying. How could a community be so heartless? And then she thought back to that day at the store when Linda and her two daughters had peered out the front door of the Troyers' store, trying to catch a glimpse of Adam driving by. She remembered their heartless words and lack of compassion for the man she now called her husband. Another memory came to mind: Gabriel trying to convince her that she did not need to fulfill her promise to marry Adam. And, of course, the horrified response of the people in her church district when Adam and Belle's wedding banns had been announced. Belle realized that the real question was not how the community could be so heartless, but how she could have not seen the truth of who they were.

CHAPTER TWENTY-TWO

"Adam?"

She peered around the corner of the barn, hesitant to step inside. She knew he preferred to work alone in both the dairy barn and the fields. But she hadn't seen him all day and was worried.

Ever since their trip to the auction on Monday, he seemed more pensive and reclusive. If she had hoped that their day at the auction might help their relationship, her hopes were soon dashed. Now it was three days later, and he hadn't been coming inside for either breakfast or dinner. Again. It was five o'clock and supper was ready, but it was clear he had no intention of joining her. Again.

"Adam? Are you in here?" Despite not wanting to seem as if she was pestering him, she stepped inside and searched for him.

She was surprised at how clean the barn was. The cows were out in the pasture, and the aisle in between the milking stalls bordered on spotless. She had never seen any Amish dairy barn kept so tidy. She walked through the main section and headed toward the back rooms. But those, too, were empty. A ladder that led to the hayloft caught her attention, and she quickly climbed it, poking her head through the hole in the floor.

There were bales of hay stacked against the far wall. He must have stacked all of them by himself, and she couldn't imagine how hard that must have been, carrying the excess bales up the ladder and then stacking them. But he had done so, and in a way that was clearly very organized and perfectly aligned. Even the floor had been swept clean, so that hardly any stray hay was scattered about.

She got to her feet and looked around, taking in the scene. It was amazingly orderly for a hayloft. Adam must spend hours up here, she thought, while making her way across the wide wooden boards of the floor. When she got to the other side she was surprised to see a very small opening that seemed to lead to a crawl space. From the outside of the building, she would never have noticed it.

It was dark in the loft, but there was just

enough light filtering through a small window to see that Adam was not there. However, when she stooped down and peeked inside the tiny room, what she saw caught her off guard.

There was a mattress on the floorboards with a woolen blanket folded neatly atop it. Above it were two pegs from which hung a pair of trousers and a shirt. It all made sense now. At night, while Belle slept alone in the house, Adam slept here. But what she didn't know was how long he'd been sleeping up there. Could it be that he'd been living in the hayloft *before* she'd moved to the farm?

Curious, she stooped and entered the little room, then swept her eyes around, looking for a light. When she spotted a small, battery-operated lantern near the mattress, she picked it up and flicked on the switch. She tried to stand up, but the ceiling was too low, so she hunched herself over and hobbled to the far corner. That's when she saw a second opening. Crawling through it, she was surprised to find that it was a larger space than the other and had a full-height ceiling. She straightened herself up and stretched, then looked around. A makeshift kitchen was in one corner, a small table and chair — everything one would need to be comfortable.

"Belle?"

Adam's voice startled her. She turned around, dropping the lantern, which hit the wooden floor with a thud. Thankfully, it was electric, not kerosene. "Oh!" She knelt down to pick it up at the same time as Adam, and they bumped heads. Adam reached out to steady her, then pulled her back to her feet. His arm was wrapped around her waist, and for a second, Belle stared up at him and wondered — no, wished! — that he might kiss her.

"What are you doing up here?" His voice, so deep and gruff, had a raspy tone that surprised her even more than finding herself in his embrace.

"I . . . I was worried."

"About?"

She let her hand fall against his chest, surprised at how bold she felt. "About you."

Stiffening, he made a noise as if scoffing at her.

"Do you find that odd?" she asked, her finger tracing the buttons on his shirt. "I hardly see you, not even for meals. I was worried something had happened to you." She glanced at the makeshift kitchen. "Am I such a bad cook that you prefer to prepare your own meals?"

"That's not it . . ."

"Then why?"

He didn't answer her.

But Belle was determined to get some answers. She needed to understand what was holding him back when it had been he, not Belle, who wanted this marriage. "Why are you avoiding me?"

He started to step backward, but she held on to his shirt.

"Adam," she said. "You told me you didn't want a housekeeper — you wanted a wife. Yet you have turned me into a housekeeper. Have you changed your mind?"

He reached up, covering her hand with his, allowing his thumb to caress the back of her fingers. They hadn't been this close to each other before. She could feel his heart rapidly beating through the fabric of his work shirt and realized he was as nervous as she was. "*Nee,* Belle. I have not changed my mind," he managed to say, his voice raspy and thick with emotion. From the pained look on his face, she could sense that he wanted to open up to her. *What's holding him back?* she wondered.

"Then what is it? Why are you sleeping in the hayloft? Why are you eating alone?"

He squeezed her hand and pulled her closer. In the darkness of the room, she could sense him leaning down, his face close to hers. His warm breath caressed her cheek, and she sighed. Lifting her head, she closed her eyes and waited for him to kiss her. But the kiss never came.

Instead, he gently pushed her away.

"You shouldn't have come up here, Belle." He turned his back to her. "I told you not to come into the dairy."

"But why?" She took a step toward him, reaching her hand out to touch his shoulder. "Why are you rejecting me? Do I have to remind you this was your idea? This marriage?" She felt his muscles twitch under her touch. "If you haven't changed your mind, why are you pushing me away?"

Before the words had finished leaving her lips, he turned around and grabbed her, pulling her against him. She could barely catch her breath, and before she realized what was happening, he pinned her against the wall, one hand holding her arms over her head. His breath was warm against her neck.

"Is this what you want?" he said, his lips just inches from hers. "To drive me insane?"

"Insane?" His choice of words frightened her. "*Nee,* but I —"

"I stay away from you, Belle," he groaned into her neck, "because I have to. I can't begin to hope that you might one day have

312

feelings for me."

She shut her eyes. "Adam . . ."

"I never imagined that I might find a woman. A woman like you."

She relaxed when she felt him loosen his hold. She let her arms find their way to his shoulders, then wrapped them around his neck. "Like me?"

"A woman who would look past my face and see my heart . . ."

She leaned her head to the side and sighed. "If only you would show me more of your heart . . ." Clinging to him, she pressed her cheek against his and felt him turn his head, just slightly. "I catch glimpses, Adam, and I see that your heart is very large. You're a special man."

He relaxed a little as she spoke. She felt him lightly trail his lips along her neckline, letting them linger near her cheek. Shivering in anticipation, Belle held her breath as she waited for her first kiss.

"A good man," she whispered.

For a moment, he stiffened, and then he pulled back, covering her hands with his and gently removing them from around his neck. He clutched them and held them against his chest. She stared up at him, longing for him to break down that final brick in the wall that he used to isolate himself from the outside world. From *her.*

"*Nee,* Belle," he said, backing away from her. He reached for the lamp and started walking toward the door. "Not like this." He shut off the light and set it down on the floor inside the door. "*Kum,* Belle. If you've supper ready, I'll join you this evening, then."

He stood by the door, waiting for her to follow him. But she hesitated, confused about what had just happened, though, for once, she asked no questions. Instead, she left his makeshift bedroom and kitchen, following him to the ladder. He reached for her hand and, when their fingers touched, Belle felt an electrical charge soar through every nerve in her body. And yet she still felt disappointment that once again he'd shut her out of his world.

"I don't understand," she whispered.

"I don't expect you to." He released her hand and stood back, waiting for her to climb down the ladder before following her.

At the bottom, he stood beside her, then reached out and brushed a stray strand of her hair away from her cheek, tucking it behind her ear. When she looked at him, she realized that she wasn't seeing the scars on the right side of his face. Instead, she saw a man who felt as conflicted as she did, a man who wanted to love but was afraid. Afraid to open his heart for fear of being hurt.

Belle reached for his hand. She lifted it to her lips and gently kissed it.

He withdrew his hand from her grasp, placing a finger under her chin and tilting her head. She had no choice but to look at him. And then, slowly, he leaned down and placed a tender kiss to her forehead. "Not yet," he whispered again. "Not here." He let his hand fall, then sought hers, and they walked hand in hand out of the dairy barn and toward the farmhouse.

CHAPTER TWENTY-THREE

Once again, Belle awoke to overcast skies. Thankfully, however, it was not raining yet. She rubbed her arms, trying to warm them, as she left the comfort and heat of her bed and got dressed. The upstairs was cold, and she wondered how she would possibly keep from catching a chill during the winter months ahead. There were no fireplaces on the second floor of Adam's house.

Our house, she corrected. Although, after having seen where Adam preferred to live, she realized that the house was basically hers alone. The thought saddened her, especially as she remembered her anticipation that he might actually kiss her. When he hadn't and had pulled away from her, she had felt such an overwhelming sense of disappointment. And yet he had held her hand as they had walked back to the house.

Despite the cold, Belle stood in the middle of the bedroom, her arms wrapped around herself. She could not deny that her feelings for Adam had changed. For over a month now, she had been his wife. She'd learned about his moods and habits, as a wife should. She knew what he liked for breakfast, how he liked his coffee, and how he liked to be left alone. Oh, how she'd learned that lesson!

She walked to the window, peering outside. The trees were starting to drop leaves, and the yard was in dire need of a raking. Perhaps tomorrow, she thought. She already had plans to clean the upstairs bedrooms, even though no one used them.

Downstairs, she hurried to make some breakfast. With the oven cooking fresh bread, the kitchen soon filled with the warm, yeasty scent that spoke of home. She had just finished making scrambled eggs when Adam walked in. She looked up and greeted him with a smile.

"It's getting cooler out, *ja*?"

He nodded but didn't speak as he crossed the room to wash his hands. She kept out of his way, but stood ready with a fresh dish towel. As he wiped the water from his hands, he gave her a quick glance. "Don't suspect it will get much warmer today." Setting the towel onto the counter, he walked over to the table and sat down.

"I should like the key to unlock that bedroom upstairs." She dished his breakfast plate and poured him a cup of coffee, both of which she carried over to the table. "I plan on cleaning the upstairs today."

He mumbled something.

"Excuse me?"

"No need to focus on those rooms." He reached for his coffee and sipped at it. "Leave them be."

Belle frowned. It was easy enough for a man not to care about the cleanliness of the house, but Belle simply could not leave any room unfinished. "And it's very cold upstairs. Do you have a propane heater, perchance?"

He grumbled something else, and Belle sighed.

"*Mayhaps* you enjoy freezing to death all winter, but I don't relish the thought!"

He gave her a stern look but kept silent.

Taking her cue from him, Belle focused on eating her breakfast, wondering why he was in such a terrible mood. The hay was cut, the corn shucked, and the farm almost ready for winter. With a clean house and full belly, he had very little to complain about.

"Sunday is council," she said at last. "Will you be attending?"

He raised his head and looked at her, his expression blank.

Belle sighed. She should have figured that he wouldn't attend. Such a strange relationship, Belle thought, between the bishop and Adam. How could he possibly never attend council or communion and still be a member in good standing? Why, any other baptized member of the church would have quite a stern warning over never attending church! In fact, anyone else besides Adam would be shunned.

"Then I'll be going alone, I reckon."

Abruptly, Adam shoved away his plate and stood up. "Got chores to do," he mumbled and stalked out of the house.

Upstairs, Belle turned the knob to the locked bedroom door. She didn't know what she was expecting for, as always, it would not open. She sighed and bent down to look at the keyhole. She noticed that there was a gap between the door and the frame. For a moment, she thought about how to open the door. She couldn't fit a hairpin into the lock, for it wasn't that kind of door. But she wondered if she might push something in that gap. Perhaps she could spring the lock and finally get the door open, whether Adam liked it or not.

"Honestly!" she said out loud. Just when

she thought they were taking a step or two forward, Adam seemed to take four or five backward. His mood swings and temper flare-ups were becoming predictable, and they hurt just a little less since she had grown to expect them. She realized with a start that she'd gone from feeling hurt *by* him to feeling hurt *for* him. If only she could understand why he acted as he did!

Downstairs in the kitchen drawer, she found a plastic card. She turned it over and saw that it was a discount card for a garden store in Liberty Village. This might do, she thought and carried it upstairs. It only took her two tries to spring the lock. "Success!" she cried out happily.

The door swung open, and Belle gasped. In her wildest imagination, she never would have pictured what she saw now.

Unlike the rest of the rooms in the house, this room was not in complete disarray. While it was dusty from what appeared to be years of abandonment, a fine layer of dust covering the dresser and nightstands, it was set up as if awaiting the return of an occupant.

The light filtered through the bottom third of the windows, the rest covered with drawn-down navy shades. A beautiful blue and white quilt covered the large sleigh bed.

Kerosene lanterns, still filled with blue kerosene, rested upon the two nightstands, one on either side of the bed. Beneath the lanterns were white lace doilies, clearly handmade by a skilled person. Belle stepped through the doorway and passed by the tall dresser, where a hairbrush and hand mirror rested. Upon the walls were dresses hanging from pegs: one blue, one green, and one black. There was also a black apron hanging on the back of the bedroom door.

Without doubt, this room had belonged to a woman who decorated with love and care.

Belle sat down upon the bed and ran her hand across the top of the quilt. The stitches were fine and almost perfectly spaced, twelve stitches to an inch. The pattern of the quilt was double wedding rings, and Belle immediately knew that it had been made for a bride. But who?

She saw a leather book on the nightstand and reached for it. The worn cover spoke of frequent reading. When Belle opened it, she wasn't surprised to see that it was a Bible. She noticed that there was handwriting on the front page: Caren Hershberger. Little slips of paper poked out from between the pages. Curious, Belle turned the pages until she found one of the marked passages: "A joyful heart makes a cheerful face, But when the heart is sad, the spirit is broken." On the other side of the page was another marked passage: "A joyful heart is good medicine, But a broken spirit dries up the bones." Belle continued flipping through the Bible to read other marked pages beyond those two verses in the book of Proverbs. It was the one in Hebrews that made her catch her breath: "Do not neglect to show hospitality to strangers, for by this some have entertained angels without knowing it."

Shutting the Bible, Belle remained seated on the bed, the Bible resting on her lap with her hand atop its cover. Those verses lingered in her mind as she stared at the wall where the dresses hung. Oh, how she understood this woman who'd underlined and marked those verses. Hadn't Belle's spirit been broken when she'd arrived at the farm as Adam's wife? And yet, in spite of her sad heart and loneliness, she had begun to find moments of joy: helping Adam in the fields, riding beside him in the buggy, cooking meals in her kitchen. *Her* kitchen. She no longer felt as if she were a complete stranger in the house. She no longer longed to return to her father's farm. In many ways, her spirit had begun to heal, but the healing was not complete. She knew that she would not find a truly joyful heart until Adam was a real husband to her. He needed to share with her, confide in her, and treat her like a partner, not a hired hand.

She sighed and set the Bible on the bed. Standing up, she wandered over to the dresser and touched the hairbrush. It moved slightly, leaving a little trail in the dust. How many years had it been since someone had entered the room? How many years since the occupant last walked out the door and never returned?

Curiosity got the best of her and she opened the top drawer. It was empty. So were the second and third. But when she opened the bottom drawer, her eyes beheld the most unexpected sight. Clothing. A dress. A *kapp.* An apron. It was curious enough just to find those items in the dresser, for they should have been hung up in order to keep them from wrinkling. However, Belle quickly saw that the clothing was dirty. Very dirty.

She reached into the drawer and pulled out the *kapp.* If it had once been white, it was now gray, with traces of black on the rim. Belle frowned and set it atop the dresser before reaching for the apron. That, too, had smudges of gray on it, and the bottom was singed. Draping it over her arm, Belle leaned down for the dress. But as she withdrew it, a piece of paper fell to the floor. It must have been tucked in the folded dress.

After picking up the paper, Belle moved back to the bed, sitting down upon the edge. The paper was folded in three. Belle quickly opened it so that it lay flat on her lap, and her eyes scanned the faded print of an old article from *The Budget,* a weekly newspaper that even her father had subscribed to in order to keep up with other Amish communities around the country. What she read, however, startled her.

A fire at the Kings' dairy farm in Echo Creek killed Caren Hershberger and seriously injured her five-year-old son, Adam. The cause of the fire is unknown, but David King says his daughter, Caren, had gone into the barn to find her young son when the roof collapsed.

Belle frowned. Kings' farm? She didn't know of any Kings living in Echo Creek. And she had never heard about a Caren King, just as she knew nothing about a Caren Hershberger. But clearly this was Adam's mother. As Belle began to connect the dots, she felt that all-too-familiar tightening in her chest. Adam's mother had died trying to rescue Adam while he was visiting his grandparents. *That* was how he had been injured. And the scars on his body only masked the deeper scars that resided in his heart.

"Oh, Adam," she whispered.

Carefully, she refolded the paper and put it back in the bottom drawer. She laid the clothes on top of it, realizing that it was best she did not disturb the room. Adam had his reasons for leaving it this way, and until she could talk with him, it was best for her to leave well enough alone.

Chapter Twenty-Four

Belle pushed the floor with her feet, the rocking chair moving back and forth and causing the floorboard to creak, as she crocheted the blanket that partially covered her lap. The fire in the fireplace bathed the room in a soft orange glow and a smoky warmth for which Belle was glad, for it was cold outside. The overcast sky and naked trees made it feel like winter. She wondered if it might snow, but realized it was too early for that.

She heard the opening of the back door, and, for just a brief moment, she paused in her rocking as she listened for the now-familiar footsteps of Adam.

"You're in here already, then?" He entered the room and stood before the fireplace, his hands out as if to warm them.

Belle stared at him, her newfound knowledge of the accident that had caused his injuries forcing her to see him with fresh eyes. The verse from his mother's Bible came to the front of Belle's mind: "some have entertained angels without knowing it." Surely the rest of Echo Creek had missed out on an opportunity to entertain an angel, she thought as she watched Adam rub his hands together.

"I've made some soup for supper," she said quietly.

"Oh, *ja*?" He glanced at her, his eyes traveling to her lap, where the blanket lay. "Good to have soup on a cold night."

"You let me know when you're hungry, Adam, and I'll fetch it for you."

"Fetch it? Are you not eating then?"

She shook her head. "*Nee,* Husband." It was the first time she had called him that, and she noticed the look of surprise on his face. Setting down the blanket, she stood up and crossed the room to stand before him. "I'm not hungry for supper."

Perhaps it was the way she said the words that caused him to stop rubbing his hands. Or perhaps it was the way she looked at him. For a long, silent moment, he stood before Belle, motionless and curious, as if awaiting her next words. But she did not speak. Instead, she reached out her hand, slowly and with care, to gently touch his scarred cheek. He started to pull away, until

Belle shook her head.

"*Nee,* food will not satisfy me, but truth will."

Adam quieted and let her hand touch his skin. "Truth?"

She nodded. "*Ja,* Husband. Truth. I feel that there is a need for truth between us."

Immediately, he became tense, and she worried that he might shut down, and possibly storm out of the room and retreat to his living quarters in the dairy barn.

Quickly, she ventured forward with the words she had practiced over and over again during the early evening hours. She had prayed, too, that God would guide her tongue as she spoke to Adam.

"When I came to your house over four weeks ago and asked you to reconsider taking away *Daed*'s farm, you told me that you wanted a wife to bear you a son." She pressed her hand against his cheek. "And you visit me in my bedroom each night under cover of darkness while I sleep. Despite those visits, I wake up alone, never knowing for certain you were there save for the thread that falls from the door."

"Thread?"

She nodded. "I suspected you were coming into the room, so I began leaving a thin, blue thread that, should the door open, would fall to the floor."

Under her hand, she felt his cheek grow warm to her touch. He swallowed and looked very uncomfortable.

"Why, Adam? Why do you do that?"

He reached his hand to cover her wrist. With a firm grip on her arm, he moved it away from his face. "I'm not ready to do this." His voice was thick with emotion, and his eyes pleaded with her to stop. But Belle knew that she must push him.

"If not now, then when?"

"Just not now." Abruptly, he released his hold upon her arm and started to move away from her.

Fearing that she might lose her opportunity to finally understand what had made him want to marry her, she heard herself say, "Your mother — Caren — would want you to talk to me."

He stopped walking, standing just before the door, with his back turned toward Belle. She watched as his shoulders lifted and then drooped as if he had taken a deep breath and then exhaled. Belle waited for what seemed like an eternity for Adam to turn around and face her. There was no color in his cheeks.

"It wasn't your fault," Belle said. "That she died."

"You don't know what you are saying."

She moved toward him. "You were just a boy, Adam. And she loved you enough to try to save you from certain death."

Something changed in Adam's face, a dark cloud passing over his expression. "My *daed* never forgave me. *Maem*'s *daed* never recovered from her death."

Belle shook her head. "*Nee,* that can't be true! You were injured, and they tended to you. They raised you. Surely they thanked God for not taking you, too."

But he shook his head. "You don't know what it was like," he said sorrowfully. "*Dawdi* King moved here to live. He couldn't bear to see the burned barn on his farm, a reminder of *Maem*'s death. And my own *daed* refused to live in the *haus.* The only time I saw him was when we worked together, for he stayed in the dairy barn."

She tilted her head. "Where you sleep now?"

He nodded his head and slowly walked over to the sofa. He sank down into the cushions and leaned forward so that his elbows rested upon his knees. He covered his face with his hands.

"We quickly learned that, with my face, I couldn't attend school or church. So *Dawdi* King taught me to read and write and do my figures. When he wasn't doing that or working with *Daed* on the farm, he just sat in *Maem*'s room, reading her Bible and staring at her dresses, which hung from the walls. He never blamed me, not out loud like my *daed* did. I would sit in there, listening to him read verses from the Bible about forgiveness and faith." A hint of a smile touched the corner of his mouth. "He was all that I had."

Belle stood in place, giving Adam the time to finish his reflection.

"When *Dawdi* King died, I was fourteen. I couldn't bear to see that room. I locked the door and hid the key." He gave a sorrowful laugh. "I don't even remember where I hid it. I just knew that seeing that room would bring back too many hurtful memories of the only two people who cared for me."

Belle could hardly imagine the pain and suffering Adam must have felt growing up. Her throat swelled and she had to swallow to keep herself from crying.

"On the day *Dawdi* King died, I went to town to fetch the bishop, because I could see that *Daed* was too distraught to do anything. The schoolchildren were playing in the yard, and when they saw me . . ."

When Belle saw that his eyes welled with tears, she had to look away. Crossing her arms over her chest, she rubbed them, more for a physical distraction than because she was actually cold.

Adam cleared his throat, and Belle knew that he was trying hard to fight the tears. ". . . they pointed at me and called me a beast. When the teacher heard the commotion, she came out and saw me. She called for all of the children to hurry inside." He gave a grief-stricken laugh. "Anyone who saw me had the same reaction, except for the bishop."

Her heart ached for the broken man seated upon the sofa. "Oh, Adam." She hurried across the room and sat beside him, reaching out her hand to stroke his hair. "That was unkind and unchristian."

"After *Maem* died, the *g'may* came to the funeral, of course, and for weeks afterward they tried to bring food and help us. But hating how everyone stared and whispered about me, *Daed* refused to let them in after a while. Only the bishop was allowed to come each week, bringing food from his wife, and speaking with me in the *haus*. Then after *Daed* died when I was eighteen, the bishop could see how isolated I had become, and he tried to convince me to come to church. But I refused. He must've been relieved, because he never made much fuss about it. He even baptized me here, at the farm. *Mayhaps* he just didn't want to admit the truth about how he and his church members lived God's Word." He lifted his head and looked at her. "Or, rather, how they didn't, not when it involved an ugly boy who killed his own *maem.*"

"That's not true," she retorted quickly. "You are not ugly, and you did not kill your *maem.*"

"She was the only person who loved me."

Belle bit her lip as she stared into a face that was so full of anguish from years of suffering. "Until now," she said in a soft whisper.

For a moment, he did not respond. Instead, he held his breath as if disbelieving the words she had just spoken.

"Why do you visit my room at night?" she asked once again in the same hushed tone. "Why do you never stay?"

"I visit your room to watch you sleep, to thank God that he sent you to my farm on that day, and to love you in solitude without risk of rejection." He swallowed and then moistened his lips before he answered the second part of her question. "I never stay, Belle, because I dread the day that you might bear me a son and leave. I'd rather never stay the night with you than risk that day I would lose you, for surely I would die."

Slowly Belle leaned forward and gently pressed her lips against his. She felt him catch his breath, and she pulled back, smiling at him. "Whether one son or ten, you will never lose me." She placed both of her hands on either of his cheeks, her eyes staring into his. "Just promise me that you will never sleep outside this *haus* again. My husband is *not* a beast that should dwell in a barn, but truly the finest of men, whose place is beside his adoring and devoted wife."

Something caught in his throat, a strangled noise, and a single tear fell from his eye. Belle reached up and wiped it away with her thumb. When she did, he wrapped his arms around her, one hand behind her neck, and pulled her into a deep, warm embrace. She felt her hair loosen and fall out of the bun at the nape of her neck. His fingers entwined in her long wavy locks as he pressed his mouth upon hers, kissing her as tears of joy ran down her own face. Putting her arms around his neck, she clung to him, realizing that she was finally his wife — and he, her husband.

CHAPTER TWENTY-FIVE

Belle slid out from beneath the covers, careful to not awaken Adam. For a moment, she stood by the bedside, pulling her robe around herself, and stared down at her husband as he slept. The quilt hardly covered his bare shoulder, and she reached forward to gently raise it so that he would not catch a chill. When she did so, he grumbled something and moved just a little, his thick black wavy locks falling over the side of his face, the stubble from his beard casting a dark shadow on his cheeks.

Belle smiled and kissed her fingers before placing them lightly against his cheek.

To her surprise, he reached up and grabbed her hand.

"Oh!"

He rolled over, the quilt covering him, and pulled her so that she had no choice but to sit on the side of the bed.

"I'm so sorry, Adam. I hadn't meant to

awaken you!" And she meant it. She had intended to hurry downstairs and make him breakfast so that when he arose for morning chores, he could have something warm to fill his empty stomach.

Putting one arm behind his head, Adam propped himself against the pillow and headboard. "Don't be sorry," he said in a low, calm voice. "I would've been disappointed to wake up and not find you here. Like awakening from a dream only to realize that it never happened at all." He reached out and tugged at the long, thick braid that hung down her back. His eyes never left her face. "But you have awoken me earlier than need be."

She bit her lower lip, chastising herself for having awoken him at all.

Adam let his hand move from her braid to her arm. Gently, he pulled her so that she had no choice but to lie down beside him. He tucked her petite body against his and then covered her with the quilt. "This is how I want to wake up," he breathed into her ear. "And not just today, but every day, Belle Hershberger."

She was glad he couldn't see her face, for she was certain that her cheeks flushed pink.

He kissed the back of her head and wrapped his arm around her waist, pressing her tight against his body. For what seemed to be a long time, they stayed like that, until he finally sighed and began to move. At that moment, Belle realized that it wasn't long enough. If only she could stay in his arms forever.

After slipping on his pants, he shuffled over to the chair where, the previous evening, he had discarded his shirt. She watched as he slid first one arm and then the other into the sleeves before he turned around and began buttoning it. Her eyes took in the strong muscles in his chest before he finished closing the shirt and tucked it into his pants.

Adam must have noticed her watching him, and he stopped. "You're staring at me."

"I am."

He raised an eyebrow. "Why?"

She smiled. "You're beautiful."

He shut his eyes as he stood before her. "Those are words I never thought to hear," he murmured. "Not with these scars."

Belle sat up, letting her legs slide over the edge of the bed. "Don't you realize that beauty comes from the inside out? In fact . . ."

She stood up and walked over to him. Placing one hand on his shoulder, she raised the other to touch his face. He did not wince as she let her fingers trace the raised skin alongside his cheek and over his eye.

". . . I don't see scars, Adam. I see the man that I love who is God's gift to me."

He tried to look away, but she refused to give him that freedom.

"God made someone very special on the day that he made you." She leaned forward, and after stepping onto her tippy toes, she planted soft kisses upon his skin, one after another, until every inch of his scars had been kissed.

"Belle . . ."

She lowered herself and stared up at him. *"Ja?"*

"I love you."

She smiled and reached up to give him one more kiss, this one on his lips. "And I love you, Adam Hershberger. I love you so much that my heart hurts with joy."

He reached up his hand, placing it on the back of her neck and pulling her into him. Lowering his mouth to cover hers, he wrapped his other arm around her waist and stepped forward, pushing her backward until her calves hit the side of the bed. He tucked one finger into the loop of her robe belt and gave it a gentle tug.

"But the cows . . ." she started to say.

". . . will wait."

By the time she finally made breakfast, the sun had risen and was shining from behind the barn. She glanced out the window, hoping to see Adam finishing up his chores. When she finally heard Shep barking, she peered outside and, upon seeing Adam throwing a stick for the dog, smiled. There was a lightness to his step as he walked from the dairy barn to the house. He paused twice, his hands on his hips as he whistled for Shep to bring him the stick for another round of fetch. The dog was only too happy to comply.

As usual, he announced his arrival by stomping his boots on the porch steps. Belle reached her hand to her hair and made certain that no stray strands hung from beneath her prayer *kapp*. Then she smoothed her hands over her apron and waited for her husband to enter.

At first, he merely glanced at her. She wondered if he felt as awkward as she did. When he shuffled across the floor, avoiding her eyes, she knew the answer to that question.

She busied herself at the stove, finishing the scrambled eggs and putting the sausage onto the platter in order to carry it over to the table. But Adam wasn't sitting down. Instead, he had gone into the other room and returned with something in his hands.

"Best sit and eat while it's hot," she said, curious about his strange behavior.

He nodded and sat down, putting the package on the floor by his chair. She didn't ask any questions, figuring that if he wanted her to know what was on his mind or in that bag, he would let her know.

When she finally sat next to him and bowed her head to pray, she noticed that Adam followed her example, his eyes shut and his hands folded before him. She smiled to herself as she silently thanked the good Lord for all of his numerous blessings. Especially Adam.

"What do you have in store today, Adam?" she asked in a soft, shy tone.

He reached for the plate of toast at the same time she did, and he quickly pulled back. "Sorry, Belle."

"No, no, you first. Take your toast. I'm sure you're hungry after working so hard this morning."

He glanced at her, a surprised expression on his face.

"With the cows," she added dryly and raised an eyebrow, waiting for him to take his toast. When he did, she pushed the butter plate toward him so that he could easily access it. "You know, *mayhaps* you might rethink your position on the dairy barn being off-limits to me."

With the conversation having turned toward cows, Adam seemed to relax. "And why's that?"

She gave a little shrug of her shoulders. "I reckon you didn't want me in the barn because you were sleeping there; didn't want me to see that."

For the first time that morning, he looked directly at her. "Is that what you reckon?"

Belle nodded as she took two pieces of toast and set them on her plate. "So since we've resolved *that* issue, there's no reason for you to milk all those cows by yourself."

"Is that so?"

She ignored the amused looked that was beginning to cross his face. "Oh, *ja*, it is. Two hands make light the work, isn't that what they always say? Besides, I always enjoyed milking the cows at my *daed*'s farm. I miss it, to be truthful."

"I'd expect nothing less than that from you, Belle."

She reached for the butter dish. "Of course. And I would only give you the truth." As she stuck her knife into the butter, she looked up at him and met his gaze. "You know that, don't you, Adam? You know that I meant what I said."

"Which part?"

"If you mean about one son or ten sons, I meant that."

"I see."

She gave him a coy look. "But if you mean about how I love you and cannot imagine living one day without you, I meant that, too."

She thought she saw a hint of a blush on his cheeks.

After a few minutes of silence broken only by the ticking of the clock and the sound of breakfast being enjoyed, Adam finally cleared his throat and pushed back his plate.

"I may not be as good with words as you are, Belle, but if I could, I'd tell you the same things." He reached down and picked up the package from the floor. "However, this might be just as good as words at explaining things." Casually, he handed it to her.

"What is this?" She wiped her hands on her apron and took the package from him. It was a white plastic bag, folded over twice. Whatever was inside was soft and squishy. "You bought something for me?"

"Just open it, Belle."

Obediently, she unwrapped the plastic so that she could slide out whatever was inside. White tissue paper was wrapped around it, and she quickly opened that.

A bolt of yellow fabric lay nestled in the white paper. It was the same yellow fabric that she had admired at the Troyers' store just the previous weekend. She caught her breath and looked up at him, her eyes wide and questioning.

"How did you know I liked this?"

Adam's face shone, delighted with her surprise as well as her approval. "I saw you standing there, running your hand over that fabric. And then you saw the price tag, I reckon, and immediately put it back with the others. But I knew that you would look especially pretty in that color, Belle. With your dark hair and dark eyes, you'd light up any room if you wore a dress made in that fabric. I want other people to feel that special light you have, just the way I feel it whenever you are around."

Belle clutched the yellow fabric to her chest, feeling a tightening in her throat. She blinked her eyes, refusing to cry, but one tear escaped, and she laughed as she wiped it away.

"For a man who says he's not good with words, you sure just fooled me, Adam

Hershberger." And then she got up from her seat and went over to him, wrapping her arms around his neck from behind and kissing his cheek. "*Danke,* Adam. You are truly the best of men and the best of husbands."

He raised his hand up to pat her arm.

"I don't know why God led me to you, Adam," she whispered into his ear. "But I'm sure thankful that he did. What a special gift *you* are, and I will spend every day of my life hoping to prove to you just how much I love you."

He tightened his hold on her arm and gently pulled her around the back of his chair and onto his lap. She reached up her hand and brushed his hair away from his forehead, tucking it behind his ear.

"Now don't go spoiling me with such fancy talk, Belle," he murmured. "If I can just see you smile and hear you laugh, once each day, that's enough to make me die a happy man."

She laid her palm against his cheek. "I think that is something I can happily give to you."

He leaned forward and gave her a sweet, soft kiss. And then she rested her head against his chest, her arms back around his neck. She sat there, listening to the gentle pounding of his heart and the steady ticking of the clock. Surely she understood God's plan now. When she had thought she might lose faith, he had shown her that faith was sometimes the only thing worth seeking — and, once found, keeping.

CHAPTER TWENTY-SIX

On Sunday morning, when she walked downstairs, she was surprised to see Adam standing in the kitchen with a cup of hot coffee in his hand. It wasn't just the fact that he had made coffee, but the fact that he was wearing his suit — the same one he had worn on their wedding day.

"What's this?" she asked as she set her shawl onto the back of a chair. "You're looking mighty fancy there, Adam Hershberger."

"And so are you, Belle Hershberger. I was right about the yellow." His eyes shone as he took in the sight of her wearing a new dress made from the cloth he'd given her. Eager to demonstrate her delight in his gift, she'd spent the previous afternoon feverishly cutting and stitching, her spirits as bright as the color of the fabric.

"And your beard! Why! It's rather becoming on you, Adam." Purposefully, she neglected to add that his facial hair covered the scars on his cheek. In truth, she hadn't noticed his facial scars for a while, but now they were almost completely hidden. His external beauty now matched what she had seen on the inside of her husband.

Adam leaned against the counter and pursed his lips as he continued to study her. "Figured my beautiful *fraa* might want some company at worship this week."

"Oh, Adam!" Smiling, she hurried over to him, and, despite his feigned protests, she hugged him. With her arms around his neck, she clung to him while he tried to set down his cup of coffee so that it didn't spill on their clothes.

"Now, Belle," he chastised lightly. "No need to get so excited."

"But I am, Adam!" She kept hold of him but pulled back enough so that she could look into his eyes. "Do you know how much this means to me? Why, I can hardly wait to sit there and look across the way at my husband! We'll be singing the same hymns together and listening to the sermon." She nestled her head under his chin, feeling the tickle of his beard. "And on our ride home, we can talk about what the preachers say. Why, this is destined to be the best Sunday ever."

He cleared his throat as if uncomfortable,

but she felt him wrap one of his arms around her waist. "Did you forget that there's a council meeting after fellowship today, too? After all, we can't have communion this month if all is not right with the church district."

She sighed. She had forgotten that there would be a council meeting today. That meant almost seven hours at worship. The regular service and fellowship would be followed by a long meeting, led by the bishop. Everyone would have to confess to their sins, and any disagreements would need to be resolved. Only then could the members do the foot washing and communion service two weeks later.

"It'll be a long day, no doubt," she said as she reluctantly extracted herself from Adam's embrace. "But I'm so pleased that we will be together."

An hour later, they arrived at the Grimms' farm, where worship was being held. The driveway was already filled with buggies, and several young boys ran over to greet them, eager to help them unhitch the horse. Belle noticed that two of the boys shied away, but she decided to ignore their reaction. She was certain that children would not be the only ones with wide eyes and opened mouths when they saw Adam enter the house with the other men.

As they approached the house, Adam's pace slowed.

When she realized that he was no longer beside her, Belle turned to face him. "Oh," she said as she stopped walking. "I reckon you best go join the men, then."

He took a deep breath, his eyes piercing hers. She couldn't tell whether he was pleading with her to stay with him or trying to tell her that everything was all right. Fortunately, before either one of them could speak, the bishop walked over and placed his strong, large hand upon Adam's shoulder.

"Adam! Belle! What a *wunderbarr gut* surprise to have you both here!" He beamed at Belle as if she had just delivered a long-lost sheep back to the shepherd. He turned to Adam. "And for council!"

Adam gave a single nod of his head. "*Ja*, I've decided that" — he hesitated and looked at Belle — "that I'll be here for communion this year, Bishop."

The bishop's eyes crinkled in delight. "Oh, that's just *wunderbarr*," he repeated, this time with a long, breathy sigh. "I knew this day would *kum*." He returned his attention to Belle. "*Danke*, Belle."

Feeling self-conscious that she was the

center of attention, for all of the men lingering near the barn were staring, Belle lowered her eyes and took a step backward in the direction of the house. "Nothing to thank me for, Bishop. Adam made up his own mind."

But she knew the bishop was still smiling at her.

Eager to escape his attention and the other men's scrutiny, she quickly changed the conversation. "Has anyone heard word from Sadie?" she asked.

"*Nee,* Belle." The bishop took a deep breath and lowered his voice. "All we can do is continue to pray for her safe return."

"Oh, dear." Belle swallowed. "That we will certainly do."

"And more, if needed," Adam offered solemnly.

"*Danke,*" the bishop said. "Both of you."

With the break in the conversation, Belle excused herself and hurried into the house, where the other women were gathered for pre-worship conversation.

No sooner did she enter and begin to pass through the circle of women, greeting each one with a handshake and kiss, than she felt a hand on her arm and the familiar voice of her sister, Susie, in her ear.

"Did I hear that your husband is here for

service?"

Barely had Belle turned around than her other sister was at her side. "Where did you get that dress?" Verna asked, her words sounding envious rather than curious.

Susie glanced down at Belle's dress and caught her breath. "Why! Didn't I see that fabric at Troyers' store? It was almost twice the price of the next best fabric!" She looked at Belle in surprise. "How on earth did you . . . ?"

Fortunately, Ella joined them, and she gave Belle a quick embrace, even though most Amish women did not greet others like that for fear of indicating a special bond between each other. "Oh, Belle! You did a right *gut* job on that dress! When your husband bought it, I told Adam that the color would suit you!"

"Adam?" Susie gasped. "He bought that fabric for *you*?"

Belle did not need to explain, for Ella appeared more than happy to do it for her. "Oh, *ja*!" Ella ran her hands down her own white organza apron that covered her blue dress. "Why, he was just delighted as could be to buy her that fabric. Wanted to surprise her." She leaned forward and lowered her voice. "I don't think I've ever met a kinder man, so devoted to his *fraa*." Suddenly, Ella

351

covered her mouth and turned toward Belle. "Oh, help. I do sound like a braggart, don't I?" There was a mischievous twinkle in her eye. "I wonder," Ella said, returning her attention to Susie, "is it a sin to brag if it's about someone else's good fortune?"

Both Susie and Verna stood there, speechless and with their mouths hanging agape. Belle, too, was almost stunned into silence. She suspected that Ella had come to her rescue, knowing that Susie and Verna had a hundred and one questions, with not one of them out of genuine concern for Belle. While she appreciated Ella's interception, Belle was still surprised that her friend had spoken up at all.

"I shall have to ask the bishop about that," Ella mused out loud, although from the sparkle in her eyes, Belle doubted Ella would do any such thing.

"Well, I suppose if one doesn't do it too often," Belle replied in a slow, thoughtful voice.

There was no more time for discussion, for the bishop and preachers entered the kitchen, making their way through the line of women, shaking their hands as a way of greeting them. As soon as the bishop and preachers were seated, the older and married women sat. Before slipping away to take her spot in the line, Belle gave Ella a look of gratitude. She knew that they would talk after the worship.

After the women were seated, the elderly and married men walked into the room. Belle saw her father for the first time since her wedding. She felt a momentary surge of happiness, especially when she saw that he walked with a straight back and bright eyes. As he started to sit on the pine bench, he looked up and scanned the room until he caught sight of her. Despite the solemnness of worship, her father smiled and winked at her. Belle could hardly wait to speak to him after the service and to hear about how his wonderful new grill had begun selling — a wonderful change of fortune for Melvin Beiler.

As usual, the worship began with the members singing a hymn while the bishop and preachers left for a side room. Belle stared across the heads of the other women seated before her, her eyes seeking out her husband. He sat between two married men, their long beards a sharp contrast to Adam's still-growing one. She tried not to smile as she watched him sing, needing to reference the *Ausbund* hymnal while other members sang the song from memory. He appeared uncomfortable but determined. And when he glanced in her direction, she gave him a small, encouraging smile.

By the time the church members had finished the hymn, the bishop and preachers had returned. It was one of the preachers who began retelling stories from the Old Testament, starting with creation and leading up to the reading of Matthew 18. Belle shut her eyes and absorbed the reading from the Gospel, especially the seventh verse: "Woe unto the world because of offences! for it must needs be that offences come; but woe to that man by whom the offence cometh!"

From years past, Belle knew that the council meeting was based upon this very verse. The children and unbaptized members would not attend the meeting. Instead, only members stayed for the meeting, which focused on correcting wrongs, discussing issues, and addressing disagreements, for the community had to be in harmony prior to accepting communion at the next worship service.

And yet, as she listened to the congregation begin singing "Das Loblieb," the hymn that was always sung after the first sermon, Belle found her mind wandering back to that verse.

How could she not bring up the matter

about Adam? How the community had wronged him for so many years? Why, she could bring up a number of examples . . . from Linda Troyer and her daughters ridiculing him as they peered out the window of their store to John Grimm not reprimanding his two small children for mocking him to Gabriel trying to get Belle to renege on her agreement to marry him. In fact, if Belle really thought about it, she could think of a dozen more people who had stared at him, whispered about him, and given him a wide berth.

All because he looked different

Her heart began to beat rapidly. She felt a conflict of love for her husband and disappointment in the church. She knew that she could not harbor such feelings in good conscience and still accept communion the following week. Surely that would be a sin, wouldn't it? As the verse in Matthew said, "It is better for thee to enter into life with one eye, rather than having two eyes to be cast into hell fire." Still, she did not want to make Adam feel uncomfortable. He had made a great step toward healing by attending the service, something she knew he had avoided for many years.

When "Das Loblieb" ended, Belle watched as the bishop stood up. It was his turn to preach the second sermon, which was usually the longer of the two. However, being that they would hold council meeting later, Belle knew that he would reiterate the message from the earlier sermon, citing that harmony among the church members was necessary before any one of them could accept communion.

So, when the bishop began to speak, she was surprised that he did not follow the format of previous sermons on council meeting Sunday.

"Just one speck of dust can blind an eye."

He paused and waited for people to understand what he had just said. Then he held up his hand, pointing one finger into the air. "Just one. It takes so little to make a person unable to see. And what is dust? It is nothing more than a tiny particle of matter, of earth. And yet, the Bible tells us that God created the heavens and the earth. He created even that tiny particle of dust that is so powerful, it can blind."

He began to pace the floor before the congregation. "Think about that. God can make a tiny particle of dust blind a man. Surely that is proof enough of his magnificence and power. But we don't ask for proof, for we have faith, and faith is all that we need. We don't need proof."

Abruptly, he stopped pacing. "At least that is what we claim when we accept our baptism."

Belle frowned, wondering what the bishop was really trying to say. His sermon was different from any other she had heard him preach. Apparently other people were making this realization, too. Not one person's attention was anything less than riveted to where the bishop stood.

"We all have a speck of dust in our eyes. Each and every one of us. We have all been blinded by this tiny particle, unable to see the truth, to hear the truth, and, ultimately, to speak the truth. In fact, we have turned this blind eye to others within the congregation, refusing to extend the hand of God because they look different, live different, behave different."

Belle caught her breath and glanced across the people between them to look at Adam.

"This is not how Christians behave. Jesus placed his hands upon the leper's wounds so that he could heal. Jesus cast out the possessed man's demon so that he could live. Jesus rubbed mud upon the blind man's eyes so that he could see. But all that Jesus asks of us is to love thy neighbor. And yet, each and every one of us is guilty of breaking this commandment. Each and every one of us has permitted that speck of dust to blind us. And you can call that speck by other names . . . prejudice, intolerance, bias, aversion, envy, fear . . . but it has the same effect. It blinds us and removes us far . . . *very far* . . . from God's loving embrace."

Suddenly the bishop opened his arms. With one hand, he pointed toward Belle, and with the other, he pointed toward Adam. "And yet there are two among you who found a way to remove that speck of dust, to use faith in God to see once again. There among you sits a young woman who saved her father's farm by marrying a man she did not know."

Belle pressed her lips together, feeling the heat rise to her cheeks. She knew that several people were looking at her. She could *feel* the weight of their scrutiny as they stared at her. It was hard not to squirm under their scrutiny. She took no pride in being called out as a role model by the bishop. In fact, she felt even more humble under his praise.

"And rather than stand by and recognize *her* faith, how many among you stood by with nothing less than idle gossip or speculation? Why, I even know a few of you who came to me, seeking excommunication of the man."

He didn't need to glance at Linda Troyer for Belle to know exactly to whom he referred.

"And why the anger, hostility, resentment toward the man?" The bishop paused again, lowering his arms. "Because he was injured as a child? Because his mother died in a fire? Where was the loving community offering to help this child who lost his mother? To help his father, who lost his wife? The grandfather, who lost his daughter? Why, David King was so distraught that, eventually, he sold his farm rather than continue living on the property where his daughter died."

The bishop's shoulders sagged. His sermon, an admonishment to the congregation, was draining him. Belle could see that right away. And while she had never seen a bishop preach like this, she knew that it was something that should have been done long ago. Perhaps that was at the core of his emotional exertion: the bishop knew that, too.

"When the child grew up — alone, mind you, for the majority of his life — he saw a way to help a family in need by offering to buy their farm. He didn't need the land, but the family was in debt. The man paid the debt and, in turn, acquired the farm where his mother had died."

Belle gasped. Several people glanced at her, equally as surprised as she was by this news.

"And yet the dust in your eyes," the bishop said, scanning the room with a stern expression on his face. "That dust blinded you to the fact that this man was helping the Beiler family. You saw it as something sinister and accused him of stealing the farm away." The bishop softened his voice. "But he was merely trying to help. Just as he was merely trying to help when he purchased a new horse and buggy for the man to replace the horse and buggy that Melvin Beiler had lost in an accident."

The bishop took his hand and pointed at the members of the congregation, his arm moving in a semicircle. "How many of you contributed to help your neighbor? To live the word of Jesus?"

Several heads bowed down. Belle knew the real reason why, for Adam had already told her of the lack of generosity on their part when the bishop had asked for contributions to help the Beiler family.

Lifting his chin, the bishop straightened his shoulders as he lowered his arm. "So today, as we prepare for fellowship before our council meeting, I want to address this issue, for the dust is blinding, and it is my responsibility to help all of you see. Remove that speck of dust and see with fresh eyes that there is beauty in every single one of God's creations, no matter how perfect or imperfect. For truly, when you can see with the heart and not just with the eye, you will realize that you are no longer blind and are finally walking in the light with God."

His sermon over, the bishop returned to his spot next to the other preachers. Almost immediately, the *vorsinger* began singing the last hymn, his voice starting the first word of the hymn so that the rest of the worshippers could join in. But Belle barely heard the words and couldn't find the focus to sing with the rest of the congregation. Instead, she found herself lost in thought for the last half hour of worship.

Afterward, the men began to convert the benches into tables while the women prepared the plates of cold cuts, sliced bread, and side salads that would serve as the noon dinner meal. Belle hurried over to help them. For the first time since the bishop had announced her marriage to Adam, she felt acceptance from the other women. Instead of curious gazes or hushed whispers, the women bestowed warm smiles on her, and a few, including Susie, gave apologetic looks that Belle acknowledged with a simple nod of her head. She still didn't understand exactly why the bishop had preached such a sermon, but Belle suspected that things would begin changing for the better now. Not just for her and Adam, but perhaps for everyone in Echo Creek.

CHAPTER TWENTY-SEVEN

After they arrived home from council meeting, Belle helped Adam unhitch and unharness the horse. Then, after quickly changing out of her new yellow dress and into her regular work clothes, she returned to the dairy barn to assist Adam with the evening milking. In silence, they worked side by side. Occasionally, Belle would talk to the cows as she milked them, gently tugging at their full udders. Twice she caught Adam smiling at her soft conversations. A blush would cover her cheeks, and she would dip her head so that he couldn't see.

When the last cow had been milked and they had been turned out for the evening, Belle slipped back inside to prepare supper while Adam finished tending to the horses.

As usual, he stomped his boots when he walked up the steps. This time, however, he paused for a minute before he walked through the door. She was surprised to see that he was only wearing his socks.

When she questioned him with a raised eyebrow, he shrugged. "Figured I'd spare you a muddy floor."

Her heart warmed at his considerate gesture. "I sure do appreciate that, Adam."

The meal consisted of reheated fried chicken and mashed potatoes. Since the Sunday fellowship meal was always light, Belle had spent time the previous day preparing something more substantive for them to enjoy after council meeting. From past experiences, Belle had suspected they would both be hungry as well as exhausted by the time they returned home from the long meeting.

And she had been correct.

For the first part of the meal, they ate in silence. But as Belle became full, she set down her fork and pushed her plate away from the edge of the table.

"Such a long afternoon," she sighed and rubbed her temples.

He nodded, still chewing. "*Ja,* 'twas."

She took a deep breath and sighed. "Who would have thought that there could be so many little issues in a town like Echo Creek?"

He gave a low chuckle as he swallowed.

"And over such trivial things," she continued. "Neighbors upset over property lines. Farmers accusing one another of breaking borrowed equipment." Running her finger along the edge of the table, she pursed her lips. "Such pettiness. I reckon the bishop's sermon went in one ear and out the other."

Adam raised an eyebrow. "For some, I reckon. But not for all. Don't sound so disappointed, Belle. People don't change overnight."

She thought of her family. With Susie engaged, things would undoubtedly change for Verna. She was the spinster of the family now and, if Gabriel took over Melvin's farm, Verna would be beholden to her sister and her brother-in-law. It wasn't a situation that Belle would have liked being in.

"I spoke with *Daed,*" she said. "He's doing quite well. Apparently the *Englische* folk love his new grill design."

"Oh?"

"Apparently someone has invested in it and that's helped him manufacturer more models." She looked at Adam, watching his reaction with great curiosity. She couldn't help but wonder whether or not Adam might have anything to do with that mysterious investor. But Adam did not flinch or make any indication that he might have been the silent backer. Perhaps it was better that she not know, she thought.

"Oh, and my sister Susie is getting married."

Adam glanced up from his plate.

"To Gabriel."

He made a noise deep in his throat. Belle knew that Adam had no love for Gabriel, especially after their words in town that one day that happened so long ago it felt like another lifetime to Belle.

"There is one thing, Adam, that has been troubling me for a while." Belle set down her fork. She hadn't wanted to bring up the subject, but she knew she deserved the truth. "When I visited Susie a while back, she told me that you had asked them not to come visit me. Why, Adam?"

For a brief moment, Belle worried that he would get upset with her for asking such a question. But he didn't. Instead, he stared at the wall as if collecting his thoughts. "Belle, I knew what you had left: a home, a family, a way of life. I asked your *daed* to give you some space. Just until you had a chance to adapt."

Fair enough, she thought. "I wish you had told me, Adam. I thought that they had forgotten me. They've been so busy with so many good changes in their lives. It was as if . . ." She was about to comment that her sacrifice didn't matter, but she no longer considered it a sacrifice. Lowering her head, she felt her cheeks grow warm. "Well, I suppose that doesn't matter anymore, does it? I don't feel that way now."

The sides of his mouth twitched as if he wanted to smile. Instead, he took a bite of the mashed potatoes she had made.

"Are you glad that you went, Adam? To worship today, I mean."

He dabbed at his mouth with a napkin and leaned back in his chair. He studied her for a minute while he reflected on her question. She wondered what he was thinking, how he had truly felt about the sermon. She still wasn't certain what she had felt.

"*Ja,* Belle," he said at last. "I am. And not just because of what the bishop said." He paused for a long, thoughtful moment. "*Mayhaps* it was a long time coming. But I'm not resentful about the amount of time it took to correct the wrong. I'm just hopeful that it was corrected."

She agreed with him. "In time, they will see you as I do, Adam."

He leveled his gaze at her. "And how do you see me, Belle?"

A soft smile played over her lips. "Let me see . . ." She pretended to think, as if searching for an answer. But she already knew how to respond. Moving closer to him, she stared into his face. "What do I see? Hmmm . . . a man with a large heart who has carried the weight of a very heavy burden on his shoulders for far too long." She leaned forward. "I see a man who loved his mother very much, so much that he wanted to keep the farmhouse where she had been born, raised, and eventually died, no matter how painful the memory was to him." Reaching out her hand, she pressed her palm against his scarred cheek. "And I see a man . . . a very, very handsome man . . . who has captured my heart — a man I'm proud to call my husband."

He leaned against her palm and shut his eyes.

"I've learned something, Adam," she said softly. "People often accuse others of the very defects they themselves are hiding. Why, all of those years of people treating you like a beast! Hiding from you, mocking you, ridiculing you both to your face and behind your back. It seems that people are more inclined to participate in poor behavior when led astray by others. And while I don't understand why, I wonder if people take delight in someone else's misfortune and suffering because it helps them forget their own character defects."

Covering her hand with his, he moved his head to plant a kiss on her palm. "Then they need our prayers, Belle."

"Prayers that they will reflect on the bishop's words, *ja*?"

He nodded. "It takes courage to sit down and listen."

"And courage to stand up against injustice."

"That's what I see when I look at you."

Surprised, she leaned back. "What is it you see, Adam?"

"Courage." Standing, he reached down and pulled her to her feet. "Great courage." Playfully, he made a scary face at her. "You tamed the beast, after all."

A laugh escaped her lips. "Oh, Adam. You're anything but a beast. I hope you believe that now."

He nodded his head. "You've shown me that, Belle."

From outside, the dog barked. Both of them glanced at the door. The sun was already setting and casting shadows on the front yard in between the house and the barn. A breeze rustled the trees, which were losing more leaves every day. But the clear sky indicated that it would be good weather the next day. They had plenty of work to do, for they needed to spread manure in the recently plowed fields to prepare for the next year's crops.

Adam exhaled and returned his attention to Belle. "I reckon it's not too early to retire for the night."

She gave a gentle shake of her head. "I reckon not."

He hesitated before he said, "After all, we've a long day tomorrow."

"*Ja,* we do."

He stretched his arms. "And I sure am tired." But the sparkle in his eyes told her otherwise. He took a step toward the door that led to the hallway, holding her hand as he led her out of the kitchen.

She paused and glanced at the plates on the table. "Give me a minute, Adam. I sure do hate waking up to a messy kitchen."

"Such a good *fraa.*" Bending down, he planted a soft kiss on her lips before releasing her. "I'll be waiting."

She tried to hide her smile as she watched him saunter down the hallway and head for the stairs. For a moment after he disappeared, she touched her fingers to her lips as if trying to recapture his sweet but chaste kiss. Oh, how things had changed! Not long ago, she never would have thought she'd long for his attentions. Now, she could hardly contain her joy.

Finally, alone in the kitchen, Belle carried the plates over to the sink and quickly washed them. Rather than dry them, she merely set them on a towel. Then, rather than joining Adam, she hurried back to the bench where she had, just minutes before, sat talking with her husband. She knelt down and folded her hands, placing them on the bench as she pressed her forehead against them.

Thank you, Lord, she prayed, *for all of your blessings. Thank you for forgiving us our sins and for giving us the grace to forgive others. May you continue to bless me so that I may live the true virtues of a good Christian. I pray that I honor your name, Lord, by setting a good example in all of my behavior, demonstrating your love for us in how I love others. And may my love for my husband continue to grow and shine, helping him with his healing as he finds himself back in the fold of your loving arms.*

Silently, she added the Lord's Prayer before she stood up. She reached for the kerosene lantern and blew out the flame. Cloaked in the increasing darkness, she glanced around the kitchen, pleased that she had made the effort to clean it so that, in the morning, when she and Adam came downstairs, they would be met with a tidy, orderly room and she could make him his breakfast before they went outside, together, to begin the morning chores.

With a satisfied heart, she wandered down the dark hallway and ascended the stairs to join Adam in the bedroom they shared. Night would pass, and come dawn, a new day would present a fresh opportunity to rejoice in the love of God and all of his blessings. As for Belle, she knew she would never have enough mornings to thank God for the blessing of his love, as well as that of her husband.

Epilogue

Belle leaned against the hoe, assessing her morning's work in the garden. Each of the rows was cleared of weeds, and tiny sprouts poked up from the small mounds of dirt. Had it only been three weeks earlier that Adam had helped her clear the patch of dirt from the previous years' growth? He hadn't wanted her to work so hard, given her current condition.

Smiling, she rested one of her hands upon her rounded belly. In two months she would give Adam the one gift she knew he most wanted: a child. She didn't care whether the baby was a boy or a girl. Deep down, she knew that Adam didn't, either. The only thing they cared about was the health of the baby.

"The little one moving around, then?"

She turned around, not surprised to see Adam walking toward her, their dog, Shep, jogging at his side. He looked thoughtful, his hands behind his back as he approached her.

Belle smiled and nodded her head. "*Ja,* I think I feel a foot right here." She reached for one of his hands and pressed it against her side. "Do you feel that? It's a heel."

Watching his face, Belle saw his eyes widen with delight. "The miracles of God never cease," he said, leaving his hand on her dress.

She leaned backward, pressing her back against his chest. "Just think, in two months, we'll be parents to a beautiful baby boy or girl."

"Beauty is in the eye of the beholder," he remonstrated gently.

Belle laughed. "Oh, Adam, this baby will be the most beautiful baby in the world, and you know it."

He managed to chuckle. "*Ja,* I reckon I do. To us, anyway." Reaching up his free hand, he removed his hat and scratched at his ear. "You think all parents feel that way about their babies?"

"For sure and certain." She turned around so that his hand now rested on the small of her back. Staring into his face, the edge of his beard almost touching her forehead and tickling her skin, Belle sighed. "Isn't it strange to think that less than a year ago, we didn't even know each other existed?"

Adam raised an eyebrow, plopping his hat back on his head so that he could wrap his other arm around her. "Oh, is that what you think?" He gave her a mischievous look. "I knew who you were, Belle Hershberger."

For a second, she thought he was teasing. But when she realized that he was not, she opened her mouth into a small O.

"*Ja,* that's right. I knew you lived on my *maem*'s family farm. In fact, whenever I went to town, I'd slow as I passed your *haus.* Sometimes I'd see you outside hanging up laundry or leading the cows in from the fields. And then there was that day —"

"What day?" she demanded, interrupting him.

He gave her a gentle squeeze. "Don't you Remember that day when you were walking home and I passed you in the buggy?"

She gasped. "I do! You slowed down as you passed me."

He nodded his head. "And you smiled at me and waved."

"I did?"

"*Ja,* you sure did." He leaned down and kissed the tip of her nose. "*Mayhaps* that was the moment I fell in love with you." From behind his back, he withdrew his other hand. In his closed fist, he held three stems of beautiful, yellow sunflowers. He handed them to Belle.

"Oh, Adam!" Her eyes widened in delight. "The patch of sunflowers behind the barn bloomed already?"

He smiled at her. "I knew you'd like them."

"Why, they're just beautiful."

"Not nearly as beautiful as you."

She blushed and lowered her gaze. "Best get them into some water, *ja*?" she said in a soft voice. "And fix you some food. It's almost noon."

Adam reached out so that Belle could take his hand. Together, they left the garden and walked to the front porch, the sunflowers gently laid across Belle's arm. As Adam and Belle disappeared inside the house, two cardinals, one male and the other female, flew overhead and headed beyond the barn. Together, they landed on the head of a giant sunflower, chirping sweetly to each other.

ABOUT THE AUTHOR

Sarah Price comes from a long line of devout Mennonites, including numerous church leaders and ministers throughout the years. Her involvement with the Amish dates back to 1978 when she wrote her first novel, *Fields of Corn,* while studying anthropology and writing at Drew University. She was drawn to the amazing culture of the Amish of Lancaster Country where Ms. Price is involved with numerous Amish communities and is considered family by some and friend by most others. *Fields of Corn* went on to become an Amazon bestseller and *First Impressions, A Retelling of Pride & Prejudice,* Sarah's salute to Jane Austen from an Amish perspective, debuted on the ECPA bestseller list. In 2014, *An Amish Buggy Ride* became a #1 Amazon bestseller in Religious Romance. Ms. Price has advanced degrees in Communication

(MA), Marketing (MBA), and Educational Leadership (A.B.D.) and was a former college professor. She now writes full-time and talks about her books and her faith on a daily live stream with readers. Learn more about Sarah and her novels at SarahPrice Author.com.